BRADLEY'S DRAGONS

PATRICK MATTHEWS

Second
Story Up

Bradley's Dragons is for everyone who ever dreamed of being more than they are. Mostly, though, it's for Helene, who already is.

CONTENTS

A LOST MEMORY

"Stop."

Bradley paused, his throwing arm in mid-motion. He and his aunt were skipping stones on a lake in the Ocala National Forest. She had the record, seven bounces. "Why?"

His aunt wasn't looking at him. She faced away from the lake, and her eyes were scanning the thick Florida woods. "We need to go."

"Antlee-een!" That was what Bradley called her. Her real name was Helene, but when he was two years old, he'd pronounced 'aunt Helene' as 'Antleen'. He'd called her that ever since.

"I know," she said. "We'll come back."

"But you're winning!"

"I'm serious, Bradley."

Bradley stuffed his skipping stone into his pocket. It was bigger than he usually threw, but flat and round. "The score doesn't count," he said. "The game's not over 'til I get my next throw."

"I know. Just—"

The palmettos rustled behind them, and she turned. A man stood at the trail entrance. He was tall and pale, with short red hair and a brown leather jacket that was too heavy for the Florida heat.

"Max?" Antleen said, her voice uncertain.

He walked toward them through the long grasses at the edge of the wood. "Helene," he said.

"What are you doing?" she asked. "You know you can't be here."

"I came for Bradley."

"Not funny." Antleen stepped forward so she was between Bradley and the man.

Max stopped. He leaned sideways and smiled around her at Bradley.

Bradley shivered. The man's eyes looked wrong, glassy and unfocused.

"Stop it," Antleen said.

Ignoring her, the man held his hand out toward Bradley and made a twirling gesture with his forefinger. "Hello, Bradley," he said. "I'm Max."

At the sound of the name, Bradley's vision dimmed. Pain blossomed behind his eyes, and the world seemed to tilt and blur.

"No!" Antleen shouted.

"Antleen," Bradley gasped. "What's happening?"

Max was out of the weeds now and walking toward them, repeating that strange twirling gesture.

Sweat dripped down Bradley's back. His chest ached, and his legs felt weak and rubbery. His vision dimmed again, and he collapsed to the ground.

"Get back," Antleen growled at Max.

Max stumbled, then regained his balance. Leaning forward as if against a strong wind, he stepped closer. "You can't stop me, not with him here."

Bradley concentrated on his aunt. *It's okay*, he told himself. *Antleen's here. She knows what to do.* His vision started to clear. The muddy grass felt warm and wet between his fingers, and the smells of lake water and dying fish filled his nose. Antleen's deeply tanned skin looked paler than usual. Her eyes were glittering angry slits.

"Why?" she demanded.

"The two of you alone?" Max asked. "How could I not?" He took another step closer.

"He's only nine!" she shouted, her voice cracking.

"He'll grow."

Panting with effort, Bradley forced himself to stand. His head still hurt, but his dizziness was gone.

"Run," Antleen hissed under her breath.

Bradley's eyes widened. His aunt was scared.

Her green eyes locked with his. "Run! Now!"

Heart pounding with fear, Bradley shook his head. "No."

"Bradley!"

"I won't leave you," he insisted, voice trembling "I won't."

"It's too late," Max interrupted from less than ten feet away. He made the twirling gesture with his hand again.

Bradley's legs went numb. He grabbed his aunt's arm to keep from falling.

"Stop," Antleen pleaded with Max. "Think about what you're doing."

Bradley reached into his pocket for his skipping stone.

"It's over," Max said. Without taking his eyes off Antleen, he held out a hand to Bradley. "Come on. Time to go."

Shaking his head, Bradley let go of his aunt and planted his feet.

"Come with me," Max said, "or I'll kill your aunt."

With one smooth motion, Bradley pulled the rock from his pocket and threw. The stone slammed into Max's forehead. Max doubled over, clapping both hands to where the rock had hit him.

Antleen flung her arms into the air, and Max's body lifted like a rag doll caught in a hurricane.

"No!" Max shouted, still holding both hands to his forehead. "Wait!"

Antleen moved her hands like she was throwing a soccer ball. Max crashed through the palmettos, slammed into the trunk of a cypress tree, then spun away over the tree tops.

"Antleen?" Bradley said. His voice was so wispy he could barely hear it. "What happened?" He lost his balance and slid down to the muddy grass.

"He's gone." She knelt down to cradle him in her arms. Tears were running down her face.

"Where'd he go? What happened?"

"Shh," she said. "I've got you. You're safe."

"I couldn't run away. I just couldn't."

She smiled fiercely at him. "You saved us."

"I did?"

"Yes."

With a sigh, Bradley relaxed into his aunt and fell asleep.

He woke with a gasp much later, then recognized his bedroom in the familiar soft blue glow of his night light. He was safe at home in Jacksonville, tucked into his bed as though nothing had happened.

His dad's voice drifted in from outside his door. "This doesn't make sense. Why would a hunter have tried for him? He's too young."

"I don't know," Antleen answered. "But the hunter's gone. He won't bother us anymore."

"You shouldn't have been out there alone," Bradley's mom said.

Antleen snorted. "How could I have known?"

"You should have known," Bradley's mom said. "We all should have known."

There was an extended quiet, and Bradley fell back asleep.

The next time he woke, it was to his mom's voice. Once again, it sounded like she was standing just outside his door.

"He's been asleep for two days," she said. "Do you think . . .?"

"No," his dad interrupted. "He'll be fine. He's strong. Remember what Helene said? He stood and fought. He didn't run."

Two days? Bradley thought. It didn't feel like he'd been asleep for two days.

"He must have been so scared," she said. "Facing that hunter . . ."

"He's going to be fine."

"Will he?" she asked. "How can we know?"

"I know," his dad said. "He's a Nash. He'll be fine."

Bradley stayed quiet. The memory of Max's glassy eyes made his heart beat faster and his hands tremble. *Hunter*, he thought. The word suited the man perfectly. *And he was hunting me*, Bradley thought. He swallowed, eyes darting to his window, half-expecting to see Max's face looking in at him. *He was hunting me!*

"We have to move," his mother said. "If one hunter found us, others can, too."

"We don't know that. Helene said she'd never seen him before," his father said. "It could've just been bad luck."

Never seen him before? Bradley sat up. That wasn't true. Antleen and Max had definitely known each other.

"You can't really think hunters found Bradley by accident," his mother said. "They must have been watching, and followed them on their camping trip."

"Stop it," his father said. "We don't know any of that."

"You know I'm right," she said. "We have to move."

"No, we don't!" his father snapped. "No more hiding. It's not natural! Not for—"

"Mom?" Bradley said. "Dad?"

"Bradley?" His mom stepped into his bedroom, turned on the light, and rushed to his bedside. "Oh, Bradley."

Bradley blinked against the sudden brightness. "Where's Antleen? Is she okay?"

"Your aunt is fine." She leaned over to kiss his forehead, and for a moment, her long black hair fell soft around his face, a comforting curtain that separated the two of them from the world. "I was so worried," she breathed against his cheek.

"It's okay," he said. "I'm okay."

"You're shaking," she said.

"I'm fine."

She straightened. Bradley's dad stood behind her, shorter

than she was, but much wider, a solid block of a man with short sand-colored hair and fierce green eyes.

"Hi, Dad," Bradley said.

His dad reached down and squeezed his shoulder. "You did me proud out there, Bradley. Real proud."

Bradley grinned as his face grew warm. "Thanks."

His mom touched his forehead, her fingers soft against his skin. "You need to sleep," she murmured, "to let your body recover."

"I'm okay," Bradley said. "I mean, I was dizzy before, but I'm not—"

"Hush."

The word was spoken softly, but it echoed in Bradley's ears and settled so deeply into his mind that it cleared away all his memories of everything that had happened at the lake. He fell fast asleep.

2

THREE YEARS LATER

"Hey, shrimp," Chris said, walking up the dirt road to Bradley's trailer. Chris was Bradley's closest friend, the only other kid his age who lived in their trailer park. "I didn't think you were getting back till tonight."

"Got back this morning," Bradley said. "Big storms in Georgia. Mom cut our camping trip short."

"So, you decided to sit here and watch lizards?"

Bradley grinned self-consciously. That's exactly what he'd been doing, sitting on his trailer's front stoop and watching a pair of lizards. It wasn't the most exciting thing, but it was better than homework. "Seemed like a good idea. Want to go out on the raft?"

The two of them had built the raft the previous year. It was tied up in the swamp behind Bradley's trailer. They went out on it whenever they could, sometimes fishing, sometimes just exploring.

"How about we go check out the Williston place instead? Someone moved in while you were gone. I heard he's rich."

"No way," Bradley said, standing. No one rich ever moved into Highwater Acres.

"Way. Come on!" Chris ran down the curving road and quickly disappeared between the trailers.

Bradley sprinted after him, but it was no use. Chris wasn't just the biggest and fastest kid in the sixth grade, he was the fastest in their school. By the time Bradley caught up to him, he was leaning casually against a palm tree on the edge of the only field in Highwater Acres.

Bradley thought the field might once have been a playground, but now it was just a big abandoned lot. The neighborhood kept it mowed short, which had the unfortunate effect of emphasizing the crumpled beer cans that littered its edges.

"Dude," Chris said. "You ever think about, oh, I don't know, exercising?"

"You know," Bradley shot back. "Freakishly big isn't really in this year. You might want to scale it back a notch."

Chris laughed. "Check it out." He pointed across the field at the Williston trailer. Months of standing vacant had filled its lawn with weeds as tall as Bradley's chest. Its roof was patched with moss, and its siding had faded to a sad pale yellow.

"It's the same as always."

"Exactly. The guy moved in just after you left on your trip. He's been here seven days, but nobody has seen him."

"That's weird," Bradley said.

"He keeps the blinds down and hasn't touched the lawn. I heard it's 'cause he can't go out during the day, that the sunlight burns him."

"So now he's not just rich, he's a vampire? Who are you hearing this stuff from?"

Before Chris could answer, an orange moving truck arrived in front of the trailer, and two men in gray uniforms climbed out.

At the sight of strangers, Bradley's stomach lurched. He moved behind the palm tree as casually as he could, trying not to look like he was scared. Chris stayed where he was.

"Just wait till you see his car," Chris said. "The guy is loaded."

"That's crazy," Bradley said, leaning his head against the tree. Being hidden from the men helped. He could almost pretend they weren't there. "Nobody with money would move here."

Highwater Acres was beyond quiet, a collection of run-down trailers surrounded by a state-protected swamp. It didn't even have a paved road. He couldn't imagine anyone moving there on purpose. *Anyone else, that is.* He'd lived there for three years, but still didn't understand why his parents had moved his family there from Jacksonville.

Chris slapped at a mosquito. "I'm just saying there was a '66 Corvette Stingray in the driveway yesterday. You know how much one of those costs?"

Bradley didn't answer. He wouldn't have recognized a Corvette if it ran over him. He moved sideways so he could peek around the tree to watch the movers, shading his eyes against the afternoon sun.

Even from this far away, and safely behind a tree with Chris right next to him, he was still scared. *Stop it,* he told himself. *There's nothing to be afraid of.*

Talking to himself never helped when the fear came, but he always tried it anyway.

"Check it out!" Chris said.

The men were struggling to move a large canvas-draped object out of the truck.

"What is that?" Bradley asked.

"I think it's a piano."

"A piano in a trailer park?" Bradley chuckled. Talking with Chris helped push the fear away. "They must love tornadoes."

"What?"

"Oh, come on. Can you think of anything that would make a trailer more likely to be hit by a tornado?"

"You are so bizarre."

"Bet they take it around back to the French doors," Bradley said.

An old man walked down the trailer's driveway to the truck. Short and slightly stooped, he had a shiny bald head without a hint of hair and wore a light blue long-sleeved shirt buttoned all the way up to his neck. His pants were dark gray with frazzled cuffs. When he reached the movers, he gestured toward the back of the trailer.

"So much for the vampire theory," Bradley said, trying to keep his voice even. *He's just an old man. There's nothing to be afraid of. Chris is here.*

"Yeah." Chris sounded disappointed. "He's not rich either. Check out those clothes."

The old man turned abruptly and looked straight at them.

Bradley ducked back behind the tree, his heart racing.

Nothing terrified him more than having a stranger look at him. Nothing.

"He's coming this way," Chris said. "I think you should talk to him."

"Chris!" Bradley hissed. His mouth had gone dry, and his hands trembled. He felt like he was going to throw up.

"I know, I know. Your condition."

"It's not my fault . . . I can't . . ." Bradley focused on breathing the way his mom had taught him: in through the nose, out through the mouth.

"Just relax," Chris said. "I got this."

Ever since he'd left Jacksonville, Bradley had been terrified of strangers. He had no idea why. Chris called it 'his condition,' like it was some kind of disease.

"Hello, young man." The accent sounded southern, but not like any southern that Bradley had heard before. He shrank back against the tree. *Stop it*, he thought desperately. *Stop being so afraid!*

"Hello," Chris said. "Nice piano."

Still hidden by the tree, Bradley swallowed a laugh. *Leave it to Chris.*

"Well, thank you. I'm mighty partial to it. I'm a piano teacher."

"Cool," Chris said.

Bradley's mom called his moments of panic anxiety attacks. Bradley didn't care what they were called. He just wanted them to stop.

"My name is Mr. Sallson." The man stepped forward to shake hands with Chris. Seeing Bradley pressed against the tree, he extended his hand. "Well, hello there."

Bradley clenched his teeth. *You can do this. He's just an old man. Besides, Chris is right here.* He took a deep breath, wiped his trembling hand on his pant leg, and held it out. The man's grip was strong, but his skin felt oddly chilled and papery.

"Bradley Nash," Bradley mumbled, pulling his hand away.

"Nice to meet you, Bradley Nash."

Bradley shivered. The man wasn't much taller than Chris, but there was something strange about his eyes. They were too shiny, and the pupils didn't seem to focus. *It's like they're made out of glass,* Bradley thought. But that was impossible. *No one has two glass eyes.*

"I'm Christopher Vaega," Chris said.

"Vaega? Is that Hawaiian?"

"Samoan."

Mr. Sallson slapped his neck. "Ow! The bugs sure are a terror." He turned his strange eyes back to Bradley. "Do you live in Highwater Acres? I'm surprised to see you out on your own."

Bradley stared at the grass, too scared to answer. He was turning twelve in a few days, and Chris was almost thirteen. Why wouldn't they be out on their own?

"Our parents don't mind us being out," Chris said. "They know where we are."

Still looking down, Bradley nodded. Chris wasn't lying. His mom always knew exactly when he and Chris were getting into trouble. It was uncanny.

"That's good to know," Mr. Sallson said. "Do you think they'd mind you two helping me set up my piano? It's quite a work of art, and I'm worried about letting the movers do it."

"Um," Chris said, glancing at Bradley. "I'm not sure that's a good idea."

"Yeah," Bradley stammered. "We . . . we should be getting home."

"I understand," Mr. Sallson said. "Mind if I accompany you? I'd love to meet your parents."

"Okay-ay," Chris said, drawing the word out like he thought Mr. Sallson was crazy.

The main road in Highwater Acres formed a wavy loop, with smaller dead-end roads that led to the homes in the middle. Each trailer had its own little lawn, and nobody had a fence. Usually Bradley and Chris cut through backyards to get where they were going. With Mr. Sallson following, they kept to the road.

The buzz of cicadas filled the humid air as they walked. Bradley's cheeks burned red. His anxiety attack had faded, but not the embarrassment of it. He hated being scared, hated feeling so helpless.

As they drew near to Bradley's trailer, his little sister banged open the front door. Anna wore pink princess sunglasses, and her blond hair bounced wildly as she jumped down the steps and ran toward them.

"Dad's looking for you," she said to Bradley. "Better go quick."

"Is this your sister?" Mr. Sallson said to Bradley.

Bradley shrugged. Except for their green eyes, he and Anna didn't look much alike. She was as pale as their mother, but with straight blonde hair instead of black. His skin was swarthier, more like his dad's, and he had curly hair the color of wet sand.

"Nice to meet you," Mr. Sallson said, bending over to hold out his hand to Anna. "I'm your new neighbor."

She backed up a step.

"Don't be scared," he said. "I'm a teacher. You like teachers, don't you?"

"Not really."

Chris laughed.

"I don't believe that," Mr. Sallson said. "You're in kindergarten, right? Spring vacation ends tomorrow. Aren't you excited to go back?"

"The school flooded," Anna said. "I get to play at Mrs. Herns' tomorrow."

Bradley's mom appeared in the doorway of the trailer. "Bradley Nash," she said sternly, walking toward them, "your father has been searching all over for you."

Bradley hunched. "Sorry."

"Told you," Anna whispered.

"Don't be too hard on him," Mr. Sallson said, straightening. "If he's late, it's my fault. I get to chatting sometimes. I'm Aaron Sallson, your new neighbor."

"Nice to meet you." She focused her blue eyes on him. "Now if you'll excuse us . . ."

"Of course. I need to get back, anyway. You know how movers can be. You have to watch them every second." He nodded his head slightly, then turned and strolled away, whistling.

"Are you okay?" Bradley's mom dropped to one knee in front of him and smoothed the sweaty hair off his forehead.

He sighed and hung his head. "It happened again. I couldn't . . . I couldn't even talk."

"It wasn't that bad," Chris said. "I don't think he noticed."

"Yeah," Anna added. "You look fine."

Bradley's mom circled her arm around his shoulders. "Don't worry. You'll get over it. I know you will."

He didn't answer. His mom had been saying the same thing for three years. He still wasn't over it.

"See you later, Chris," she said. "Bradley's dad needs to talk to him."

"Okay. See you, Bradley."

Bradley's mom guided him into the trailer. "Wash your face first, then go see your dad."

"Can I come, too?" Anna asked.

"I don't think so." She scooped Anna up into her arms. "It's almost three o'clock, and you're really sleepy."

"No!" Anna said, wiggling to get free. "I don't want a nap!"

In the bathroom, Bradley scrubbed the sweat tracks off his face. He could hear Anna through the wall, arguing that she didn't need a nap.

"Hush, dear," his mom said.

Anna's voice fell quiet.

Bradley smiled at himself in the mirror. His mom always knew when Anna needed a nap.

He turned off the water and dried his face, then heard the front door of the trailer creak open and bang closed. *That's weird,* he thought. *Where's Mom going?*

The door banged closed one more time. "Dad?" Bradley called. "Mom?"

No one answered.

3

THE BOOK

Putting down the towel, Bradley looked out of the bathroom. The trailer was quiet. He peeked in his sister's room. She sprawled face-down on her bed, asleep.

"Mom? Dad?" he called.

Their trailer wasn't that big. One end held his and Anna's bedrooms, along with the bathroom they shared. The other end held his parents' bedroom and bathroom. The kitchen and den lay in the middle, a single space divided into two rooms by furniture. It only took a glance for him to see that his parents weren't there.

"Mom?" Bradley called again, checking his own bedroom. "Dad?"

It wasn't like them to leave him and his sister alone. He jogged through the kitchen to knock on his parents' bedroom door. No answer. He checked out front. His dad's pickup truck was in the driveway, but there was no sign of either of his parents. Returning inside, he went to the sliding glass door at the back of the trailer. The porch was empty, except for their two faded plastic chairs. Beyond it, the little yard sloped down to the chain link fence that separated Highwater Acres from the swamp.

The fence's gate was just behind their yard. Could his parents have gone out there? It was filled with a network of rivers that his dad sometimes liked to walk along. His mom wasn't such a big fan, but it still seemed worth a check.

He grabbed the handle of the sliding glass door and pulled. The door stuck, as always, but Bradley braced his feet and forced it open, then stepped onto the porch and slid the door closed.

"Dad?" he said, moving forward to the edge of the small slab of concrete that was their porch.

Nothing moved in the tall grasses and saw palmettos beyond the fence. Everything was still and quiet.

"Mom? Are you guys out here?"

There was no answer.

Turning to go back inside, he spotted a book on one of the plastic chairs. It had a bright yellow sticky note on it, with his dad's blocky handwriting: *Bradley, an early birthday present.*

He picked it up. The book's covers were two unevenly cut pieces of wood, painted black and rough to the touch, held together by rusty metal rings. A red leather strap had been wrapped around it to keep it closed, and the covers didn't have any writing on them at all.

Is that where they are? Preparing an early birthday surprise?

Dropping into the plastic chair, he untied the red leather strap and opened the book. The pages inside were thick paper, off-white and stiff. The first page held a painting of a bright yellow dragon flying over a pine forest. Beneath it were four words, written in heavy red brush strokes: *Mastering the Gallu Draig.*

Bradley ran his fingers over the image of the dragon. The paint felt smooth and cold. He turned the page. The next one was blank, except for a single sentence written in the same red paint used for the title: *The most important part of your journey is choosing your direction.*

A splash sounded from the swamp, and Bradley looked up. He couldn't see the river. There was too much greenery in the way. The splash had sounded large, though, bigger than what a turtle or otter might make.

"Dad?" he called, standing.

The air around the chain link fence shimmered, as if with the heat.

It's not that hot out here. Bradley squinted, holding one hand up to shield his eyes.

The shimmering seemed to outline a shape above the fence. It was huge, bigger than a pickup truck.

What's going on?

As he concentrated, moving his focus along the edges of that strange shape, it wavered and gained form and color: a giant gray-green lizard head, covered in scales. The head hovered over the fence, its edges shimmering.

Bradley's mouth went dry, and his hands started to shake.

I'm losing my mind. I'm going crazy.

The shimmering expanded outward, revealing more and more of the creature. The head was unmistakable now, with bony hairless eyebrows that jutted over bright green eyes, and an elongated snout that ended in two flared nostrils. A ridge of mud-colored spikes started just behind the creature's eyebrows and ran down its neck between two dark wings that lay folded against its body.

Bradley's heart pounded and his breath came in quick ragged gasps.

It's not real. It's not real. It's not real.

The creature was so big that the six-foot-high chain link fence didn't even reach up to its belly. Gaze fixed on Bradley, it stepped over the fence, placing one taloned foot carefully on the grass near the concrete porch. The foot was jointed like a bird's, with four toes facing forward and one back. Black claws curved out of the tip of the toes, each one longer than Bradley's leg.

Bradley ran to the sliding glass door and pulled on its handle. The door didn't budge.

"No! Not now. Not now!"

He glanced over his shoulder.

The dragon's lips peeled back, revealing triple rows of long pointed teeth. Its breath puffed out, warm and smelling of old fish. The pupils of its eyes were shaped like a cat's, but dark green.

"Mom," Bradley yelled.

The dragon tilted its head and looked Bradley up and down.

"Help!" Bradley shouted. He pulled the handle of the sliding glass door with both hands. It still didn't move.

The dragon's talons scratched on the concrete porch behind him.

"Mom!" Bradley's voice cracked as he pounded on the glass door. "Mom, Dad!" Pulling at the door handle again, he threw his back into it, straining with all his strength. It still didn't move.

"Dad!" he shouted. "Dad, help! Help!"

No one answered. Nothing moved inside the trailer. The blurry reflection of the dragon in the sliding glass door raised its head and spread two giant leathery bat wings that blocked out the sky.

"Daddy," Bradley screamed. "I need you!"

The dragon lowered its head next to Bradley's ear, so close that its foul-smelling breath tickled his hair. "Yes?" it whispered. "What is it?"

Bradley fainted.

4

FAMILY SECRETS

B radley woke on the couch in the den, his head resting on his mom's lap. The back of his skull throbbed with pain. The wooden dragon book lay on the coffee table. On the other side of the coffee table, his dad's green reclining chair was empty. Bradley heard the front door open and close, and felt his mom shift.

"Aww, Gayle," his dad said from the door. "Don't be mad. We agreed we'd tell him."

Bradley closed his eyes, hoping they hadn't noticed that he was awake, and tried to figure out what had happened on the porch. The memory of that giant scaled head set his heart pounding. *Dragons aren't real,* he thought. *They're not real!*

"I leave you alone for two minutes, *two minutes,*" his mom said. "And you scare the boy half to death. What were you thinking? You know how scared he gets!"

"He's fine. He's tougher than he looks."

"He fainted!"

"Well . . . It was better than how my dad told me."

"Your dad," she said, stroking Bradley's hair, "threw you out the castle window and shouted 'fly, fly' while you fell to the rocks below."

Bradley tried not to wince under his mom's hand. The smell of stale hamburger grease and burned eggs filled his nose, as much a part of his mom's waitress uniform as its mustard color.

"Yeah, well," his dad said. "Dad never was the smartest—"

"You broke a leg, an arm, and cracked two ribs."

"This wasn't so bad, then, was it?"

"William Nash," Bradley's mom said.

Bradley recognized that tone. He coughed and opened his eyes before his dad got in any more trouble. "What happened?"

His mom patted his shoulder and helped him sit up. "All better now?"

The world spun when Bradley moved, and the pain in his head temporarily blacked out his vision. Reaching to the back of his head, he felt a large lump under his fingers. "Ow!"

"Hold on there, Sleeping Beauty," his dad said. "Let me get some ice for that. You took quite a fall out there."

"What were you guys talking about?" Bradley asked. "What castle?"

"You heard, huh?" His dad was wearing loose sweatpants and a t-shirt. He pulled an ice cube tray from the freezer and cracked some ice into a paper towel. "That's how my dad told me."

"Told you what?"

"Guess."

"Dear," his mom said. "We have something to tell you, something that's going to be hard to understand."

"Don't baby the boy, Gayle." His dad handed him the paper towel with the ice inside. "You're a dragon, kid. We all are."

Bradley forced a smile. Clearly, this was some weird practical joke. Or maybe he was dreaming. Maybe he was still sitting on the porch.

His dad chuckled. "You should have seen your face!"

"William!" his mom said sharply.

"What?" His dad spread his hands wide. "He's finding out he's a dragon. This should be the best day of his life!"

Cold water seeped through the paper towel in Bradley's hand. *Definitely a dream.* He held the ice to the bump on his head. *Maybe I fell asleep reading the weird book.* His eyes focused on it, sitting innocently on the coffee table.

"Honey," his mom said. "Are you okay?"

"Huh?"

She laid a gentle hand on his shoulder. "It's true, dear. You're a dragon. We all are."

"A dragon?" Bradley felt like his mind was moving at half speed. The words his parents were saying weren't making any sense to him.

"That's right!" his dad said excitedly. He opened the freezer and lifted out an ice cream cake. The top of it was decorated with a black dragon breathing bright red frosting. "Ta-da! I got you a congratulations-on-being-a-dragon cake!"

His mom stood and walked to the kitchen. "That does look good."

"I . . . um, I–" Bradley took a breath. The ceiling fan

spun lopsidedly over his head, its pull chain clacking with each revolution. "Where's Anna?"

"Your dad took her over to Chloe's while you were asleep." His mom pulled some paper plates out of the cupboard and helped his dad divide the cake into three huge pieces and one tiny one. She put the tiny one back in the freezer. "Don't worry. I'm saving a piece for her."

"Come on, kiddo!" His dad handed him a plate of cake and a fork. "Aren't you excited? You're a dragon. Don't you have questions?"

Bradley glanced at his mom, who was leaning against the wall, taking a bite of the ice cream cake. "You're telling me you're a dragon."

"Yep," his dad said.

"A dragon who works as a car mechanic and lives in a trailer." Bradley took the ice off his head and put it on the plate next to his cake.

His dad chuckled. "Don't believe me?"

"Not so much."

"That's going to be awkward," his dad said, still smiling, "what with you becoming one and all."

"Be nice, William," Bradley's mom said.

His dad glanced at her. "Okay," he said. "Let me try it a different way. You've studied animals in school, right?"

"Well, yeah, real animals, not dragons."

"What about frogs or caterpillars? Cicadas?" His dad gestured with his plate. "What about those bugs that look exactly like fireflies but aren't? The ones that eat fireflies? Or the birds that lay their eggs in other birds' nests so that they don't have to raise their own kids?"

"Stop," Bradley said. His head hurt too much for one of his dad's lectures. "We learned all that."

"Okay, then let's talk tadpoles. They look like fish but turn into frogs, right? Well, we start out looking like people, but turn into dragons."

"I don't understand."

"Show him," Bradley's mom said. "I know you want to."

His dad grinned. Putting down his cake, he pulled off his shirt and moved to the center of the den.

"What are you . . .?" The question died on Bradley's lips as his dad's hair pulled back into his scalp and his skin melted into small gray-green scales. *What is happening?* Bradley's stomach clenched, and beads of cold sweat formed on his back. The scales were the exact same color as the dragon that Bradley had seen out back.

His dad's head elongated into the shape of a lizard's. His chest and arms grew massive, swelling with bands of muscle beneath the small scales. Black claws sprouted from the ends of his fingertips, and his baggy sweatpants were suddenly tight. The only part of him that did not appear to change were his feet. They remained in their sneakers.

Bradley leaned back into the couch, speechless. His dad was a monster.

The creature that he had always thought of as his dad crossed his arms and spoke. "I call it my Halloween body. It's hard keeping the size so small, but it's great for putting down uppity nobles." He grinned, revealing rows of needle-sharp teeth. "'Course we don't have many of those these days."

Bradley wasn't really hearing the words. His dad was like something out of a horror movie.

"The best part is how tough it is," the creature said, stepping closer to him.

Bradley sat motionless, too scared to even run away.

"These scales would stop a bullet." His dad paused. "Well, some bullets. I wouldn't want to try them against the really high caliber military stuff."

"Are you okay, Bradley?" his mom asked. "You look kind of pale."

"Um." He swallowed, not able to take his eyes off his dad. "Um."

"It's amazing, isn't it?" she said, turning her eyes back to her husband. "Other dragons just have two shapes: human and dragon. Your dad is the only one I've ever met that can do a third."

Bradley smiled weakly. His dad's head was a smaller version of the dragon head he'd seen on the porch. Even small, it was terrifying. "It's great."

"Thanks." His dad changed back into a human as he walked back to his chair. He put his shirt on and picked up his ice cream cake.

Bradley sat on his hands to stop them from shaking.

"Aw. You're shivering." His mom sat next to him on the couch. "It's okay, dear." She put an arm around his shoulders. "We're still your parents. We're not going to hurt you."

Bradley flinched when her arm touched him. *She's a dragon, too.*

"Don't worry, Gayle. He'll be fine. Besides, it's not like we had any choice. If he's going to hatch, he needs to know this stuff."

"H-hatch?"

"Yes," his dad said, sitting down in his reclining chair. "Baby dragons look just like humans, but we call 'em eggs. Hatching is when they turn into dragons."

"Your power arrived a couple days early," his mom added. "Most dragons don't show it until they're twelve."

Bradley licked his lips. He felt like he was in a dream. If he hadn't just seen his dad turn into a monster, he wouldn't have believed any of it. *But I did just see it*, he thought. "Like a tadpole turning into a frog?" he asked.

"Not exactly," she said.

"But . . . we're all dragons?" Bradley asked. "Anna, too?"

"Pretty cool, right?" his dad said. "Bet you never dreamed you were a dragon!"

Bradley couldn't think of anything to say. He stared at his cake.

"Okay." His mom patted his knee and stood up. "I think you're going to be all right."

"Wait!" Bradley grabbed her hand. He wasn't ready to be alone with his dad, not after seeing his monster body.

She smiled down at him, the same gentle reassuring smile he'd seen all his life. "I know, dear," she said. "It all seems very scary, but it's not. Your parents are dragons." She pulled her hand away from his. "Believe me, you couldn't be any safer than you are with your dad."

"Where are you going?"

"I've got to get to work. I'm sorry. Talk to your father. He'll tell you everything." She gave Bradley's dad a serious look, then left. Bradley listened to their pickup truck sputter to life in the driveway and drive away.

"Mom's a dragon," Bradley said in the quiet that followed. Thinking about it now, she seemed more like a dragon than his dad. She was the more serious of the two, and always seemed to know . . . well, everything. He smiled. "I should have guessed."

"I'll tell her you said that."

An unlikely laugh bubbled up inside Bradley as he pictured his mom's reaction.

"So," his dad said, leaning forward in his chair, "you okay now?"

"I think so," Bradley said. He took a bite of ice cream cake. It tasted sweet and chocolatey, with a layer of strawberry in the ice cream. *I'm turning into a dragon.* The more he thought about it, the more exciting it seemed. Best of all, if he was a dragon, he'd never have to be scared again. *No more panic attacks.*

"Any questions?" his dad asked.

"So many. How do we change shape? Why didn't you tell me sooner? What about—"

"Woah!" His dad held up his hands. "Pick one to start."

Bradley thought for a second. "Can we breathe fire?"

"Ha!" His dad slapped his knee. "Now we're getting somewhere. Not all dragons can, but you're going to be a swamp dragon, just like me, and swamp dragons can breathe fire."

"So . . . how do we do it?"

"Swamp gas. You belch it out, then scrape your back teeth together to make a spark, and boom! Instant ball of fire. Just remember not to inhale. That hurts something fierce."

Belching swamp gas didn't sound so great. "Our teeth spark when they scrape together?"

"If we want them to."

Bradley clicked his teeth together, but nothing happened.

His dad laughed. "You can't do it as a human. You'll need your dragon body to breathe fire, and you won't get that until master your power, your *gallu draig*. It'll let you do just about anything, if you want it badly enough. That's why my dad threw me out the castle window. He figured that would make me want to fly, and that if I was a real dragon, I would."

"But you didn't," Bradley said. He'd never met his grandfather. Neither of his parents ever talked about their parents.

"No. I fell like a rock, almost died when I hit the ground. My dad had it all wrong. Turning into a dragon isn't about willpower."

"What's it about?"

"You need to decide who you are, what's important to you." His dad pointed at the black wooden book. "Read that. It'll help."

"Help with what?"

"Hatching! Haven't you been listening?"

"Yeah, but I don't . . ." Bradley trailed off. He had so many questions, he didn't know where to begin.

"Okay," his dad said. "I'll slow down. The thing that makes dragons different from humans is the *gallu draig*. Dragons have it. People don't. Think of it like an energy that dragons create. Your body has just started making it. We know, because your mom and aunt can see it. To them, it's like a glow."

Bradley examined his hands. He didn't see any glow.

"Don't worry," his dad said. "I can't see it, either. Neither could my dad."

"Why not?"

"I don't know, but it's not important. What is important is that your *gallu draig* is all crazy. It's not under your control. Your body's pumping it out, but your mind doesn't know what to do with it."

"And I won't hatch until I get it under control?"

"Exactly. Hatching isn't easy. It's different for everyone. Some people hatch quickly. Others take a long time. Some never make it. You're going to have to work to turn into a dragon, but once you do . . . that's when the real fun begins. Everything you do will be easier, and you'll be able to switch between dragon and human form."

Bradley examined his hands again. It was hard to imagine them changing into the kind of claws he'd seen on his dad. "Can I tell Chris?"

His dad hesitated. "Let's hold off on that until after you've hatched."

"Why?"

"Right now, with your *gallu draig* the way it is, you're a target for dragon hunters."

"Dragon hunters?" Bradley shook his head. "C'mon, Dad!"

"Just stay quiet for now. You'll have plenty of time to talk after you've hatched."

"What about Anna? I can tell her, right? I mean, she's a dragon, too."

"She's only five years old, just an egg. We won't know if she's a dragon until she gets older, until her body starts creating *gallu draig*."

"What do you mean? You and mom are dragons. That makes Anna and me dragons."

His dad stood and tossed his paper plate into the trash. "Most eggs don't manifest the *gallu draig*. Without that, they can't hatch into dragons: no extra power, no dragon body, nothing. They're just humans. That's why we haven't told you about this before now. Until your *gallu draig* showed up, we didn't know if you even could hatch."

Something about the way his dad said the words "just humans" sent a chill up Bradley's spine.

The doorbell rang, startling him. He jumped up to answer it.

"Bradley," his dad said. "Hold on a moment."

"Yeah?"

"That's probably Chris. You can go out, but remember what I said about keeping this quiet."

"Okay."

Not like Chris would believe it, anyway, Bradley thought, turning back to the door. *I'm not even sure that I do.*

5

INVESTIGATIONS

B radley pulled open the front door. "Hey, Chri—"
He froze mid-sentence. A boy about his age stood
on the front step. Almost as tall as Chris and deeply tanned,
he had dark blue eyes and blonde hair that reached to his
shoulders. He wore blue-flowered board shorts, an overly
large gray T-shirt, and flip flops.

Bradley's hands shook as the anxiety attack took over, just
like it always did when he came face-to-face with a stranger.
His knees felt weak, and he could barely breathe. He gripped
the door with both hands.

"Hey," the boy said. "Are you alright?"

"Kevin!" Bradley's dad said, reaching past Bradley to
shake the boy's hand. "You're early."

"Caught a tailwind."

Bradley's dad snorted. "Your timing's perfect. I just
finished giving your cousin the dragon talk."

"C-Cousin?" Bradley asked.

"You remember my brother Cedrych?" his dad said.

"Kevin's his grandson. He's going to be your bodyguard until you hatch."

"I can't . . ." Bradley swallowed hard. "I can't." *I will not be afraid. I will not!*

"Wasn't my idea, either," Kevin said, "but hey, it'll be fun, right? Your mom even got me signed up at your school. I was supposed to start at the beginning of the school year, but they're letting me come in late."

"I don't want a bodyguard," Bradley said. His panic had started to fade, much more quickly than usual. *Probably because Dad's here*, he thought.

"Then let's just be friends."

Bradley's hands had stopped shaking, and his heart was slowing down. He nodded.

"Good," Kevin said. "You sure you're okay? You don't look so good."

"He's fine," Bradley's dad said. "Why don't you two get to know each other while I go check on Anna?"

"But—" Bradley started.

"Show him around the neighborhood," his dad interrupted, pushing him gently out the door, then following. "If he's going to be your bodyguard, he needs to know his way around." He pulled the door closed and locked it.

"I'll keep him safe, Uncle William," Kevin said.

"Just stay out of trouble," Bradley's dad said, walking down the driveway. "Or if you get into it, make sure you get out again. I'll be with your sister at Chloe's."

"Dad," Bradley said. "I can't. I'm not . . ." He trailed off.

His dad stopped. "You have your phone?"

"Yeah." Bradley had a cell phone that was supposed to be used for emergencies only.

"Call if you need help," his dad said. "You're fine."

"But—"

"Have fun," His dad strode away, ignoring him.

"Huh," Kevin said, once the two of them were alone. "I guess it's just you and me."

Bradley took a deep breath, in through his nose, and out through his mouth. He had recovered from his panic attack much faster than usual. He didn't know if it was because he was hatching or because Kevin was a relative. Either way, he'd take it.

"You sure you're okay?" Kevin asked.

"Yeah." Bradley glanced at the door, then sat down on the stoop, where the trailer shaded him from the Florida sun. "I can't believe he locked us out."

"It's a dragon thing," Kevin said, sitting next to him and stretching out his legs. "Never a good idea to let another dragon into your home."

"That doesn't make sense. He trusts you with me, but not with being inside?"

"Don't sweat it," Kevin said. "If I were him, I'd do the same thing."

Bradley picked up a pebble and tossed it into the street. "I feel like all this is a dream," he said. "Dragons are real?" He shook his head. "And I'm going to be one?"

"I know. It's crazy. You must have a ton of questions."

"Too many. I don't even know where to start."

"Fire away," Kevin said. "I've been a dragon for a few years now. I can probably help."

"A few years?"

"I'm older than I look—seventeen, actually." He flashed a lopsided grin. "Hard to believe, isn't it?"

"Seventeen? No way."

"It's true. Come on," Kevin bumped his shoulder against Bradley's. "You've got to have questions about more than just me."

Bradley flicked a stone off the stoop. High overhead, two vultures drifted lazily across the pale blue sky. "Dad said there were dragon hunters," he said. "That's not a real thing, is it?"

Kevin turned to him, startled.

"What?" Bradley asked.

"It's just . . . Of all the questions you could ask, that's the strangest. How could you not know about hunters? You were almost grabbed by one three years ago."

"I was *what?*"

"I don't know the whole story, but it was the family buzz for months. You and your aunt were out camping and a hunter tried to snatch you."

Bradley's mouth fell open.

"It's true. Aunt Helene fought him off. If she hadn't been there, you'd be toast."

"No way. Not Antleen. She wouldn't fight anyone."

"Maybe not as a human," Kevin said, "but as a dragon?"

Bradley shook his head. "I'd remember something like that."

"Yeah. You'd think so."

"Tell me," Bradley said. "Tell me everything. Maybe I'll remember."

"I don't know anything more than that."

"What do you mean?"

"That's the whole story," Kevin said. He pitched his voice

to imitate someone Bradley didn't know. "Did you hear about William's boy? They tried to grab him when he was only nine. Can you imagine? Nine?" He shrugged and switched back to his own voice. "That's pretty much where it ends."

"Then tell me about the hunters!" Bradley said, frustrated. "What are they? What do they do? Why do they hunt dragons?"

"Hunters are eggs that manifested the *gallu draig* but never managed to hatch. Eventually, their bodies stopped producing the *gallu draig*, and they lost their chance to be dragons. They reached the point of being able to see and use their power, but then it went away. So, they search for unhatched eggs to siphon."

"What happens to an egg that gets, um, siphoned?"

"The hunter keeps it alive, but unconscious. They say a hunter can get *gallu draig* out of an egg for three or four years." Kevin shrugged. "Then he kills it."

Bradley's breath whooshed out of him. *That almost happened to me.*

"That's why you guys are here, instead of in Jacksonville," Kevin said. "After the attack, your mom took your family into hiding. Your dad didn't like it, but he couldn't argue much. Once the hunters find your eggs, you don't have many choices."

"So that's why we moved! I wish they'd told me."

"It's really weird that you don't remember the attack. Unless—nah."

"What?"

"Your mom's a seriously powerful sky dragon. She could have wiped your memory."

"Wiped my memory?" A hollow fear settled in Bradley's stomach. "She can do that?"

"Probably. Different dragons have different powers, but sky dragons are known for messing with people's minds."

"She wouldn't have," Bradley said. "Would she?"

"I don't know."

"But why?" Bradley asked. "Why erase my memories?"

"Still don't know. Sorry."

Bradley sat in silence, trying to sort out his thoughts. *It's not right*, he thought angrily. *People shouldn't mess with people's minds.*

"Don't be too hard on her," Kevin said. "I'm sure she was just worried about you. I mean, that's why I'm here, to keep you safe from hunters."

Bradley nodded. *Safe from hunters*, he thought, remembering Mr. Sallson's strange eyes. He turned to Kevin. "Could you recognize a dragon hunter?"

"Yeah. Most dragons can see *gallu draig*, and all hunters have it," Kevin said.

"You just said that hunters don't have it."

"They don't have enough to use, but they still have a little. It takes *gallu draig* to see *gallu draig*. A hunter who goes completely dry wouldn't be a hunter anymore."

"Can we go check out the new guy that just moved in?" Bradley stood. "I met him today. He's really creepy."

"Sure." Kevin stood up. "One rule, though. If I say run, you run." His face grew serious. "I can beat a hunter without any problem, but I can't do it at the same time that I'm stopping him from draining your *gallu draig*. If we see a hunter, you run, I fight."

"You expect me to run away?" Bradley asked.

"I *require* it," Kevin said.

Bradley clenched his teeth. "I'm not some little baby! I can fight, too!"

"As a human," Kevin said, "you're right, but as a dragon, you're not even a baby. You're an egg."

"I won't—"

"You don't understand," Kevin interrupted. "With you here, I have to pick between using my *gallu draig* to fight, and using it to keep you from being drained. You choose. Do I keep us alive, or do I keep you from being drained into a coma?"

"I'm—" Bradley stopped himself. He had no way of knowing if Kevin was right or not, and they both knew it. "Fine. If you say run, I run."

"Then lead on," Kevin said with a gesture. "Take me to your creepy stranger."

Bradley led him along the dirt road toward Mr. Sallson's. The late afternoon sun burned bright overhead, and the air hung with the faint odor of rotten eggs that always filled the swamp.

"Is it always this hot?" Kevin asked.

"You get used to it. Summer's tons worse. Wait a sec." He guided Kevin off the road to stand in the bushes next to Mr. Alders' trailer. Peeking around its corner, he pointed across the field toward Mr. Sallson's trailer.

"You've got to be kidding me," Kevin said.

"What?" Bradley craned his neck around. A shiny black limousine with silver trim had pulled up into the driveway. A tall man stepped out of the back. His hair was bright red, and his skin was almost as pale as Mr. Sallson's. He wore a brown leather jacket, way too heavy for the Florida heat.

"Nothing," Kevin said. "Just surprised to see a limo here. Is that the creepy guy? He's got no *gallu draig*. Definitely not a hunter."

"I have no idea who that is," Bradley said. *A limousine in Highwater Acres?* He wished Chris was there to see it.

The door to the trailer opened, and Mr. Sallson stepped out. The two men shook hands and spoke. Bradley saw the shape of a man sitting in the driver's seat, waiting. Mr. Sallson and the red-headed stranger walked down the road, away from where Bradley and Kevin were hiding.

"They're just humans," Kevin said. "No big deal."

"Humans with a limo," Bradley said.

"Yeah. That is weird. I can see the driver from here, though. He's not a hunter either."

"Can I see the *gallu draig*?"

"Most eggs can't, but go ahead and try with me. Do I look any different from anyone else?"

"No," Bradley said. "You look just like any other thirteen-year old."

Kevin grinned, and in the blink of an eye his appearance changed. Instead of a gangly thirteen-year old, Kevin was older and thicker, with scraggly blonde stubble on his jaw line and cords of muscle on his arms. A thin scar ran down the side of his neck, and a black tattoo of a dragon skull showed prominently on his left wrist. Even his eyes were different, less friendly and more squinty. "How about now?"

Bradley jerked back in surprise and bumped into Mr. Alder's trailer.

"You can never trust your senses around a sky dragon," Kevin said, his voice deeper than it had been before.

"Playing with people's minds is kind of our specialty." His appearance faded back to the younger version.

"Wow." Bradley leaned against Mr. Alders' trailer.

"I know what you're thinking," Kevin said, smiling. "Which one is the real me?"

"Actually, I wasn't thinking that."

Kevin laughed. "Your mom is tons better than me. For the most part, I can only affect human minds. She's powerful enough to mess with dragons, or even the fae."

"Fae? That's another word for fairies, right?"

"The fae are where the fairy stories come from. They're made of pure energy," Kevin said. "Really tough. Don't mess with them. They live even longer than dragons."

First dragons, now fairies. Bradley tried to keep his voice sounding casual. "Are there any other mythical creatures out there?"

"If there are, I don't know about them."

On the way back to Bradley's trailer, they spotted Mr. Sallson and the red-headed man walking on the road.

Bradley pulled Kevin behind clump of palmettos so they could watch. Mr. Sallson was gesturing as he talked. The red-headed man listened attentively, occasionally giving a slight nod. Except for the paleness of their skin, the two men couldn't have looked more different. Mr. Sallson was old and slow and slightly stooped. The red-headed stranger was taller, and moved like he owned everything around him.

Bradley wished he was closer, could hear what they were talking about. Something about the red-headed stranger seemed familiar, though he couldn't figure out what it was.

"This has been fun," Kevin said after the men left, "but I

gotta fly. Ton of stuff to do to get ready for school tomorrow."

"You're not staying with us?" Bradley asked.

"Nah. No telling how long you'll take to hatch. You'd get pretty sick of me." He smiled. "Is your dad nearby? I'm pretty sure I'm not supposed to leave you alone."

"This way." Bradley led the way to Chloe's trailer.

As they drew near, Kevin stopped. "I think you're good from here. See you tomorrow morning?"

"Sure," Bradley said, holding out his hand. "Thanks."

Kevin tilted his head and grinned, then vanished right before Bradley's eyes.

"Right," Bradley said to the empty air. "Sky dragons like to play with people's minds. Got it."

I just hope he's wrong about Mom.

6

FRIENDS

Bradley found his dad and Mrs. Herns sitting in rocking chairs in her backyard, watching Anna and Chloe play tag. The two girls looked so much alike they could be twins: straight blonde hair, pale skin, thin faces, and infectious smiles. The only thing that set them apart were their eyes. Anna's were sparkling green, like Bradley's. Chloe's were sky blue.

"What happened to Kevin?" his dad asked.

"He said he had stuff to do for tomorrow."

"Bradley!" Chloe shouted, running to him. She wore green sunglasses, with frames shaped like frog eyes. Reaching out, she slapped his arm as she ran past. "Tag!"

"No fair." Anna skidded to a stop, then backed away. She had her ladybug sunglasses on, red with black spots. "You're too big."

"Too fast, you mean." He lunged and tagged her.

She pointed at Chloe. "I'm gonna get you."

Chloe squealed and ran behind Bradley. "Save me!"

"Save you?" he said, twisting to try to get her out from behind him. "No! Get away! She's just going to–"

Anna tagged him and the two girls danced away. "Bradley's it! Bradley's it!"

Chloe's mom laughed. "They got you."

"They always get me."

Mrs. Herns was tall and slender, with big brown eyes. She smiled. "It happens to the best of us."

"Bradley," Chloe said. "Come on! Let's play."

"He won't play now," Anna said, teasing. "He's too–"

"Tag!" Bradley shouted. His fingertips just brushed her hair as she jumped away.

"Hair counts!" said Chloe, running from Anna.

Bradley moved to stand by the adults. "I'm taking a break."

"Aww," Chloe said. "It's more fun with you."

"I hate to break up the game," Bradley's dad said, standing up, "but we should get going. It's almost dinner time."

"Wait," Chloe shouted. "You can't go yet!" She ran into the trailer.

"What's she doing?" Bradley asked.

"You'll see." Mrs. Herns winked at him. "She's been working on it all week."

Chloe emerged from the trailer, holding something behind her back. She glanced at her mom.

"Go on," Mrs. Herns said. "You spent all that time on it. You might as well show it to him."

Chloe's cheeks flushed pink. "It's a map," she said, holding out a poster board, "so you don't, you know," she bit her bottom lip, "get lost again."

Bradley took the board. Chloe had drawn a picture of Highwater Acres on it, with a thick gray line marking the fence around it. Green trees and rivers of blue glitter crowded around the trailer park, showing the swamp. Glued sand marked the road between the trailers, and a pair of heart-shaped sunglasses indicated her trailer.

"She heard about you and Chris getting lost on your raft a couple weeks ago," Mrs. Herns said. "She wanted to make you a map."

"Next time, you won't get lost," Chloe said. "Just head for the sunglasses."

"Wow!" Anna said, lifting her sunglasses up and peering around Bradley at the map. "Look at the clouds. You even drew clouds!"

Bradley didn't know what to say. Chloe must have spent hours making the poster.

"It's fantastic," Bradley's dad said.

She nodded, her eyes on Bradley.

"I love it," he said. "I really do. I'm going to hang it on my bedroom wall."

Chloe's smile transformed her whole face. "No more getting lost. Promise!"

"I promise," he said. On the walk home, he held it so that none of the glitter or sand would slip off. It was glued on, but even so, some still fell away.

At the trailer, he went to his bedroom and placed it on his dresser, then sat down and stared out the window. It hadn't even been a full day since he'd learned that he was a dragon. So much had happened, he felt like his brain was overstuffed. He wasn't even sure he believed it. He had a hundred questions to ask his parents, but couldn't say anything while his sister was around.

The evening routine of dinner and homework passed in a distracted blur.

As soon as Anna was in bed, he knocked on his parents' bedroom door. He decided not to mention the kidnapping, at least not yet, not before he figured out how he felt about it, and if he believed that his mother really had erased his memory.

His dad opened the door. "What's up, egg?"

"Hey Dad," Bradley said. "I, uh . . . Kevin and I saw this guy in a limo at Mr. Sallson's tonight."

His dad leaned on the doorjamb. "Okay."

"Kevin said they weren't dragon hunters, but . . ."

"Sallson's not a hunter," his mom said, appearing behind his dad. "I checked him twice, once when I met him, then again later, while your dad was giving you the dragon book."

"How can you be sure?"

"All hunters have a little *gallu draig*. They're never totally empty, even when they have too little to use, it's still there. Sallson didn't have any. He's not a hunter."

"And Kevin saw the man in the limo?" Bradley's dad asked.

"Yeah. He said he isn't a hunter, either. He said neither of them are."

"Then we're fine," his mom said. "Kevin's a sky dragon like me. There's no chance we both missed it. They're not hunters."

"But . . . it was a limo," Bradley said. "Here! Isn't that suspicious?"

His dad smiled reassuringly. "Relax, kiddo. All new

dragons feel this way. Your world's changing. Everything's strange and frightening, but trust me, not everything that happens is about you."

"It doesn't make sense," Bradley said. "No one with that kind of money would live here, not unless they had another reason . . . Wait. Do hunters ever work with regular humans?"

"You mean, do hunters hire humans to steal eggs for them?" his mom asked. "I suppose, but it wouldn't make much sense. They can't see the *gallu draig*, wouldn't know an egg from a human. Even if they were given a specific target, they wouldn't be able to spot any dragons that might be nearby."

"But maybe they sent Mr. Sallson here just to look around? To report back what he saw?"

"Stop it," his dad said. "You saw two men today. Did they do anything other than talk?"

"Well . . . they walked around some."

"So, there's no reason to think we've been found." Bradley's dad glanced at his mom as he spoke. "No reason at all. We're fine right here. We can't pack up and move every time someone says hi to Bradley."

We are hiding! Bradley thought. *Kevin was right.* But did that mean he was right about everything? Had Mom really erased his memory?

"Bradley's instincts might be right," she said. "I don't know . . ."

"I do." Bradley's dad turned to him. "You're a new egg who just found out about dragon hunters. It's natural for you to be jumpy."

"But—" Bradley started.

"Not to mention," his dad continued, "your little problem."

Bradley reddened and his mouth snapped shut.

"Dear!" his mom said. "That is not his fault. You know he can't help it."

"What I know," he said, "is that we are not going to pack up and move just because Bradley saw two men talking on the street. We've done enough running. *I've* done enough running. It's not natural."

"I wasn't saying we should move," Bradley said, his temper rising. "Just that they were acting weird."

"You worry about hatching," his dad said. "Let your mom and I worry about the hunters."

"Would you?" Bradley challenged. "If you thought someone was hunting you, would you hide behind your parents?"

"That's enough," his mom said.

"But—" Bradley started.

"This is not a fight you want to have." She took his arm and guided him to his room. "Go to bed, Bradley."

He slammed his door behind him, then flopped onto his bed. His parents were treating him like a baby. *Just like Kevin telling me to run away if we saw a hunter*, he thought. They were all treating him like a baby.

7

NIGHT VISIONS

Bradley tossed and turned on his bed, unable to sleep. Finally, he turned on his flashlight and went to look at the poster Chloe had given him. It was one of the nicest things anyone had ever done for him. He remembered how wide she'd smiled when he said he'd liked it. *I can't wait to tell her I'm a dragon*, he thought, *that she doesn't have to worry about me getting lost ever again.*

"But to do that," he muttered, "you have to hatch."

He picked up the dragon book and stretched out on his bed, opening it to a random page. It had a painting of a dark cave beneath a bright blue sky. Two red dragon eyes peered out of the cave, above gray writing: *The hardest shell to break is the one you cannot see.*

Bradley read it again. "I don't get it. What shell?" He'd been hoping to find a step-by-step guide to hatching, a clear plan he could follow to control his *gallu draig.* Instead, each page seemed to be a different cryptic quote.

He flipped back to the beginning of the book, to the first

page he hadn't read. It showed an open ocean with a long black serpent swimming in it. Above the ocean were the words, *Before you can hatch, you must master your gallu draig.* Turning the page, he found a golden dragon flying through a colorful dawn sky. Text was penciled beneath it: *Before you can master your gallu draig, you must decide on the dragon you wish to be.*

"That's more like it."

Finally, he had a clue he understood. He knew exactly what kind of dragon he wanted to be: big and powerful, just like his dad, the kind of dragon that no one ever messed with.

Except Mom. Did she really erase my memory? It was hard to believe, but then, so was being a dragon.

The next page had a painting of a very serious dragon head staring straight at him. The scales were red and black, and white smoke drifted up from its nostrils. Beneath the painting, black letters had been written in heavy brush strokes. *Do not emulate. Create.*

"Okay." He read the words again, trying to figure out what they meant. Finally, he flicked off his flashlight and rolled over to stare at the dark ceiling. *Why can't they just give it to me in steps?* With instructions like these, it was no wonder some dragons never hatched.

His mind returned to Mr. Sallson and the stranger, walking along the road while their limo sat in the driveway. He flicked the flashlight on and off, watching the light play on the ceiling. *What if I'm right?* What if the two men were working for a dragon hunter? *It doesn't matter,* he thought. *Mom and Dad won't believe me.*

He sat up and swung his legs over the edge of the bed. *I wouldn't believe me, either.* Who would? He was the kid who was scared of strangers, the one who sat in the back of the class so he could hide if a new student came in. *I'm pathetic.*

"Stop it," he whispered to himself. "You're not pathetic. You're just . . . You have a condition."

A condition of being a dragon.

"Maybe that's why I'm scared of strangers!"

He grabbed his phone and called his aunt.

"Bradley?" Antleen answered. "Are you okay?"

Suddenly, Bradley felt tongue-tied. He wanted to ask her about being a dragon, ask if that was why he was scared of strangers, ask if she'd ever been afraid of strangers. Instead, it all seemed too ridiculous to say. He felt embarrassed and silly. "Yeah," he said glumly. "I'm fine."

"Good." There was an extended pause. "Did it happen again?" she asked, at last.

"Yeah, with this old guy in the neighborhood. It doesn't make any sense!" He punched his mattress. "There's nothing scary about him at all. Nothing! He's just an old bald guy, but I could barely even talk to him."

"I'm sorry. I wish I could help."

"Is it true, Antleen?"

"Is what true?" she asked.

"Are we really dragons? Did you really save me from a hunter when I was little? Did Mom really erase my memory?" It all came out in a rush of words, each overlapping the other. When it ended, he heard his aunt take in a long breath.

"Yes," she said. "And no."

That was the last thing he'd expected to hear. "What do you mean?"

"Yes, we are dragons, but no, I didn't save you from a

hunter. To be honest, it was the other way around. You saved us both."

"I did what?"

"The hunter was draining your *gallu draig*, using it against me. I was in human form. I couldn't fight him and stop him from draining you at the same time." She hesitated. "I'm not so good with that. I was doing the best I could, but he was ripping the *gallu draig* out of you, killing you right in front of me." She gave a short grim laugh. "Then you picked up a rock."

"I . . . what?"

"Most beautiful throw I've ever seen," she said. "Smacked him right between the eyes, broke his concentration. That was all the distraction I needed."

Bradley fell back on his bed. *I saved us.*

"I should have been more careful," his aunt continued. "But you were so little. I didn't even know you had any *gallu draig* yet. Somehow, the hunter did, and he was able to pull it out of you. You throwing that rock was one of the bravest things I've ever seen." She paused. "I was really mad when your mom said she erased your memory."

"Wait a minute. You knew she did that?"

"Not until after it was done. Your dad didn't know either. Your mom made the decision on her own. She was worried that what had happened would scar you, that it would leave you afraid, jumping at shadows, not able to sleep at night."

"But I *am* afraid!" Bradley hissed. "Every time I see a stranger, I can barely keep from puking, I'm so afraid!"

"I know. I'm sorry."

"Why didn't you tell me?"

"She's your mom," Antleen said. "And your dad didn't want me to say anything, either. I had to respect that."

Bradley didn't say anything.

"Come on, Bradley," Antleen said. "You know I would have told you if I could."

"Is that why we left Jacksonville?" Bradley asked.

"Your mom thought it wasn't safe, that hunters were tracking you. They left to keep you safe."

"But Mom and Dad are dragons! I saw Dad. No one would mess with him."

"The problem with hunters is that they're sneaky. The ones you see coming are easy to deal with. The others . . . Well, they can be difficult."

Bradley tried to turn his mind away from what his mom had done to him. "That's why they hired Kevin as a bodyguard."

"Yep. For when you're at school."

"Do hunters ever hire regular humans? You know, people without any *gallu draig*? People dragons wouldn't spot as hunters?"

"I suppose they could. Why?"

"I saw these two guys today. One's the old bald guy I told you about. The other was super rich. He had a limo and everything. They were walking around the trailer park."

"I don't know," Antleen said. "I doubt a hunter would walk around a dragon's neighborhood. That's a pretty high risk move, and it doesn't sound like they were trying to stay hidden, not with a limo."

Bradley sighed with relief. She was right. Anyone who knew his dad was a dragon would stay as far out of sight as possible. "That makes sense. Thanks."

"No problem."

After the call, he sat in the darkness. His mom really had erased his memory. Everything about that seemed wrong. *Still*, he thought, *Antleen said she did it to keep me from being scared.* He slammed his hand on the mattress. *What if Mom was right? How much worse would I be if I actually remembered what happened?*

Standing, he paced to the window and pushed the curtains aside to look out. He froze. On the street, clearly visible in the moonlight, stood Mr. Sallson. The man smiled, touched one hand to his forehead, and pointed at him.

Bradley dropped to the floor, breathing hard.

Staying beneath the level of the window, he scrabbled across his floor and into the hallway. His parents were in the den, reading.

"Mom!" he hissed, "Dad! He's out there! Mr. Sallson's out front!"

Dropping her book, his mom jumped off the couch, slid open the porch door, and disappeared into the darkness.

His dad strode to the front door. "Come on."

"Out there?"

His dad already had the door open. "I don't see anyone."

Bradley ran to the door. Highwater Acres had no street lights, but the moon shone bright enough for him to see the empty street. A chorus of crickets and frogs filled the air. He looked up and down the street. Light glowed from the windows of nearby trailers, casting long shadows, but nothing moved.

"Are you sure he was there?" his dad asked.

"Yes." Bradley pointed. "He was standing in the road, looking in my window. He even smiled at me!"

"Sounds more like a bad dream."

"Da-ad!"

"Okay. We'll check it out." He guided Bradley out of the trailer, then closed and locked the door behind him. "Hon," he said. "I'm with Bradley. Let me know when you're back."

"Are you talking to Mom?" Bradley asked. "Where is she?"

His dad winked and pointed up at the night sky. "Good luck spotting her, though."

Oh yeah, Bradley thought as he gazed up at the empty sky. *Mom's a dragon, too.*

"Why don't you take me to where Mr. Sallson was?"

Bradley led him to the center of the street. "Right here. When I looked out my window, he smiled and . . ." He trailed off. With the moon shining, and his bedroom lights off, his window looked like a black mirror. *There's no way that he could have seen me from here.* He spun around, examining the trailers and trees nearest the road. *And if he was here, where'd he go?*

"Sallson's trailer is dark and empty," Bradley's mom whispered.

Bradley jumped and spun. His mom was nowhere to be seen.

"The road is empty, too," she continued. "I'm back in the trailer with Anna."

"Wha–how? Where is–" Bradley sputtered.

"When a dragon doesn't want to be seen, it isn't seen," his dad said. "That's even more true with your mom."

"He was here," Bradley said. "I know he was."

"I doubt he's hiding behind a tree," his dad said. "Are you sure it wasn't just a bad dream?"

"Yes!"

"Bradley," his dad said gently. "There's no one out here. Come on. Let's go back inside."

"The swamp!" Bradley said. "He must have run to the swamp."

"If you say so." His dad gestured. "Lead the way."

Together, they walked around the trailer to their backyard, to a gate in the chain link fence that separated Highwater Acres from the swamp surrounding it. Bradley reached up and lifted the latch.

Beyond the fence, Spanish moss draped the branches of oak, pine, and cedar trees, swaying slightly in a breeze that had the palmettos clacking their leaves together. Frogs peeped and croaked in the darkness, and Bradley's bare feet squelched on the wet ground. He didn't mind. He loved the swamp, and had spent more than a few afternoons floating through it on the raft that he and Chris had built.

He and his dad walked down the slope to the edge of the river. The normally brown water was black in the night, murkily reflecting the trees and bushes on its far bank. Bradley examined the bank, peering up and down the river, and searching the ground for footprints. He didn't find anything.

"I know I saw him," he insisted. "It wasn't a dream."

His dad nodded. "I believe you."

Bradley sighed and listened to the reassuringly familiar sounds of the swamp. *Maybe it was just a bad dream.* "Did you ever have nightmares like this when you were hatching?" he asked.

"Me? Nah. Your aunt did, though. Your mom might have, too. I don't know. It's different for everyone. Ready to go back in?"

"I guess."

They started walking back to the trailer.

"Dad," Bradley said, "where would we be if we weren't hiding?"

His dad stopped. "What do you mean?"

"Well, we're dragons, right? If we weren't hiding, where would we be? Are there like dragon cities, or something?"

His dad smiled. "Actually, there are. My uncle Li lives in one in the mountains. I'll take you for a visit once you've hatched."

"Why aren't we there now?" Bradley asked. "Wouldn't that be safer?"

"You'd think so, wouldn't you? But I grew up in one, and believe me when I say that dragons aren't any more or less trustworthy than humans."

"But there wouldn't be any hunters, right?"

His dad shook his head. "The cities have humans, too, and are a prime target for hunters. Living out here, in the middle of nowhere, anyone with *gallu draig* sticks out like a sore thumb. You're safe out here, Bradley. There's nothing to worry about. Now, let's get you back to bed."

It was a long time before Bradley managed to fall asleep. Try as he might, he couldn't stop thinking about Mr. Sallson. The only way the old man could have been on the street is if he'd been able to hide from both of Bradley's parents.

Impossible, Bradley told himself. *Nobody can hide from two dragons.*

It didn't matter how many times he said it, though. The knot of fear that had settled in his stomach wouldn't go away.

8

SCHOOL

Bradley woke to the sound of someone pounding on his bedroom door. "I'm up. I'm up!" he shouted.

"Time to go," his dad said through the closed door. "Your mom's at work, and your sister's already at Chloe's. Hurry up. Kevin will be here any minute."

Stumbling out of bed, Bradley grabbed a clean pair of jeans and a green t-shirt. His dreams had been filled with red-headed men chasing him through the swamp, while Mr. Sallson watched from the shadows.

"What about me?" he shouted, pulling on his clothes, "and, um, my egg-ness? Is it safe for me to go to school?"

His dad laughed. "You're not getting out of school *that* easily."

Bradley snagged a pair of socks from the drawer and pulled them on, then jammed his feet into his sneakers and hurried out of his room. His dad stood at the front door of the trailer, waiting for him. "But what if someone spots me?" Bradley asked. "Can't hunters tell I'm an egg?"

"Relax. Just stay away from strangers, and you'll be fine. Besides, Kevin will be with you the whole time, and you've got your phone. Call me at work if you need help." He opened the front door and looked outside. "Now, where is that . . . aha! Come here. I want to show you this."

Bradley grabbed his backpack and went to the door. His dad was staring into a bright blue morning sky.

"What are we looking at?" Bradley asked.

"Right there." His dad nodded at the sky. "Look harder."

"The cloud?"

"If a dragon doesn't want to be seen, a human won't see him. Human minds don't have the focus to get past our willpower. All a dragon has to do is *think* that he doesn't want to be seen, and instead of a dragon, humans will see a cloud, or a truck, or even a plane. That's if they even look at all. Most just look away without realizing it." He clapped a hand on Bradley's shoulder. "But you're not a human. You can do this. Look. Force yourself to see the truth."

Bradley examined the cloud. *Not a cloud,* he thought. It did seem to be drifting through the air faster than the others, and now that he focused on it, he saw that its edges were moving up and down. He squinted and clenched his jaw. "See it," he muttered. "See!"

Suddenly, the cloud wasn't a cloud. Instead, it was the strangest dragon Bradley had ever seen, one without any scales or ridges. The creature's blue skin glistened smooth and reflective in the sunlight, and its wings were more like an eagle's than a bat's, complete with over-sized gold and brown feathers. *Feathers? What kind of a dragon has feathers?* "Is that Kevin?"

"Now you've got it," his dad said proudly.

"He's kind of small, isn't he?" Kevin wasn't even half the size his dad had been.

"Ha!" His dad slapped him on the back. "Not many dragons as big as me. You may be, though. Who knows?"

Kevin swooped low over the trailer, giving Bradley a better view. He had a short snout on his lizard head and powerful looking talons on his feet. Bradley saw a leather backpack clutched in one of those talons before the dragon disappeared behind the trailer. A few moments later, Kevin walked around to the front door in human form, wearing knee-length shorts, sandals, and a pair of earbuds connected to a device in the pocket of a red print Hawaiian shirt. The leather backpack was slung over one shoulder. "Hey," he said.

"You're late," Bradley's dad said.

"Sorry."

With only two kids in middle school, Highwater Acres didn't get its own bus stop. Instead, Bradley and Chris used the one outside Winter Creek, about a mile up the street. Usually, they met each other at the front of the neighborhood, but Chris was probably already at the bus stop by now.

"I've been thinking," Bradley said as they left his trailer. "Cedrych is my dad's brother."

"Yeah," Kevin said. "So?"

"And you're his grandson."

"Yeah."

Bradley smiled. "Doesn't that make me your uncle?"

"No."

"I'm pretty sure it does."

"Listen, *cuz*," Kevin said. "If you think I'm going to call you uncle, you're crazy."

Bradley laughed.

"You seen your mom this morning?" Kevin asked.

"She was already out when I got up. Come on. We're really late."

Mr. Sallson was pushing his lawnmower across his lawn as they jogged past. He waved and smiled. Kevin waved back. Bradley just shivered and sped up. *The old guy may not be a hunter, but he still gives me the creeps.*

On the main road, they slowed to a fast walk. "There's one thing I don't get," Bradley said. "Why do dragons turn back into humans? I mean, why not just stay dragons?"

"A few do," Kevin said. "Mostly, though, we all stay hidden. Nobody wants a war with the humans. There are billions of them, and maybe a couple thousand of us. It'd be bad."

"War? Why would there be war?"

Kevin snorted. "Haven't you read any history? If humans discover dragons are real, they'll either try to kill us or capture us."

"Not everyone would," Bradley said. "You make us sound evil."

"Nah." Kevin waved a hand. "It's just good sense. Imagine if the government knew about your dad. He's too dangerous to leave alone."

"Dad?" Bradley thought about his own reaction. Kevin was probably right.

"Besides, can you imagine shopping for groceries as a dragon?" Kevin grinned. "Or buying a house? Everything's easier as a human. Tons better than swooping down on cows."

Bradley couldn't tell if his cousin was joking or not. "So, you mostly stay human, but when do you turn into dragons, you stop people from seeing you?"

"It's not so bad. Actually, I like living with humans. They may be weak-minded, but they're fun to play with."

"Weak-minded?"

"Don't get all defensive. It just is what it is," Kevin said. "If it makes you feel any better, you're pretty weak minded, too."

"Thanks," Bradley said drily. He had a sour taste in his mouth. *Chris is a human*, he thought. *So's Chloe. They're not weak-minded.*

"We're almost at the bus stop. You got any other dragon questions?"

"Yeah," Bradley said. "Do all dragons look down on humans like you do?"

Kevin looked at him out of the corner of his eyes. "Your parents sure don't, if that's what you're asking. Your dad, in particular. Nobody messes with humans when he's around."

"My dad?"

"You would not believe the stories I've heard about him, and every one starts and ends with him saving humans."

"Really?"

"Yeah. Now, go on ahead. I'll catch up. I've got a phone call to make."

When Bradley reached the bus stop, Chris was already there, standing a little distance from the other kids. Neither Bradley or Chris had ever felt like they fit in with the kids at

Liberty Middle School. Sometimes, Bradley wondered if anyone ever felt like they fit in at school.

"Dude," Chris said. "Why so late? You forget about school?"

"Nah," Bradley said. "Dad and I were up late last night, out in the swamp."

"Night fishing? Did you catch anything?"

"No. Just–"

"You were in the swamp?" Andrea interrupted, walking nearer.

Bradley swallowed. If ever he had wanted to have a girlfriend, Andrea would be it, a tall hazel-eyed soccer jock who ate peanut butter and blackberry jelly sandwiches for lunch.

Chris moved a half step away from him, not even trying to hide his grin.

Bradley smiled weakly as he tried to come up with something to say. "Yeah, I was fishing on the raft."

"A raft?" Andrea said. "Aren't you afraid of alligators?"

"Nah," Chris said. "He's more afraid of the snakes."

"Thanks a lot," Bradley growled.

"Hey," Kevin flashed a smile at Andrea as he approached. "I'm Kevin."

She looked at him without answering.

"I'm Bradley's cousin from Chicago," Kevin said. "My folks transferred me to your school. I was supposed to start at the beginning of the year, but I couldn't. We're moving into your neighborhood next month."

"Our neighborhood?" she echoed.

Chris and Bradley glanced at each other, and Bradley felt his ears redden. Andrea lived in Winter Creek, a sprawling golf community filled with well-manicured lawns, carefully painted fences, and kids who carried more money in their pockets than he saw in a year. There was no way Bradley's family could afford a house in Winter Creek.

"I didn't mean it like that," she said quickly, noticing their expressions. "I just . . . Oh, never mind. I'm Andrea."

The bus arrived in a cloud of diesel fumes, and Bradley and Chris headed for the back, where they always sat. Kevin sat next to Andrea, three rows up. He held out an ear bud for her to listen and she put it in her ear. Bradley put his forehead on the back of the seat in front of him so he didn't have to watch them.

"Your cousin?" Chris whispered.

"Yeah," Bradley said, without lifting his head. "I've never even heard of him before, and now I have to show him around."

Chris chuckled. "Your life stinks."

During school, Bradley fell back into his normal classroom routine, hurrying into classes early so he could sit in the back. That way, if he had a panic attack, no one would notice.

Kevin was in all his classes. *Mom must have set that up*, Bradley thought. The teachers knew about Bradley's condition, had seen his anxiety attacks. He even had a weekly check-in with the school counselor. If his mom told them his cousin's presence would help prevent his anxiety attacks, he was sure they'd cooperate.

During morning math, Bradley ignored the teacher and wrote down quotes he remembered from the dragon book. Then he made a list of features describing exactly the dragon he wanted to be: brave, powerful, flying, fire-breathing, and strong. He ran out of ideas after strong, and abandoned the list in favor of trying to see his own *gallu draig*.

"I'd forgotten how boring middle school was," Kevin whispered. "How do you get through this?"

"Shh!" Bradley said. "You'll get us in trouble."

Kevin rolled his eyes.

During Language Arts, Bradley went back to his list and tried to add some less obvious traits: kind, courageous, smart, not afraid of strangers, immune to anxiety attacks. He underlined the last two items three times.

Kevin spotted the list and chuckled. "You'll get there, cuz," he whispered. "Don't worry."

On the way to lunch, Kevin grabbed Bradley's arm and held him back until the crowd had passed. "Are you always this . . . alone?" he asked in a whisper.

"Well," Bradley said. "Chris isn't in any of my classes, and I don't really know anyone else."

"But you've lived here three years. You must know somebody."

"I do, but we're not what you'd call friends."

"I've seen you talk to people, and they all know your name."

"I know, but . . . Look. It's not easy for me, okay?"

"Okay, okay," Kevin said, holding up his hands. "I'm just trying to help."

Bradley sighed. "Sorry." He glanced around. The hallway had emptied, and the classroom doors were all closed. "None of that matters right now. I'm trying to figure out how to hatch, but I have no idea how to even begin."

"Hatching's easy. Just try stuff you can't do."

"What do you mean?"

"Every dragon uses the *gallu draig* in a different way. Each of us has some special talent, something impossible that we can do. Want to hatch? Try stuff that's impossible. When you find something you can do, you'll hatch."

Bradley considered. It made sense, in a weird sort of way. "That sounds kind of easy."

"It is. I hatched in four days. Piece of cake."

"Four days," Bradley echoed. "Think I can do it that quick?"

"Who knows?" Kevin asked. "Probably depends on how much you want it."

"I want it pretty bad," Bradley said.

"Good. Let's go get lunch. Andrea asked me to sit with her." Kevin bobbed his head and grinned out of the corner of his mouth. "She's really cute."

"I know," Bradley said sourly as he walked away.

At the cafeteria, he found Chris at their usual table. He tossed his bag lunch on the table. "You would not believe who Kevin likes."

"Andrea."

"Andrea!" Bradley said, dropping into a chair. "Can you believe this?"

"Your life stinks, dude. Haven't you noticed that before?"

"Gee. Thanks."

"What's up with your cousin, anyway?" Chris asked. "I've never heard of him."

"Me neither," Bradley said, "at least not before yesterday. He's actually my uncle's grandson. Lives in Chicago, but transferred down here."

"Why?"

"Who knows? He doesn't seem too bad, though, except for, you know . . . Andrea."

Bradley's phone buzzed and he pulled it out of his pocket.

Mrs. Herns' voice filled the phone, screechy and intense. "Bradley," she yelled. "Thank God! Where's your dad? I need to speak to him."

"I'm at school, Mrs. Herns. Dad's at work, same as every day. What's going on?"

"No one's answering. Not your mom or your dad or Chris's dad, or anyone." She took a deep breath. "Can you find him for me?"

"Okay, Mrs. Herns, I'll get him, but—"

"Have him call me right away." The phone went dead.

"What's going on?" Chris asked.

"I don't know. That was Mrs. Herns. She wants me to get my dad." He dialed his dad, but there was no answer. He tried his mom next. No answer.

"Are Chloe and Anna okay?"

"Chloe and . . ." Bradley trailed off. He'd forgotten that the girls were with Mrs. Herns. "Oh, no."

He called Mrs. Herns back, but the call went straight to voicemail.

Chris crammed the rest of his sandwich in his mouth. "Let's go."

Along with every other kid at Liberty Middle, Bradley and Chris had long ago mastered the art of escaping the cafeteria. They paused just long enough to not be noticed by any of the cafeteria monitors, then darted outside. Kevin joined them as they reached the street.

"What are you doing here?" Chris asked.

"Gotta stick with my cousin."

Bradley ran down the road. Chris easily caught up, then loped along beside him, his face closed and worried. Kevin followed a few paces back. A car whizzed past, trailing a cloud of dust.

They reached *Nash Automotive* in half the time it usually took. His dad was outside, working underneath a red two-door coupe with the music blaring. Behind him, an open garage held two more cars.

Panting, Bradley turned off the music.

His dad rolled out from under the car. His eyes took in the three boys. "What's wrong?"

"Mrs. Herns," Bradley held out his phone. "She wants to talk."

His dad grabbed the phone and dialed. "Susan, it's William."

"I hope they're okay," Chris said to Bradley.

"Who?" Kevin asked.

"Chloe and Anna," Bradley said, watching his dad.

"No," his dad said into the phone. "Of course not. I'll be right there. Don't worry, Susan. Don't worry. I'm on my way." He covered the mouthpiece and tossed a ring of keys to Bradley. "Lock up. We're leaving."

Bradley caught the keys and started to run to the garage door.

"Kevin," his dad said. "I've got Bradley. You get back to Highwater Acres right away. Look for a little lost girl: pale skin, blonde hair, blue eyes."

At the words, Bradley stumbled, then stopped, looking at his dad.

"Yes sir," Kevin said. He turned, took six running steps

toward the road, then leaped into the air. His body quadrupled in size, ripping out of his clothes and turning blue as it grew giant gold-feathered wings. Those wings flapped powerfully, driving him into the sky. His torn clothes fluttered to the ground.

"Where'd he go?" Chris asked, wide eyes focused on where Kevin had jumped into the sky. "He . . . he just vanished!"

"Bradley!" his dad barked.

"Sorry." Bradley ran to the open garage doors.

"But where's Kevin?" Chris asked, still staring.

"I know, Susan," his dad said into the phone. "I'm on my way. Don't worry. We'll find her. You called the police, right? Good. I'm on my way. Wait! Can I talk to Anna? Thanks."

Bradley pulled the garage doors closed and locked them, then locked the front door and flipped the "open" sign to "closed."

"Chris," he shouted. "Come on! Get in the truck!"

Chris shook his head. "But . . . but . . . Okay." He ran to join Bradley.

"No, Anna," his dad said into the phone, opening the door to his pickup. "Listen to me. Don't leave Mrs. Herns. Do you understand? Don't leave her. Don't go with anyone else, not the police, not a neighbor, nobody." His voice intensified as he climbed into his pickup and turned on the engine. "You stay with Mrs. Herns."

Chris jumped into the back seat, and Bradley slid in next to his dad. "What is it? What's happened?"

"Chloe's missing." His dad handed him back his phone. "Mrs. Herns thinks someone took her. She said something about a black SUV. Hold on."

The truck sped onto the road as Bradley's stomach lurched. *Someone kidnapped Chloe?*

"Oh no," Chris whispered.

Bradley's phone rang again and he answered.

"What's going on?" his mom asked. "Is Anna okay?"

"Mom?" Bradley said. "How did you—"

"Is Anna okay?" she repeated.

"She's fine. We're—" Bradley braced himself against the door as his dad swung a turn way too tight and bumped over the edge of the road. "We're on our way to Chloe's place right now."

"Stay close to your father. I'll see you at home."

Bradley put his phone back into his pocket. His family only had one car, the truck his dad was driving. How was his mom going to get to Highwater Acres? Was she going to borrow someone's car or . . .? A small thrill went up his back. *She's going to fly.* He shook his head. *Mom's a dragon.*

His dad tapped the brakes, examined an intersection in front of them, then floored the gas pedal. The truck's engine grunted and shook as it sent the pickup racing beneath the red light.

Bradley put his hands on the dashboard. "Mom said she'll meet us there," he shouted.

"Good," his dad answered. "When we get there, stay close. Don't go anywhere I can't see you. Your mom, Kevin, and I will do what we can to find Chloe. Don't wander off, and don't trust anyone you don't know. Stay close to me."

"But Dad, I can help!"

His dad pulled the wheel sharply again, flinging Bradley against the door. "No, you can't," he shouted over the engine. "Your mom and I need to have you and Anna safe. That's the only way we can help look for Chloe."

"What about school?" Chris said.

"I'm sure your father won't mind," Bradley's dad answered. "Until we find out what's going on, you're both staying where I know you're safe."

Bradley opened his mouth, then closed it without speaking. *If Chloe's been kidnapped,* he thought, *Kevin and my parents are the best chance she has.* He watched the road out the windshield, willing the truck to go faster. *I'm holding him back,* he realized. If he and Chris weren't there, his dad would already have changed to a dragon and flown home.

Behind him, Chris rode in silence, his knees braced against the seat.

A single police car was parked in Mrs. Herns' driveway when they pulled up. Mrs. Herns stood in front of her door, crying as she spoke to two uniformed police officers. Anna clung with both arms to her leg.

The hollow pit of worry in Bradley's stomach intensified at the sight of the police. Having them there made the whole thing more real.

Chloe really was gone.

9

THE SEARCH

As soon as she saw them, Anna ran to her dad. She was wearing her balloon sunglasses—white plastic, but covered with colorful stickers of balloons.

He caught her in a hug. "Shh. It's okay. I'm here."

"She's gone!" Anna wailed. "She's gone!"

"Shh," he said, patting her back. "We're going to find her. You know we will. Can you stay with your brother while I talk to the police?"

"No!" Anna wailed, wrapping her arms around his neck.

"I should have known better." He adjusted her position and glanced over his shoulder at Bradley. "Stay by the truck. I'll be back in a few."

Mrs. Herns had stopped talking, and stood with her arms tightly crossed. Tear tracks streaked her face, and her back was hunched as if she were cold. As Bradley's dad approached, the two policemen turned to him. He walked around them and stood next to Mrs. Herns, positioning himself so he could see Bradley and Chris. The policemen, wearing the dark green uniforms of the Florida Sheriff's office, each reached out to shake his hand.

"Can I borrow your phone?" Chris asked. "I gotta call my dad."

Bradley handed it over as he watched his dad and Mrs. Herns talk to the police. *Why would someone kidnap Chloe?* It didn't make sense. Her family didn't have money. No one in Highwater Acres had money.

Chris gave him back the phone. "Not answering. He's probably teaching a class."

Bradley pocketed it without looking at it. Across the street, neighbors peeked out of their trailer windows. "Look at them," Bradley said. "Why aren't they out here?"

Chris jumped up to sit on the hood of the truck. "They probably don't know what's going on."

Bradley paced, jittery and anxious. One of the policemen, the younger of the two, was taking notes on a clipboard. The other, an older man with gray hair and a large belly, stood with his thumbs hooked in his belt, talking. What were they talking about? What could be so important that they weren't already out looking for Chloe?

"Whoa, dude," Chris said. "Chill. There's nothing we can do."

"Yes, there is!" Bradley gestured at the neighborhood. "We should go look for her. We know this place better than anyone."

"But we're not going to," Chris said, "because if she was kidnapped, whoever snatched her is still out there."

"So what? You're a freakin' giant, and your dad's been shoving martial arts down your throat since you were four." Chris's dad taught martial arts in a strip mall. Chris took lessons almost every day. He'd become so good that he helped teach the classes.

"First of all, I'm only a 'freaking giant' in middle school. Secondly, if the guy's got a gun, none of that matters. Just relax. Let the police do their thing."

Bradley continued to pace. His heart raced and his skin felt like it was on fire. *Am I hatching?* he thought wildly. *Is this what it feels like?*

"Hey," Chris shouted. "We have to wait for your dad."

Bradley blinked. He'd been so caught up in his thoughts that he hadn't realized he'd walked down the street, away from Chris and the truck. He jogged back. "Sorry."

"Who do you think could have done it?" Chris asked.

"Sallson," Bradley said without hesitation. He remembered the creepy old man standing on the street in the moonlight. "Had to be."

Chris nodded. "Yeah. He's the only one new to the neighborhood, not to mention the whole come-see-my-piano thing he did with us. Still, how could he have caught her? He's like a hundred years old."

"Maybe he tricked her."

"Maybe." Chris didn't sound convinced.

Bradley waved at the police, who were still talking to his dad and Mrs. Herns. "I can't believe they're just talking." He rubbed his forearms. The sensation of burning skin was fading. "We can't wait for them," he said. "We need to go now, before he moves her."

"We're not going anywhere without your dad." Chris leaned forward, resting his elbows on his knees. "If you really think Sallson grabbed her, go tell the cops."

Bradley slumped against the truck. He knew what would

happen if he tried to talk to the police. As soon as he got close, he'd have another anxiety attack. He'd end up looking like a complete idiot. *Like I always do around strangers.*

Chris sighed and slid off the truck. "Come on."

The four adults stopped talking as Bradley and Chris approached. Anna kept her face buried in her dad's shoulder.

Bradley felt a familiar wave of fear as he saw the policemen's eyes focus on him. His mouth dried out and he swallowed reflexively. *No!* He thought furiously, balling his hands into fists to stop them from shaking. *Not now! You will not be afraid. Chloe is too important!*

The policeman with the clipboard looked at Bradley's dad, then back at Bradley. "Take it easy, son. We'll find her."

"We were just talking," Chris said. "Have you guys checked out Mr. Sallson? He moved into the neighborhood last week. He's the only new person here."

"Mrs. Herns already gave us that information and we called it in. Thanks."

"Why are you just standing here?" Bradley blurted out. He couldn't quite make himself meet the policeman's eyes, but he refused to stare at the ground. "Why aren't you out looking for her?"

His dad laid a hand on his shoulder. "Bradley," he said quietly. "We're doing what we can."

"We've already searched the immediate area," the older policeman said. "And called for help. A detective's on his way, and more officers. Once they're here, we'll get search parties organized."

"We need to find Chloe," Bradley insisted, his voice

cracking. He was rocking from foot to foot, too scared to talk, but too angry not to. "We need to start looking now!"

Fresh tears appeared in Mrs. Herns' eyes.

Bradley's dad shifted Anna in his arms, then set her down. "My son's right," he said. "I'm not doing anything useful here."

"Yes, you are," Mrs. Herns said.

"Now hold on," the older policeman said. "This is a police investigation."

"I understand," Bradley's dad said as he walked away. "We'll stay out of your way."

Bradley grabbed Anna's hand and they hurried after him. Chris strode along beside them.

"Mr. Nash," the older policeman called. "Where are you going?"

"To knock on some doors. These are my neighbors. They know me."

"Stay away from Mr. Sallson."

"We will."

Bradley squeezed Anna's hand as they followed his dad. "What happened? Did you see anything?"

"We were playing hide-and-seek. It was my turn to hide, but Chloe never came to find me. I asked Mrs. Herns, but . . ." Anna wiped fresh tears off her face.

"Think she went to the swamp?" Chris asked.

"We can't open the gate."

The two boys nodded. The chain link fence around Highwater Acres was six feet tall, and the gate's latch was on the top bar.

"What about her trailer?" Bradley asked.

"We looked there first," she cried. "We looked

everywhere!"

"Don't worry." Bradley squeezed her hand tighter. "We'll find her."

They started with the nearest neighbors, knocking on doors and explaining that Chloe was missing. Most of the people living in Highwater Acres were retired. As soon as they heard the news, they were eager to help. By the time the police detective arrived, the neighborhood was buzzing with people calling Chloe's name. They looked under every bush and tree, poked sticks into the weeds under trailers, even checked under cars and in the storm drains.

Bradley, Chris, and Anna tried to join in the search, but whenever they started to drift away from Bradley's dad, he called them back. They spent the rest of the day at his side, talking to neighbors, and calling out suggestions.

More police arrived, and more civilians. Chris's dad, Mr. Vaega, showed up. As big as Chris was, his dad was even bigger, with short gray hair and a wide expressive face that showed just how worried he was.

After giving Anna a hug, he shook hands with Bradley's dad. "Sorry I didn't check my messages earlier. Thanks for keeping an eye on Chris."

"He's been a big help," Bradley's dad said. "Always is."

Chris's dad smiled, and he and Chris left to search their home.

By evening, the search had fanned out as far as Winter Creek. A police helicopter flew overhead, and a K-9 unit went from trailer to trailer. As the sun set, the search tapered off. Highwater Acres simply wasn't that big, and the swamp around it was too dangerous to search at night.

Quiet returned to the trailer park. Bradley, Anna, and his

dad found Mrs. Herns sitting shaky and red-eyed on her front step. Anna gave her a hug, and Bradley's dad leaned in close to say some quiet words.

"Thanks." She didn't look at them, just stared hollow-eyed at her lawn.

Bradley's dad straightened. "We'll find her, Susan. You know we will."

She didn't respond. After a few uncomfortable minutes, they left her and headed home.

Bradley's mom greeted them at the door. She gathered Anna into her arms and carried her to bed.

"Oof," Bradley's dad said, lowering himself into his green chair. "What a horrible day."

"Where's Kevin?" Bradley asked, sitting on the couch.

"I sent him home," his mom answered, returning from Anna's room. "We didn't find anything in the swamp."

"We didn't find anything in the trailer park, either," his dad said. "The police even searched the trailers." He glanced at Bradley. "Including Mr. Sallson's."

She nodded. "Susan called Chloe's dad, but he wasn't there. She left a message."

"You think he did it?" Bradley asked.

"No," she answered. "He's in Gainesville with his new family. He didn't take her."

"Susan saw a black SUV with tinted windows last week." his dad said. "It drove slowly through the neighborhood twice without stopping." He went to the refrigerator and took out two bottles of beer and a soda. He handed the soda to Bradley before returning to his chair. "Whoever was driving is a more likely suspect than your Mr. Sallson."

"I still don't trust him," Bradley said. "Even if he's not a hunter, he's still creepy."

"Be that as it may," his mom said, taking one of the beers and sitting on the couch next to Bradley. "It doesn't mean he took Chloe."

"It's a nightmare," his dad said. He took a long drink. "Nothing's worse than losing a child."

She nodded.

"Isn't there anything we can do?" Bradley asked.

She shook her head. "I tried to reach Chloe's mind, but no luck. She's either too far away or unconscious."

Reach Chloe's mind? Bradley thought. *Just how powerful is she?*

"I got nothing," his dad said. "No ideas at all."

Bradley looked back and forth between his parents. "But you're dragons!" he said. "There must be something you can do."

"If you think of anything, tell us," his dad said.

Bradley's heart sank. He'd never heard his dad sound so defeated, and his mom looked to be on the verge of tears.

"But—"

"I'm sorry, Bradley," his mom said. "We've done all we can. It's up to the police to save Chloe now."

"But . . . you're dragons," Bradley repeated, more softly.

"Maybe when you hatch, you'll have some way of finding lost girls," his dad said roughly, "but I don't. Now, go get some sleep. Tomorrow's sure to be a long day."

10

MOM

B radley woke just after midnight. In his nightmares, he'd been trapped inside a tiny metal box. His parents had called for him, but no matter how much he yelled back, they hadn't heard him.

He sat on the edge of his bed in the darkness, his head in his hands.

"Just a dream," he said. "That's all."

In his heart, though, he knew it was more. If he was caught by the hunters, he'd end up just like Chloe, trapped and powerless.

His only hope was to hatch. *Once I'm a dragon, I'll find the black SUV. I won't stop looking until I find Chloe. I don't care how long it takes.*

Picking up his flashlight, he opened the dragon book and read. *Your gallu draig is governed by your willpower.* There was no illustration on the page, just large black letters.

"That's clear enough." He turned the page to find a

painting of a lump of clay, misshapen and gray, along with the words, *As you shape it, it will shape you.*

"What does that mean?" He closed the book and flopped back onto his bed. *Maybe I don't have to worry about it. After all, today is my twelfth birthday.*

His parents had said that most dragons started to hatch when they turned twelve. He closed his eyes, wondering how the change would happen. Would the scales come first, or the wings? Visions of his dad's Halloween body floated in the darkness.

No more being afraid of strangers. He couldn't imagine being afraid of anything once he was a dragon.

"Bradley?" his mom whispered from the other side of the door. "Are you awake?"

"Yeah," Bradley sat up.

She pushed quietly through his door, leading the way with a plate full of leftover fried chicken she had reheated. "Worried about Chloe?"

"Yeah."

"Me, too." She settled on the end of his bed and put the plate between them. The steam coming off the chicken smelled hot and rich and greasy. "But that's not why I'm here." She sighed. "You look so much like your father did at your age."

"I do?" Bradley reached for a piece of chicken. He loved late night snacks.

"When I met your father, he was just a little younger than you are now. I was on the run, traveling with some gypsies across Wales—"

"Gypsies?" Bradley interrupted, licking his fingers. "I thought you were from Chicago."

"We lived there for a while, but no. Your dad was born in Wales in the late 1500s. I was born in Scotland some time before that."

Bradley's mouth dropped open. "But you're only like forty-something!"

"Forty!" She stretched out her hands and studied their backs. "I'd say I look like I'm in my thirties, at the most."

"Mom!" Bradley said, exasperated.

"Oh, relax." She finished a chicken wing and dropped the bone on the plate. "After we reach eighteen or nineteen, our human bodies age very slowly, about one year for every thirty actual years."

Bradley tried to do the math in his head. *One year for thirty,* he thought. If his mom looked forty years old and her aging had slowed when she was nineteen, she was really over six hundred. He shook his head. Dragon or not, there was no way his mom was that old. *That would make her older than the United States!*

She smiled. "Don't believe me?"

"Okay," he challenged. "If you're so old, why don't you talk funny? Where are the 'thee's and 'thou's and 'wherefore's?"

"We're dragons, not idiots. Keeping up with language is easy."

"But in the movies—"

"Do *not* get me started on the movies." She wiped her hands on a paper towel and tossed it in the trash can.

Bradley wasn't sure he believed her, but he also couldn't see a reason she'd make something like that up. He decided to change the subject. "I know I'm supposed to figure out how to hatch on my own, but how does it work? When will my body start to change? Will I get wings first, or scales?"

"For goodness sake, Bradley! You're not a tadpole. You don't grow your body in pieces." She shook her head in dismay. "What did your dad tell you?"

"He said we can click our teeth together and make fire."

"*You* might be able to, maybe, but not me. I'm no swamp dragon."

"That's right. Kevin said you were a sky dragon."

"I am. There are four kinds of dragons: swamp, cave, sea, and sky. Swamp dragons have green eyes and smelly breath, and can breathe fire. Cave dragons have sonar, just like bats, and are usually brown-eyed."

"Sonar?" Bradley asked.

"Sea dragons," his mom continued, "have gills that allow them to stay under water indefinitely, and hazel eyes that change color with their mood. Sky dragons are the best flyers. We can stay in the sky for weeks at a time. We can even sleep on the wing."

"No way."

"It's true. And most of us have blue eyes," his mom said. "Like mine, and your cousin Kevin's. Some don't, though." She touched his cheek. "Who knows? You could be a green-eyed sky dragon."

"Do I get to pick? How do I choose?" He was pretty sure he wanted to be a swamp dragon, but cave dragons sounded cool, too.

"You just worry about you," she said. "The key is to decide what you care most about. Once you have that, stick to it. Stay focused. Then, one day, your body will arrive." She picked up a drumstick and took a bite. "When that happens, you'll discover more power than you know what to do with. Your body will be whatever you need it to be, and you'll do things that you can barely imagine now."

"How did you change?" Bradley asked.

Bradley's mom stilled. "That's a sad story."

"Please?"

She put her piece of chicken back on the plate and wiped her hands together. "I turned into a dragon when my mom and I were running from a mob. They thought my mom was a witch."

"Why didn't she turn into a dragon?"

"She wasn't one. My dragon parents, whoever they were, left me with her when I was an infant. She raised me as her own, and I think of her as my mom."

"Your parents left you?"

Bradley's mom folded her hands in her lap. "That's what most dragons do," she said softly. "We didn't do this with you and Anna, but usually, dragons don't raise their own kids."

"What?"

"You have a baby, leave it with some humans, and keep an eye on it from a distance. Once it reaches thirteen or fourteen without developing any *gallu draig*, you know it'll never hatch, so you move on." She paused. "It's not easy, but that's the way it is."

Bradley felt a cold lump settle in his stomach. "Move on?"

"Most dragon eggs never hatch, Bradley, and an unhatched dragon egg is just a human. What are we going to do with a human? Live with it for fifty years? Try to explain that it's nothing more than an unhatched egg?"

"So . . . the parents just . . ." Bradley trailed off. The idea was horrifying: dragon parents abandoning their kids just because they weren't dragons. *Weren't good enough,* Bradley thought. *That's what she really means.* "What about Anna? What if she never hatches?"

"It's something your dad and I have talked about. We won't just disappear when she comes of age, that's for sure. But how long will we stay in touch? Twenty years? Thirty? I don't know. It'll be hard to leave her, harder even than the others. I just hope she hatches."

"Others?" The word landed in Bradley's mind with a dull thump. "You mean we're not your first kids?"

"No, but you're the first we've raised ourselves. None of our others hatched." She blew out a breath. "It was hard, Bradley. Even though they never knew us, even though they were better off without us, it was still hard walking away from our children. That's why we decided to try raising our own kids this time, hoping that at least one of you would hatch."

Bradley bit into a drumstick. Suddenly, being a dragon didn't seem so exciting.

"We've tried dozens of times over the centuries," she continued. "But never with any success."

"Oh." He wondered what would happen if he didn't hatch. Would he wake up one day to find them gone? *Will she make me forget everything about them?* The thought terrified him. He wanted to ask her, but couldn't form the words.

Silence filled the bedroom. Bradley looked at Chloe's poster hanging on his wall, with its heart-shaped sunglasses over her trailer. He couldn't imagine what he'd do if his parents just vanished.

Finally, he spoke. "Why'd they think she was a witch?"

"Who?"

"Your mom. You said they were chasing you because they thought she was a witch. Why did they think that?"

"She was one." Bradley's mom held up her hand to stop his questions. "Let me finish. After her husband died, my mother didn't have any way to support us, so she pretended to be a witch. We created little charms and potions and fake spells. They didn't do anything, but people paid for them, and as long as we kept a low profile, everyone was happy to have us around. As I grew older, though, the spells started working. Without realizing it, we had been tapping into my *gallu draig.*"

She stopped talking, gazing into space.

"Go on," Bradley said.

"I don't know what happened to my real parents, my dragon parents. They never showed up to explain anything to me."

"So, you had the *gallu draig*, but didn't know, and you were using it by accident?" Bradley asked.

She nodded. "It wasn't long before our magic started causing problems. We moved from village to village, but everywhere ended the same, with us sneaking away. The last time, we didn't leave soon enough. They burned our house down and chased us into the woods. We ran, but they had bows. An arrow hit my mother's leg." She stopped speaking for a moment. "She stumbled. I caught her, sort of, but I was barely strong enough to drag her behind a tree, let alone carry her."

"What did you do?"

"I threw everything I had into a glamour to hide us. That's what we called our spells: glamours. I didn't think it would be strong enough, but I had to try something. As I shouted out the words, I turned into a dragon."

"Did the spell work?" Bradley asked.

His mom picked at a fleck of dirt on her skirt. "Yes. The mob charged right past without seeing us." She stopped, eyes glistening. She wiped their corners with her fingertips. "I'm sorry," she said. "It's strange that it still gets to me after all these centuries." She cleared her throat. "Remember I said your dragon body will come with more power than you ever dreamed of? I wasn't lying. My spell worked." She met Bradley's eyes. "But when my mom saw my dragon body, she was terrified. She never spoke to me again, except to scream at me to get away."

"Jeez, Mom!" Bradley stood up. "That's horrible! I can't even–wait, you were fourteen? I thought dragons hatched at twelve."

"That's one of the dangers of letting someone else raise your kids. Before a dragon hatches, its power is uncontrolled, available for anyone to take. That's what my mother had been doing, though she didn't realize it. Without it, I couldn't hatch."

"But you did hatch."

She nodded. "Yes. Once I realized what I wanted, what I *truly* wanted, I hatched."

"What was that?" he asked. "I mean, what did you want?"

His mother stared levelly at him, and he blushed. He knew that look. It was her how-could-you-be-so-stupid look, and this time he deserved it. A mob had been charging to murder her and her mother. He knew exactly what she had wanted. She'd wanted to disappear. "Kevin and Dad both mentioned the power thing," he said quickly, "about dragon eggs not being in control of their power, and how other people can steal it."

His mom stood and brushed off her skirt. "Good. Then you understand why we're hiding here in this trailer park."

"Yeah, because that hunter tried to grab me." Bradley held his breath, waiting to see how his mom would react to him knowing.

"Kevin told you about that, did he? We're safe now. Only your aunt Helene and uncle Cedrych know we're here," she said. "And now Kevin, of course. But that's it. Even your grandfather and granduncle Li don't know. There aren't any other dragons here, and no dragon hunters either."

Bradley let out his breath, disappointed. His mom didn't seem upset that he knew about the kidnapping, but he didn't know what that meant. *Did she erase my memory, or not?* "Do you think Chloe was taken by a hunter trying to get to me?"

"I don't know what happened to her, but I don't think it has anything to do with us."

"How can you be sure? Maybe they want to blackmail us?"

"For what? The trailer?"

"For . . ." Bradley trailed off. She was right. It wasn't like his parents would trade him or Anna for Chloe. There was no reason for a hunter to kidnap her.

"I know you're worried about Chloe," his mom said, "but you need to relax and focus on hatching. That's what's most important, now."

"Not more important than Chloe!"

"For you, it is," his mom said. "You can't afford to risk missing this chance. You *need* to hatch."

Bradley felt a chill run down his back. What would happen if he didn't hatch? Would they leave him, like they'd left their other children? Would he be left all alone, living in constant fear of strangers, while his *gallu draig* slowly faded away?

His mom walked to the door, carrying the plate of leftover fried chicken. "Get some sleep, Bradley. You're too wound up."

"Come on, Mom! I've got more questions."

"You've also got a long day at school tomorrow."

"Just one more!"

She tilted her head, waiting.

"What does your dragon body look like?"

She laughed. "Whatever I want it to. Controlling perceptions is my particular talent, Bradley. All those years of making glamours taught me well. I can make people, or dragons, see or hear whatever I want. Sight, sound, taste, touch, and smell are all under my control. Over the centuries, my powers have grown. I can't read minds, but if I concentrate hard enough, I can sometimes get surface thoughts. That's what I tried to do today, to find Chloe through her thoughts . . . I can also influence people, cause them to want to do things, but I can't change their thoughts. I don't have enough control to change memories, but I do have more than enough power to erase them."

Bradley's heart sank. *She did erase my memories!*

She met his eyes. "It was for the best."

He clenched his jaw. "It wasn't right."

"Sometimes what's necessary is more important than what's right. Now get some sleep. I've got to go check on Mrs. Herns."

She left, closing the door behind her.

Bradley glared at the door. *It wasn't right.* His memories were his. She had no right to take them away. *No right at all.*

He fell back on his bed. The more he learned about dragons, the more complex and frightening they seemed. *And I'm going to be one.* He rolled over and closed his eyes. *But not like her. I'd rather not be a dragon at all, than be like her.* He punched his pillow. He felt angry and empty at the same time. Had he ever really even known his mom? *I'm going to be a swamp dragon like Dad, strong and straightforward. No illusions. No playing with people's minds.*

11

DREAMS OF THE PAST

I n Bradley's dream, he glided on giant invisible wings through a night sky that sparkled with a thousand stars. Below, a village of mud and wood huts, most with thatched roofs, huddled on the edge of a dark forest. He swept down, talons extended, and slammed into a building. The rock and wood collapsed beneath his weight, and he launched himself back into the sky.

Hot rage filled him, mixed with the deepest sadness he'd ever known. He banked and swooped. The humans were running out of their huts, shouting. Some had bows, but it didn't matter. Even if he hadn't been invisible, their arrows wouldn't have been able to penetrate his scales. Claws extended, he dove down to crush another building.

This is a dream, he thought, horrified at the destruction. *I'm not really doing this. This isn't me.*

He flew low and fast, knocking over chimneys and ripping off roofs with his massive talons.

Stop! he screamed at himself. *Stop! Don't do this!* He didn't stop, though. It was as though he was in someone else's dream, unable to control what was happening. *Or someone else's memory,* he thought. *The medieval village, the forest . . . this is all from Mom's story of when she turned into a dragon.* Cold dread filled him. *This is Mom's memory.* He didn't know how he knew that, but he knew it as certainly as he knew he was dreaming.

Over and over, he raked the village, until not a single building was left standing and all the humans had fled. Then he flew into the woods and landed, silent and invisible in a field of shattered trees. A woman slept on the ground near one of the stumps, a piece of bloody cloth tied around her leg. Next to her, a broken arrow lay on the dirt.

He landed and turned back into a human. Every part of him wanted to reach out, to run to her and wrap her in a hug, but he knew that he couldn't. To her, he was a monster. She would never hug him again.

Crying, he walked away, into the darkness.

12

CRACKING THE SHELL

B radley woke up before his alarm went off. Exhausted by his dreams, he stumbled into the bathroom and splashed cold water on his face.

Today, I'm twelve years old.

He examined himself in the mirror, but nothing looked different. There were no scales or bigger muscles or anything. He checked again in the shower, but he hadn't changed at all. Disappointed, he dressed and went to the kitchen.

His dad was at the kitchen table, reading a book and eating cereal. "Happy birthday, kiddo. You're up early."

Bradley grabbed a bowl and the box of cornflakes out of the cabinet. "Morning."

"What's wrong?"

Bradley didn't meet his dad's eyes. "So many things."

His dad laughed.

Bradley pulled a carton of milk from the refrigerator. "What's so funny?"

"I felt the same way when I was your age. Just be patient. I needed three weeks to find my body. Antleen took two years."

Bradley groaned as he poured milk on his cereal. *Two years?* "Any news about Chloe?"

"No. Your mother and sister are over there now, keeping her mom company."

"I talked to Mom last night," Bradley said. "She told me how she became a dragon." He hesitated. "And then I had this dream." Even thinking about it made him want to cry.

His dad closed his book. "Are you okay?"

"I guess so. I mean, it just . . ." He met his dad's eyes. "I dreamed Mom destroyed a village. Did that happen?"

"Yes. More than one, in fact. She had a dark couple of decades. She blamed humans for what happened to her."

Bradley poked at his cornflakes with his spoon, trying to reconcile the mom he knew with a dragon who destroyed entire towns. "And she erased my memory," he said. "After that dragon hunter tried to kidnap me."

His dad took a deep breath. "I'm sorry, kiddo. Yes, she did that."

"But why?"

"She didn't want you to be scared all the time, imagining hunters in every shadow, seeing death behind every corner."

"Well, that sure didn't work."

His dad barked a bitter laugh. "No. No, it didn't. And believe me, there's not a day that goes by that she doesn't regret it."

"It's not right," Bradley said. "She shouldn't mess with people's minds. Erasing memories isn't right."

"We didn't even know if you would be a dragon," his dad

said. "You were way too young to show any signs of *gallu draig*." He shook his head. "I don't know how the hunter saw it, or how he was able to control it, but your aunt saw him pulling it out of you. You slept for two days after the attack. We didn't know if your body was too damaged to ever start producing *gallu draig* again."

"That still doesn't give her the right to take away my memories!"

"You're right. I feel the same as you." His dad opened his book again. "You need to talk to her. She did what she thought had to be done."

"But . . ."

"I'm sorry, kiddo, but that's all I can give you. The memories are gone. There's no going back."

"Da-ad!"

His dad closed his book and met his gaze. "Give your mom a break, Bradley. Since that attack, she has worried about you every day. Every night, she flies out to search the area for any sign of *gallu draig*. Every new arrival to the neighborhood, every new kid at your school. She examines all of them. While I was showing you my dragon body, she was flying over Sallson as he walked home, examining him."

"And now she got me a bodyguard," Bradley said. *She's not protecting me*, he thought angrily. *She's babying me, not letting me make my own choices.*

"That was your uncle Cedrych's idea. When he heard you were going to hatch, he offered to send Kevin to help. Your mom thought it was a great idea."

"I don't need a bodyguard," Bradley snapped. "I need someone to help me hatch."

"Help you hatch?" his dad laughed. "It doesn't work like that."

"Why not?" Bradley stood up. He hated being laughed at. "Just tell me what to do!"

His dad sobered. "I can't, Bradley. I know it's hard to understand, but if anyone helps you, you won't end up," he hesitated, looking for the right word, "well, you won't end up *you*, if that makes any sense. Believe me. We'd help if we could."

Bradley hunched his shoulders. Dragon hunters wouldn't be a problem once he hatched. *And I'd be able to find Chloe*, he thought. He was sure that he would.

"Read the dragon book," his dad said. "Your granduncle Li wrote it exactly for this situation. It helps the dragons in our family hatch, but in a way that doesn't change them."

"It's not helping me!"

His dad sighed. "Kevin won't be here for another ten minutes. Why don't you go out back and cool off?"

Bradley stormed outside, through the backyard gate, and into the swamp. He was so angry at his parents, he was shaking. He walked to the edge of the water. *They could tell me how to hatch if they wanted to.* He picked up a stone and flung it into the water.

He took a deep breath and let it out, trying to calm down. It didn't help. It never helped. *Stupid Mom with her stupid ideas.*

Kicking off his shoes and socks, he swung up into his favorite climbing tree, a huge old oak that had tipped over and now jutted out over the water. *Fine*, he thought as he walked along the trunk, *if they won't help me hatch, I'll do it Kevin's way.*

He sat cross-legged on the trunk and glared at the brown river water. What was it Kevin had said? *Try stuff that's impossible.* He ground his teeth together, trying to think of something impossible.

An alligator drifted beneath him, only the top of its head and the curve of its back visible in the water. The creature made no more ripples than a floating piece of wood. Bradley watched it. According to his dad, one inch of nose equaled one foot of body length. *I wonder if that includes the tail?*

The alligator floated higher in the water, revealing itself to be at least ten feet long, including the tail.

Bradley sucked in a breath. *Did I do that?*

He concentrated on the creature, willing it to come back, but it sank back into the water and disappeared.

Bradley squinted at the river. He held out his hand, fingers spread wide. *Come to me!*

The sounds of the swamp stretched out around him, buzzes and chirps and the lapping of water. A mosquito bit his neck. He slapped absently at it, but stayed focused on the river.

"Come to me," he muttered.

A second mosquito buzzed in his ear. A third landed on his cheek near his eye. A cloud of gnats swirled around his head. Something big and leggy landed in his hair.

Spider!

He surged to his feet, shaking his head and swatting at his hair, but his foot slipped off the tree. He balanced briefly on one leg, then tumbled into the air.

"No, no, no!"

He splashed face-first into the river. Water, warm and bitter and smelling of rotten eggs, filled his nose and mouth.

He thudded into the muddy bottom. After a frantic moment, he got his feet under him and pushed.

Sputtering and coughing, he looked frantically around for the alligator. The water was only chest high, but too brown for him to see anything in it.

He charged for the shore, grabbed his shoes, and ran home.

His dad opened the sliding glass door for him. "Trouble?"

Too excited to answer, Bradley shoved past him.

"Better get a shower," his dad said. "Kevin'll be here soon."

Bradley washed quickly, then dressed and closed himself in his room with the dragon book.

"Hey, birthday boy," his dad called. "Hurry up!"

"Just a second!" Bradley found his place in the book, and opened it to read the painted script: *It is the unconscious mind that has the greatest power.* Below the script was the back of a dragon's head, making it look as though the dragon were reading the text.

Bradley scratched at his mosquito bites. That didn't make any sense. He didn't have an unconscious need for bugs. He turned the page to find a vibrantly painted thunderstorm. *What you need is always more powerful than what you want.*

The book was driving him crazy. The one time he'd tried to use his powers, he'd called bugs. He didn't need bugs. He wasn't some kind of weird bug dragon. He turned to the next page. It had no illustration, just the words *Decide what you need,* written in red.

He slammed the book closed. What he *needed* was to

hatch. What he didn't need was half-baked life advice from some ancient wooden book.

13

DEDUCTION

At homeroom, Bradley's teacher announced a special two-part assembly before classes started. Part one was titled "How to Avoid Being Kidnapped." Part two was about dealing with stress.

Students were directed to the auditorium, where row after row of old musty chairs were bolted to a floor that sloped down to the stage. Kevin, Bradley, and Chris sat in the back row, nearest to the exit.

"This's going to be fun," Kevin muttered. "Think anyone would see if we snuck out?"

Chris, sitting on the other side of Bradley, nodded toward the teacher standing at the backdoor.

Kevin groaned, then slumped in his chair.

As the school's security officer walked onto the stage, Kevin leaned close to Bradley and whispered, "Step one to stopping a kidnapper: turn into a dragon. Step two: eat the kidnapper."

Bradley snorted.

"Will you shut up!" Chris hissed at Kevin. "You're going to get us in trouble."

"Oh, relax," Kevin whispered back. "It's not like anyone would try to kidnap you." He elbowed Bradley. "At least not without a small army."

"Seriously?" Chris said. "Chloe's been kidnapped and you think I'm worried about myself?"

"Shh!" Bradley said. "Both of you. I'm trying to listen."

Actually, he wasn't listening. He was trying to hatch. While the security officer outlined strategies for avoiding dangerous situations, Bradley concentrated as hard as he could on the next impossible thing he'd decided to try, turning invisible.

Nothing happened.

Just as well, he thought. He wasn't sure invisibility was his thing. Next, he tried to make a fire appear on his palm. When that didn't work, he tried ice. No luck.

Onstage, the security officer finished his speech to polite applause. The principal took the stage, gave a brief speech about the importance of recognizing your feelings, then introduced the school counselor. "I think you've all met Mrs. Whitfreeh. Today, she's going to share some ideas to help us get through this difficult time."

"No way," Kevin whispered. "The school counselor is called wit-free? That's just too easy."

"Hush," Bradley said.

Maybe mind powers, he thought. He focused his gaze on Chris, trying to reach out with his mind to hear what he was thinking.

In contrast to Kevin's slouch, Chris sat upright, hands resting on his knees. His face had settled into what Bradley had come to think of as a meditative expression. It's how Chris looked whenever a teacher was lecturing. Others often misinterpreted the relaxed features and steady gaze, but Bradley had learned that they meant Chris was forcing himself to stay focused.

Chris glanced at him, then shifted in his seat. "Dude, what is wrong with you? Stop staring at me!"

"Sorry," Bradley said, embarrassed.

"What's going on?" Kevin asked.

"I'm trying to help Chloe," Bradley whispered back. "If I can just . . . you know . . . I can go get her."

Kevin laughed. "Good luck with that."

Anger flashed through Bradley. What else was he supposed to do? It wasn't like his parents were doing anything–or Kevin, for that matter.

By the time the assembly ended, Bradley had gone through all the superpowers he could think of. He'd even tried to levitate. Nothing had worked.

As they crowded out of the assembly, they met Andrea waiting in the hall. "How's your sister doing?" she asked Bradley. "She knew Chloe, right?"

"She *knows* Chloe!" Bradley said hotly. "Chloe's not dead!"

"Oh, right. Sorry."

"Don't mind him," Kevin said. "Chloe was playing hide and seek with his sister when she disappeared."

"Oh no!" Andrea put her hand to her mouth. "That's horrible. She must feel so guilty!"

"Guilty?" Chris asked.

"'Cause she was there," Andrea said, "when it happened."

"No, she wasn't," Bradley snapped. "She was hiding." He turned away. "I've got to get to class."

As details of the kidnapping spread around the school, Chris and Bradley became the focus of every conversation. People stared at them as they walked by, and suddenly stopped talking when they walked into rooms.

At lunch, they sat at a table by themselves. Kevin sat with Andrea.

"I hate this," Chris said. "I can't believe Chloe's gone."

Bradley picked at his hamburger. "I know. Me, too."

"You still having your birthday dinner?"

"I think so," Bradley said. It was hard to get excited about his birthday with Chloe missing. "Can you come?"

"Yeah. Dad and I'll be there."

"It'll be weird without Chloe. I hope Mrs. Herns comes."

After lunch, as Bradley was getting his books for afternoon classes, Kevin stopped by. "Andrea was pretty upset. Why'd you blow up like that?"

"I know," Bradley said. "I need to apologize. It's just . . . she was talking like Chloe's dead."

"So what if she was? It's not her fault Chloe was kidnapped."

"I know."

"And even if Chloe is dead," Kevin continued. "Why are you so upset?"

Bradley's mouth dropped open. "What?"

"You've got to stop thinking like a human," Kevin said. "Human's die. It's what they do. You can't get too connected."

"How could you say that? Look at her." He waved at a picture of Chloe someone had posted on the wall. "You know it could have been my sister, right? They were playing together when she was snatched. The creep could just as easily have grabbed her!"

Bradley stopped. He looked at the poster of Chloe again. She looked almost exactly like Anna, especially with the sunglasses on.

"It was a mistake," he whispered.

"What?" Kevin asked.

"A mistake," Bradley repeated. "They wanted Anna, not Chloe."

"Why?"

"Cause she's a—", Bradley dropped his voice, "dragon egg."

"Nah. She's too young. No way to tell if she'll ever develop. Nobody wastes time on those."

"Someone did with me," Bradley said.

"If you're right," Kevin said, shifting his backpack to his other shoulder. "Chloe's a goner. There's no reason for a hunter to keep a human."

"You mean—oh, no!"

"Relax. No hunter would make a mistake like that. Chloe was snatched by a regular human."

Sallson, Bradley thought. Mr. Sallson had seen Anna when he was moving in, but she'd been wearing sunglasses, hiding the only easy way to tell her apart from Chloe. "Are you sure Sallson's not a hunter?" he asked.

"Yeah," Kevin said. "Your mom and I both checked him out. He's human. Come on. We've got to get to class."

"Could he be working for a hunter?"

"I guess." Kevin shrugged as he walked away.

Bradley trailed after his cousin, still thinking. The police had searched Sallson's trailer. Could they have missed Chloe?

The thought gnawed at him all day. He twisted and turned it every way he could imagine, but it made too much sense to go away. The police were focused on the black SUV, but what if they were wrong? What if Sallson was working for a hunter and he'd mixed up Anna and Chloe? What if he hadn't been in the street that night looking for Bradley, but for Anna, and had run away when he realized he was looking in Bradley's window?

The bus ride from school buzzed with gossip and speculation. Chloe had been snatched by a biker. No, she'd been taken by her deadbeat dad who had rented a black SUV. No, she'd gotten lost in the swamp and been eaten by an alligator.

Bradley shared a seat with Chris at the back. Both boys kept their heads down and tried to ignore all the nonsense.

Finally, the bus arrived at Winter Creek, and the group of anxious parents waiting for their kids.

"You nervous?" Chris asked Bradley as the bus drove away.

"Just worried about Chloe."

"Ready to go?" Kevin asked Bradley.

"Where?" Chris asked.

"I'm gonna walk you two home."

Chris snorted in disbelief.

"No," Bradley said quickly. He liked Kevin, but he didn't want him around for what he was planning. "That's all right. We'll be fine."

"Sorry, cuz," Kevin said. "I don't have any choice."

"We'll be fine." Bradley repeated.

Kevin shrugged, but didn't leave Bradley's side.

"What's going on?" Chris asked.

"My parents are worried," Bradley said. "They asked Kevin to keep an eye on me."

"But he's hardly any bigger than you are!"

Kevin grinned. "Yeah, but I'm wiry."

"They just want us to stay together," Bradley said, "a kidnapper's less likely to try for two people."

"Dude," Chris said to Bradley. "Your life stinks."

"Gee, thanks. Can we go home now?"

Chris picked up his backpack. "Sure."

"This way," Bradley said quickly, leading them to the swamp. They walked along the overgrown footpath, stepping over cypress knees and leaping over muddy pools of brown water. After the second bridge, Chris took the lead, followed by Kevin and Bradley.

"Really?" Kevin said, swatting at a mosquito. "The swamp? Why aren't we walking on the nice dry road?"

"It's safer out here," Bradley said. "Nobody knows this place better than Chris and me."

"True," Chris said.

Kevin's foot sank ankle-deep in smelly black muck.

"Careful," Chris said with a cheerful grin over his shoulder. "You don't want to lose your shoe."

Kevin's eyes focused on the larger boy's back, and for a moment, Bradley saw through his cousin's illusion. While the illusionary Kevin still appeared smiling and happy, the real Kevin, the older tattooed Kevin, had his eyes narrowed and his jaw clenched.

Bradley stepped forward and used his backpack to push a

saw palmetto out of the way. "Watch out for these," he said. "They can slice right through your clothes."

Kevin pulled his foot out of the muck. "Thanks."

The three continued through the swamp in silence, until they reached a little wooden bridge that led across a narrow spot in the river that bordered Highwater Acres.

When the trailer park came into view, Bradley stopped. "Okay," he said to Kevin. "We're good."

Kevin tilted his head. "What are you up to?"

"Nothing. I just don't want anyone to see you walking me home. It's embarrassing."

"Can't argue with that," Chris said.

"I guess we're close enough," Kevin said, turning back up the trail. "I'll see you guys tomorrow."

"Thanks," Bradley said.

After he left, Chris faced Bradley. "Okay, let's hear it. Why did we really walk through the swamp? What are you planning?"

Bradley squatted on the edge of the bridge. "The kidnapper," he said. "I think he grabbed the wrong girl."

"What?"

"He meant to grab Anna, not Chloe."

"What are you—" Chris's foot slipped off a rock and splashed into the edge of the river. "Aw, crud. What are you talking about? Kidnapped the wrong girl?"

"I saw Mr. Sallson Sunday night, watching my trailer," Bradley said. "Then, the next day, Chloe is kidnapped? I didn't put them together until today, but Anna and Chloe look exactly alike. I know Sallson is the one who took her. I just know it."

"No, you don't."

"Okay, I don't, but he's the most likely guy. The week he moves in, he meets Anna. The next day, a girl who looks exactly like her is kidnapped." Bradley threw his hands up. "This isn't rocket science!"

"No," Chris said. "It's not. I think they call it 'making things up'."

"I'm telling you, it was him. Didn't you see his eyes? They looked all . . . well, they looked wrong. Mean, somehow."

"Mean eyes. Right. Cause that's what kidnappers have."

"No," Bradley said. "I just . . . Look, I just know, okay? I just know he did it."

"Okay. Let's say you're right. Let's ignore what the police think, pretend we never heard about the black SUV, and go with your theory of a crazy piano teacher. So what? There's nothing we can do about it."

"I just want to talk to Sallson, that's all. I want to ask him some questions."

"Questions like 'why did you kidnap Chloe?' and 'give her back before my giant friend here smashes your head?'"

"No! I want to ask questions like 'why didn't you help search yesterday?' and 'where were you when she disappeared?'"

"I'm sure that'll go over much better. Besides, if you think he's such a bad guy, why the heck would we go talk to him without our parents? Isn't that just a bit insane?"

"Don't tell me you're scared," Bradley said. "The guy's like ninety years old." *Besides*, he thought. *Mom already told me he has no gallu draig.* "I thought I was the one who was scared of strangers."

After a long pause, Chris said, "You still haven't said why we walked through the swamp."

"'Cause if I'm wrong about it being Sallson, whoever kidnapped Chloe could still be out there."

"You," Chris said as he crossed the bridge, "are the only guy on the planet who feels safer in a swamp than on a road."

Bradley felt his ears turn red. "Well," he said defensively. "What I told Kevin was true. Who knows this swamp better than us, right?"

Chris laughed.

As he opened the gate in the fence around Highwater Acres, Bradley asked Chris, "How about it? You gonna go with me to talk to Mr. Sallson?"

"This isn't fair," Chris said. "You're not even going to be able to talk to him. We're going to get there, you're going to go all pale and shaky, and it's all going to be on me."

Bradley flushed with embarrassment. "I'm getting better. Did you see me with the police? I almost talked to them."

Chris sighed. "Okay. But let's do it quick. My dad rearranged his classes. He's going to be picking me up at your place in like half an hour. If I'm late, he'll be really upset."

"Thanks!"

Chris folded his arms. "I'm still not beating anyone up for you. If you want to thump some random old guy, you're on your own."

14

A BAD IDEA

The two boys dropped their backpacks by Bradley's front door and ran to Mr. Sallson's trailer.

They slowed as they approached. The window blinds were closed, and no car sat out front, but the gentle plunking of piano keys drifted on the air.

"That's got to be him," Bradley whispered.

"This is a bad idea," Chris whispered back.

Bradley rang the doorbell and waited, fidgeting.

Please don't let it happen again, he thought. *I've seen Mr. Sallson. There's no reason to be scared. He's just an old man.*

Nobody answered. The piano music didn't falter or pause.

Heart racing, he rang the bell again. *Chris is here*, he told himself. *There's nothing to be afraid of.*

"Dude," Chris whispered from the step behind him. "This is stupid. Let's just go. He's not going to answer."

"He has to," Bradley said. "He has Chloe. I know he

does. Why else would he be ignoring us?" He rang the bell again.

"Cause you're insane," Chris said. "I wouldn't open the door either. Besides, he probably can't hear the doorbell over the piano."

"We can't chicken out," Bradley said. "What if I'm right? What if he's in there right now, playing his piano, with Chloe tied up in the corner?"

"Then we should call the police."

"The police were already here." Bradley balled up a fist and knocked on the door. "Mr. Sallson!" he shouted. "Open up!" He pounded harder.

The door shifted in its frame and drifted open.

Chris groaned. "Oh man, you've done it now."

Bradley hesitated. The doors in Highwater Acres often didn't latch properly. Over time, the swamp's humidity caused door frames to warp, which made the doors stick. You had to pull hard to close them, or else they wouldn't lock. Mr. Sallson was new to the trailer park. He probably wasn't used to closing his door hard enough.

"Mr. Sallson?" Bradley called, peering inside.

No lights were on. Heavy green curtains hid the French doors on the back of the trailer, and a thick oriental rug covered the floor. Two folding chairs sat in the corner of the room. The only other piece of furniture was a black grand piano. Though no one was near it, the piano's keys moved up and down as though it were being played.

"Cool," Chris whispered. "I heard about these. You record a song, and it can play all by itself. You can even download music to it."

"Lights off, piano playing itself. He's not home." Bradley stepped into the trailer.

Chris grabbed his arm. "What are you doing? You can't break in. You'll get arrested."

Bradley took another step. "If we get in quickly and close the door, no one will ever know."

Chris didn't move.

"Come on, Chris. All I want to do is look around, see if there's anything that can help us find Chloe. I know he's involved. I just know it!"

Chris took a deep breath and blew it out. "Okay, but hurry." He closed the front door and moved to the kitchen window to peek through the blinds. "I'll keep an eye out."

In the dimness of the trailer, Bradley studied the piano. Instead of having open space beneath it, this piano's sides extended all the way down to the floor, forming a cabinet beneath the instrument. "Why's it so big?" he whispered.

"Probably holds the computer that plays the music," Chris answered.

"Or," Bradley said, striding over to it, "Chloe's inside." He bent down and yanked open the cabinet doors. A tangled mess of wiring and circuit boards filled the inside of the cabinet.

"So much for that genius idea," Chris said.

Bradley closed the piano cabinet and walked into the kitchen. The only furniture was a small table with a folding chair next to it. He opened the cabinets and pantry, but all he found was a pair of opened potato chip bags.

The master bedroom held a large bed and two bureaus, both of which were empty.

"This is weird," Bradley called out. "No pictures on the walls, and there's hardly any furniture."

"That's not sneaking," Chris hissed back. "That's yelling."

Bradley jogged to the other side of the trailer. One bedroom had two beds, leaving no room for anything else. The third bedroom had been converted into an office. "Hey Chris," Bradley called. "I found his office."

"Just hurry up. I want to get out of here."

Bradley pulled the rolling chair around and sat down at the computer. The machine was in sleep mode, not even powered down. He touched a key and it woke up.

"Hey Chris," he called. "He doesn't have a password!"

"It's in his home," Chris said. "Why would he use a password on a machine in his own home?"

Bradley opened the email program. There were only two emails from the past week, one with the subject "re: information needed" and the other "let's meet for lunch." He clicked the first one.

```
To: Aaron Sallson
Subject: Re: Information Needed
From: Chicago Team
Attachment: Nash_genealogy.doc
Attached is the genealogy you requested. We
have no record of a sister. Please let me
know if there's anything else you need.
```

Holding his breath, Bradley opened the attachment.

It was a text document, filled with names and places. Bradley found his own name halfway down the page: *Bradley*

Nash, Egg, son of William and Gayle. Status: Hatching, Location: Highwater Acres, Florida.

Several of the names had "deceased" written next to them. Others were listed as "human" or "hatched." One sent a shiver of fear down his spine. *Abigail Nash, Egg, son of William and Gayle. Status: In custody, Location: Littleton, New Hampshire.*

He'd never heard of Abigail, but it wasn't hard to figure out that she must be one of the kids his parents had left behind, one of the eggs they thought hadn't hatched. He clicked the button to print, and ran over to catch the pages as they spilled from the printer.

"You're printing something?" Chris called from the other room. "What did you find?"

Outside, tires crunched on the dirt driveway.

"What's that?" Bradley asked.

"A car with two guys!" Chris said. "Hurry!"

Bradley grabbed the last of the pages and ran to the den. Chris was sliding the curtains back from the French doors on the back of the trailer. He pulled opened the doors.

Car doors slammed out front. Bradley flinched.

"Hurry up, shrimp!" Chris hissed.

Clutching the papers, Bradley raced outside. Chris followed, closing the doors behind him. The curtains fell back into place, covering their retreat, and they sprinted back to Bradley's home.

15

OUTCLASSED

The moment Bradley opened the door to his trailer, he knew he was in trouble. His mom stood just inside, looking angry enough to spit nails.

"Oh, uh, hi Mom," Bradley said, glancing over his shoulder. "We were just, um—"

"Get inside this trailer," she snapped.

Heads down, Bradley and Chris stepped inside and closed the door behind them.

"Is this your version of staying out of trouble?" she barked. "Leaving Kevin in the swamp? Trying to confront Mr. Sallson?" She uncrossed her arms and leaned forward. "Breaking into the man's home?"

"Wow," Chris said. "How'd you know all that?"

"Enough!" Bradley's mom shouted.

The word rolled Chris's eyes back in his head. He fell to the ground, unconscious. Bradley staggered against the door, rocked by the power in her voice.

"What do we have to do to get through to you?" his mom

demanded, leaning over him. "Against a dragon, or even a half-competent hunter, you have no chance!"

Bradley stared wide-eyed at Chris's body. "What—"

"No," she interrupted, jabbing his chest with her finger. "You don't talk now. I talk now. Do you understand?"

He nodded numbly, still staring at his best friend lying in a crumpled heap on the carpet.

"To a dragon hunter, this human," his mom nudged Chris with her toe, "is not even strong enough for a full sentence. One word, one thought, is all it takes. If Sallson had been working with a hunter, Chris would be dead right now, and you'd be unconscious. You'd spend the rest of your life in a coma, serving as a battery for some deranged hunter."

"But . . ." Bradley fought back tears. He'd thought he and Chris could at least run away, even if they couldn't fight, but this? This was impossible. "You said he wasn't a hunter, just a human."

"And that makes it okay to break into his house? What would have happened if you were arrested?" Her voice cracked. "How can I keep you safe when you're in prison?"

"But I found something on his computer, a file with all our names." He held out the pages.

She snatched them from his hand and examined them. After a few seconds, her face softened. The muscles in her arms relaxed. "This," she said, looking up to meet his gaze. "This was good work."

The breath Bradley hadn't realized he was holding whooshed out of him.

"You can't worry me like that," his mom said, stepping forward to gather him into a hug. "You just can't."

Bradley stiffened at first, then relaxed into the hug and hugged her back. "I'm sorry. I wanted to help Chloe. I didn't know another—"

"I know." She held him at arm's length. "Your dad says I worry too much, that you're turning into a dragon and can take care of yourself. He says you think I'm smothering you."

"No! I . . . um," Bradley glanced down at Chris, uncomfortable. "How *did* you know where we were?"

She smiled gently. "The day after Chloe is kidnapped, and you didn't think I'd be keeping an eye on you?"

"You were watching me?"

She released him. "Going through the swamp was a good plan. That's probably the safest place for you, especially if you are a swamp dragon."

"Wait a minute," Bradley said. "You could *hear* us?"

"I was right overhead. I've been flying lower since Chloe was kidnapped." She turned back to the papers, her lips pressed together. "This is bad, Bradley, really bad."

"What is it?"

"This is too much information for one person to gather, and it goes back too far. We're not dealing with a single hunter. We're dealing with an organization." She chewed her lip as she read. "I wonder if Sallson could have hidden his power from me. I've never heard of anything like that, but maybe . . ." She inhaled sharply. "Abigail!" Her voice hardened, and her eyes turned dark. "We thought she died in a car accident."

"Mom," Bradley said, uncertain.

She slapped the papers on her leg. "Our whole family's in danger. Your Mr. Sallson may not be a dragon hunter, but he's definitely working for someone who is, someone who is coming after us."

"Did you hear what I told Chris about Chloe? I think Sallson meant to grab Anna." His eyes widened. "Where is Anna? Isn't she with you? What if Sallson tries–"

"She's with your father at the garage." His mom said. "As for Sallson, we'll find out tonight. When your dad comes home, he's going to have a chat with him." She walked to her bedroom, her bare feet slapping the linoleum floor. "I've got to get dressed. Wake up Chris while I'm gone."

"Dressed?" Bradley asked. His mom had on a loose blue sun dress. She wasn't wearing shoes, but she was definitely dressed.

"Dragons don't wear clothes, dear. When I saw you safely out of Mr. Sallson's place, I came here and changed to this body, but I didn't have time to pull on more than this dress." She grinned. "And I generally prefer to wear underwear."

Bradley's face turned bright red and he looked away as fast as he could.

He heard his mom's bedroom door close, but waited until the heat left his face before bending down to shake his friend's shoulder. "Chris," he said. "Chris, wake up!"

"What?" Chris asked. "What happened?"

"You fainted."

Chris shoved him away and stood up. "No way. I don't faint."

"You did this time," Bradley said. "Maybe you were scared of my mom."

"Yeah, right."

Bradley's mom returned from her bedroom, her hair tied up in a bun, white sneakers on her feet, holding a folder. "Are you okay, Chris? That was a nasty fall you took. I'm sorry if I scared you."

"I'm fine, Mrs. Nash. I just tripped is all."

"I trust you've learned your lesson about breaking into people's homes? If you'd fallen like that at Mr. Sallson's, you'd have woken up in the back of a police car."

Chris hung his head. "Yes, ma'am."

"Good. I need to see Mrs. Herns. Come along. We'll call your dad to let him know you're there with us."

"Yes, ma'am."

They followed her out the door and down the street.

"She's going to tell my dad," Chris whispered to Bradley. "I am so dead."

"Not this time," Bradley whispered back. "She's gonna cover for us."

"Why?"

"Because I'm so nice," Bradley's mom said. She turned her head just enough to pin them with one sparkling blue eye. "Right?"

Bradley and Chris exchanged a nervous glance.

"Yes, ma'am," Chris said.

16

THE FAE

B radley spent the rest of the day at the Herns' trailer. Mrs. Herns cried most of the time, and when she wasn't crying, her face held a vacant, lifeless expression. Bradley wanted to scream. Forbidden from leaving the trailer, he didn't even have the dragon book to distract him. All he could do was worry about Chloe.

As the sun was starting to set, he and his mom walked Mrs. Herns to Chris's trailer, then returned home.

"We have leftover chowder," his mom said. "I'm sorry I didn't have time to make chili."

"It's fine." Chili was his traditional birthday dinner, but with Chloe missing, it was hard to be upset about food. He pulled the kettle of fish chowder out of the fridge and put it on the stove. While he cooked, his mom set the table for dinner and cleaned up the den.

Bradley was pushing the ladle through the milky liquid, watching the gray chunks of fish bob and bounce, and wondering what dragons ate, when Mr. Vaega arrived with Chris and Mrs. Herns.

Chris joined Bradley at the stove.

"Have you heard what your dad got you?" Chris whispered to him.

Bradley shook his head.

"Private lessons."

"No way!" Bradley had been begging his dad for martial arts lessons for years. He went to every one of Chris's competitions, had watched him win countless matches. He'd never been able to take classes, though, not with his anxiety attacks. He pointed at Chris. "I'm so gonna kick your butt."

Chris laughed. "Sure you are, shrimp."

"That's birthday shrimp to you." Bradley turned to Chris's dad. "Thanks, Mr. Vaega!"

"Don't thank me," the big Samoan man said. "Your dad bought the lessons."

Tires crunched on the gravel driveway out front, and Bradley's mom jumped to her feet. "Excuse me. It sounds like William's here." Holding a folder of papers in her hand, she hurried out the door.

"Dude," Chris whispered. "Are those the papers you stole?"

Bradley and Chris watched through the kitchen window as Anna and Bradley's father climbed out of the truck.

Bradley's mom hugged Anna, then handed the folder of papers over to his dad. His dad examined the first page, his expression hardening. After a few seconds, he met Bradley's eyes through the kitchen window.

"Are they?" Chris repeated.

"What? Yeah, I think so." Bradley shook himself. "My

mom's been holding onto them." Out front, his mom and dad walked toward the trailer. Anna trailed along behind them. She didn't have any sunglasses on. "I'll tell you about it later."

"But we're gonna get in trouble," Chris said, glancing over his shoulder toward his dad. "If Dad finds out I broke into Sallson's trailer, he'll flip!"

"Don't worry. Mom'll cover for us."

As soon as Bradley's dad opened the front door, Mrs. Herns rose to greet him. "Have you heard anything?"

"No." He touched her shoulder gently. "I'm sorry."

She forced a smile, but couldn't hold it.

Mr. Vaega guided her back to a chair at the table. "That chowder smells good, Bradley. Think it's ready yet?"

"Not quite," Bradley's dad said. "I'm sorry. I have to run one more errand. It's just up the street, shouldn't be long."

Anna tilted her head at him, "Up the street?"

"For Bradley's birthday," Bradley's mom interrupted smoothly. "Why don't you get the cards. We'll play Go Fish while we wait. Your dad'll be back in no time."

Bradley turned back to the chowder so no one would see his face. *Don't any of the others hear how fake my mom sounds? Unless . . .* He stole a glance at her. *Is she making them believe it?*

"Want me to come with you?" Mr. Vaega asked Bradley's dad.

"No thanks. I'll just be a moment."

The idea of his dad facing Mr. Sallson alone suddenly terrified Bradley. He ran to follow, but his mom caught him at the door. "Bradley Nash," she said, "just where do you think you're going?"

"But . . ." Bradley stood in the doorway, unable to

take his eyes from his dad's silhouette as it strode away. The sun had finished setting, and the moon hung overhead, half-full and surrounded by stars. "We can't let him go alone," he whispered. "What if Sallson knows I was on his computer? What if he's waiting for him?"

"What if he is? Your dad can handle it." She pushed the door closed. "You know that."

"What's wrong?" Mr. Vaega asked.

"Nothing," Bradley lied.

"Your dad'll be fine," Mrs. Herns' said. Her hands crossed and uncrossed on the table in front of her. She didn't seem to notice.

Bradley's mom settled in the chair next to her. "Of course, he will. Anna, do you need help?"

"Nope," Anna said, dealing the cards.

Bradley stayed at the kitchen window. With the sun down, it looked like a black mirror. He leaned over the counter to open it. Outside, Highwater Acres sat quiet in the clear moonlit sky, its trailers casting dark shadows in the night. He ground his teeth together. He was certain his dad was walking into an ambush.

A brilliant golden light flashed across the sky.

"What was that?" his mom asked, joining him at the window.

"I don't know." Bradley stared at the sky. Big heavy clouds were appearing out of the darkness, blocking out the stars and the moon. Lightning flickered behind them. "Looks like a storm's rolling in."

"Fae light," she muttered. "But why would a fae be here?"

Bradley remembered Kevin's explanation of the fae, that they were made of energy.

"Is everything okay?" Mr. Vaega called from the table.

"Just fine," Bradley's mom answered. She glanced at Bradley. "You stay here." She handed him the folder, her eyes serious. "Keep this safe."

Bradley's pulse quickened. "Where are you going?"

"Outside," she whispered so quietly he could barely hear her. "Stay near the humans." She nodded toward Chris and Anna, who were showing their cards to each other. Across from them, Mr. Vaega and Mrs. Herns sipped iced tea. "If we fall, hide among them."

"If you fall?" Bradley couldn't believe his ears. "Mom!"

"If the fae are here, it's time to grow up. Playtime's over." She walked to the front door and pulled it open. "Go ahead and start without me," she said in her normal voice to Mr. Vaega. "I'm going to bring William back before the storm really gets going."

"Are you sure?" he said, standing.

"I'll just be a moment." She closed the door behind her.

Bradley dropped the folder on the counter and watched his mom walk down their driveway. When she reached the street, she disappeared.

Lightning flashed, highlighting the thunderclouds.

A deep low rumbling sounded, then a loud sharp crack. More lightning flashed.

This isn't right, he thought. Where was the rain? How had the clouds arrived so suddenly? None of it made sense. *It's an illusion*, he thought. He concentrated on the sky, trying to ignore the clouds.

Pain throbbed behind his eyes as he focused. Sweat

beaded his forehead. His vision blurred and cleared. *See through it*, he thought. *You're a dragon, not a human. You can do this!*

Then, with a sigh that he felt more than heard, the storm faded away. Instead of heavy clouds, he saw a clear night sky dotted with stars and dominated by the moon. A dragon soared overhead. The creature's body was massive, bigger than a school bus, with a neck and tail to match.

That's my dad, Bradley thought. Broad leathery wings extended from the dragon's sides, and a ridge of triangular scales ran down the center of its back to its long spiked tail.

Bradley couldn't stop grinning. He'd never seen anything so magnificent in all his life.

Below the dragon, a golden light the size of a golf ball darted erratically through the air.

That must be the fae. Bradley didn't see why his mom had been worried. The little light didn't stand a chance.

His dad banked and blasted a column of fire toward the fae. It zipped out of the way, moving so fast that Bradley's eyes could barely keep up.

"Wow," Chris said from beside him. "Did you see that lightning? See how it went horizontal and not vertical? That's heat lightning."

"Um," Bradley said. "Okay."

Something heavy banged the roof, and the trailer creaked and swayed.

"What was that?" Chris said.

Anna jumped and ran to Bradley. He swung her up into his arms, and then onto the counter to sit.

At the table, Mr. Vaega and Mrs. Herns stood, their expressions tense. Quiet filled the trailer as everyone waited to see what would happen next. When there weren't any more noises or movement, they sat back down. "Probably just a gust of wind," Mrs. Herns said.

Keeping his arm around Anna, Bradley gazed through the open kitchen window. Up in the sky, an eye-piercing lance of golden light flashed from the fae toward his dad. The light burned straight through his dad's wing. His dad roared and flapped, slashing at the air with his talons.

The fae fired again, sending another beam of light through his dad's shoulder.

Bradley shuddered, suddenly scared.

"You okay?" Chris said. "It's just a storm."

"I know. I . . . I'm just worried about my folks. That's all."

"They'll be fine. We've had worse storms than this. Remember the year before last, when the swamp flooded? This is nothing."

Outside, another beam of light burned through his father's back leg. It hung limp beneath his body. Bradley's arms tightened around his sister. *Dad,* he thought desperately, *get out of there. Fly away.*

A beam flashed through his dad's wing and hit a tree across the street.

Anna squealed and twisted out of Bradley's arms to kneel on the counter and point. "Did you see that? The lightning struck the ground! Right there!"

Heart pounding, Bradley kept his eyes focused on his dad. *I can't just stay here. I can't just stand here and watch Dad be killed!*

Mr. Vaega and Mrs. Herns crowded behind them to peer out the window. "Where?"

"Look at that tree," Chris pointed. "See the hole?"

Bradley ignored the tree. *Mom,* he thought desperately. *Where are you?* He'd never seen his mom's dragon body, but he knew from his dream that she was powerful, and that she could make herself invisible. *Maybe she could make Dad invisible.*

His dad dove and circled, twisting through the sky, snapping at the fae. The fae spiraled around him, shooting from all angles.

Mr. Vaega put his arm around his son's shoulders. "I've never seen lightning do that before."

Bradley wanted to scream. The fae was clearly winning. As far as he could tell, his Dad hadn't hit it even once.

"What's wrong?" Anna asked him.

Bradley didn't answer.

His dad hovered in the sky, pumping his wings. He opened his jaws and spit bursts of fire at the fae. The fae dodged and fired more beams of light, puncturing his dad's wings and torso.

His dad spat more fire, but the tiny light moved faster than he could turn his head.

Bradley held his breath to keep from shouting. His hands gripped the counter's edge.

A beam of golden light struck his dad in the center of his chest. His dad's head jerked back, his wings went limp, and he dropped like a stone.

Bradley gasped.

The fae followed his dad, sending beam after searing beam through the limp dragon body. It slammed into the dirt road with a thud that reverberated through Bradley's feet.

A hush fell over the crowd at the kitchen window. Anna grabbed Bradley's hand.

"What kind of a storm is this?" Chris asked.

"I've never seen anything like it," Mrs. Herns said.

Outside, Bradley's dad lay motionless on the road, glowing in the golden light of the fae that hovered above it.

Tears filled Bradley's eyes. *Dad,* he thought. *It can't be. It can't!*

"Are you okay?" Chris asked him.

Suddenly, a second dragon appeared in the sky above the fae. Folding its wings, it flew straight down, belching out a torrent of fire. The flames engulfed the fae with a roar. There was a brilliant golden flash so bright that Bradley had to shield his eyes, then silence. The dragon spread his wings and landed on the dirt road.

Bradley peered into the darkness.

Both the dragon that had crashed earlier and the fae were gone.

"What was that?" Anna slipped off the counter to stand on the floor, holding tight to Bradley's hand.

"I don't know," he said, wiping his eyes.

"Are you crying?"

"No!"

Even with the moon as bright as it was, the night was too dark for Bradley to make out any details of the dragon. He could only see its silhouette. The shape changed as he watched, shrinking down into a human who stumbled and fell. Another human shape raced out of the darkness to help.

As Bradley watched the two figures, his mom's voice sounded like a whisper in his ear, too quiet for anyone else to hear. "It's over. We won."

"But how?" he whispered back. "I saw Dad . . ."

"As soon as I had a chance, I made your father invisible and created an illusion of him. While the fae fought the illusion, your dad moved invisibly to get into position, then attacked."

"Wow," Bradley said.

"I'll say," Mr. Vaega put a hand on his shoulder. "What a crazy storm."

Outside, Bradley's parents had vanished. *Probably gone to get their clothes*, he thought with a giggle.

Anna and Chris exchanged a look. "What's so funny?" Chris asked.

"Nothing, it's just my parents. That's all."

"What about them?" Mrs. Herns asked from behind him.

"What do you mean? Oh," Bradley pushed away from the counter, remembering that the others hadn't seen anything but a freak storm outside. "Nothing."

"Think it's over?" Anna asked.

"I do," Mr. Vaega said. "That last bit of lightning was the end of it."

The front door banged open, revealing Bradley's parents. His dad's skin was unnaturally gray, his face a tight mask of pain. Half his shirt had been converted into a sling. The other half was tied tightly around his chest. Blood stained most of the fabric, as well as the left leg of his pants. He leaned heavily on Bradley's mom, who wore the same blue sun dress she'd been wearing earlier.

Mr. Vaega ran to help. "My God, William! What happened?"

Anna screamed and ran to her father, but Mrs. Herns caught her in a hug.

"Let go!" Anna shoved at her, squirming to get away.

"Sh," Mrs. Herns said. "Not now. He's too hurt."

While Bradley's mom dialed the phone, Mr. Vaega and Chris helped Bradley's dad to the couch. "Stupid tree fell on me," he said. "What are the odds?"

"A tree?" Bradley repeated dumbly.

His dad flashed him a warning look. "In that freak storm. You know that oak on the corner by the Alders' place? One of its branches cracked and fell, jabbed right into me." He coughed and winced as Anna, who had finally escaped from Mrs. Herns, hugged him. "Shoulder, leg, chest." He forced a smile. "I'm just lucky it didn't hit anything important."

Bradley's mom hung up the phone. "I just let the hospital know we're on our way. Andrew, could you help me get William to the truck?"

"I can get there myself." Bradley's dad gently moved Anna to the side and pushed himself to his feet, then collapsed. Chris and Mr. Vaega caught him before he hit the ground, then carried him to the passenger seat of the truck.

Bradley still hadn't left the kitchen counter. Things were moving too fast for him to follow. First his dad was dead, then he wasn't, and then he was horribly injured.

The hospital? Do they even treat dragons there?

17

THE HOSPITAL

Three minutes later, as Bradley's mom was backing the truck out of the driveway, she glanced over her shoulder. "Hush."

Anna slumped in her seat, unconscious. Sitting next to her, Bradley looked from his sister to the back of his mom's head, horrified. "Why?" he demanded. "Why did you do that?"

"She needs the sleep."

"But—"

"Not now." Her gaze met his in the rearview mirror. "Or you'll be next."

Bradley opened his mouth to yell back at her, but stopped himself. She would do it, he thought. *She'd knock me out.*

His mother sighed. "I'm sorry, Bradley. I didn't mean that. I just have to focus on getting your father to the hospital right now. Also, he and I need to talk—"

"About what?" Bradley interrupted.

"Why the fae attacked." His dad stopped abruptly. "Sorry. It hurts to talk."

The raspy thinness of his dad's voice frightened Bradley. Worse, though, was the wet bubbly noise his dad made when he inhaled.

"This is a big deal," his mom said. "Dragons and fae don't fight. It just doesn't happen."

"Kevin said the fae are made of energy?"

"Yes," his mom said. "They use light primarily, but also electricity. Any energy will do."

"But Dad burned it. If it was just energy, why would fire hurt it?"

"Energy can be disrupted, just like anything else," his dad said. "Hit it, burn it, submerge it . . . the pattern'll break, and the fae will die. The problem is how quick they are." He coughed. "They're crazy fast."

Bradley's mom talked over her shoulder to him. "At night, when the moon or stars are shining, they're at their most dangerous. They can turn even that small amount of light into a deadly weapon."

"Why not during the day?" Bradley asked.

"The sun's too bright," she said. "Its energy burns them out. Before the sun comes out each day, they use the energy from the light they've gathered to create physical bodies for themselves. They stay in those bodies until the sun sets, walking around like regular humans."

"It sounds like Mr. Sallson could be a fae," Bradley said.

"Could be," his mom answered.

"During the day," his dad rasped, "all you have to do is break the fae's body. Once the sunlight gets through the shell, the fae will die."

Bradley shuddered. "That sounds more like a vampire than a fairy."

"They've been called that, too," his mom said, "but they don't drink blood. And before you ask, they don't use *gallu draig*, either."

"But—"

"Stop," his mom said. She looked sideways at her husband. "What did you do to get the fae angry?"

"Nothing!" Bradley's dad shifted in his seat, wincing. "I was walking down the road when the thing attacked." He coughed. "I wasn't even near Sallson's trailer."

"So we don't know," Bradley said. "We don't know if the fae was Mr. Sallson, or with Mr. Sallson, or anything."

"If it was," his mom said, "we're in trouble. Fae working with hunters?" She shuddered.

"Maybe it didn't know Dad was a dragon."

"It had plenty of chances to run away. We have to assume it knew your father and wanted him dead."

"It almost got its wish," his dad said. "I was getting torn apart before you cast that illusion." He shook his head. "I never would have guessed I'd be fighting a fae. Those light beams went right through my scales. I've got to reconfigure, find a way to stop a laser."

"Heal first," his mom said.

"You mean we're really going to the hospital?" Bradley asked.

His dad coughed again. "I'm hurt pretty bad, Bradley."

"But what about being a dragon? Don't you heal when you change shapes?"

"No," his mom said. "Whatever injuries you have in one shape become injuries in the other." She paused. "Actually, it's worse than that. There's no way to tell what'll happen when you change. I've seen dragons with minor torso injuries change shape only to discover that one of their vital organs didn't work anymore."

"What?!" Bradley said.

"I never would have risked changing back into a human, tonight." His dad's voice was getting weaker, the words starting to slur. "But I didn't have a choice. Granduncle Li is the only healer I know, and he's too far away to help."

"You were lucky," Bradley's mom said, her voice thick. "I'm amazed those gut shots didn't kill you."

His dad smiled. "They probably would have, if I was some namby pamby sky dragon."

After a moment of quiet, Bradley's mom spoke. "We're not at the hospital yet, dear."

Bradley's dad's smile grew wider. He closed his eyes.

"Dad," Bradley said. "Dad!"

"Shh," his mom said. "He's sleeping. It's exactly what he needs. Your father heals better than anyone else I know, but only when he's asleep."

"Will he be okay?"

"I hope so. It's a race. If the hospital can keep him alive long enough for his own healing to take over, he'll be fine. If not . . ." Her hands tightened on the steering wheel. "I don't want to think about that."

"He'll be fine, Mom. I'm sure he will. He's Dad."

"I'm sure," she said. "Either way, I have to call a Gathering." She glanced at Bradley's dad. "Not tomorrow night," she muttered. "Maybe the night after. Cedrych and Luanna should be able to get here by then. Li, too, I hope, and Helene. Definitely Helene."

"Why Helene?"

"She's the only one of us who was ever kidnapped by a dragon hunter."

Bradley's eyes widened. "Antleen was kidnapped?"

"It happened when she was thirteen, a few years after your dad and I were married, and before your uncle Cedrych was born. A hunter named Max pretended to be Helene's friend, then kidnapped her. Your grandfather can't see the *gallu draig* any more than your father can, so he had no way of knowing that Max was a hunter. When he discovered they were gone, he chased them down. He saved Helene, but Max got away."

"Wow," Bradley said. "Do you think Max could be one of the hunters that's after me?"

"No. Hunters may be able to use the *gallu draig*, but they're still human. It's been hundreds of years since Max kidnapped Helene. He couldn't still be alive. Even so, of all of us, she has the most experience with dragon hunters."

"What about with fae?"

"Nobody knows the fae. Dragons and fae don't have anything to do with each other."

Bradley slumped back in his seat. *If the fae don't care about dragon eggs, why would one attack Dad?* He looked out the truck window at the lights of the highway speeding by. *Maybe we're overthinking it.* "Mom," he said. "What about money? Could the hunters have paid a fae to attack Dad?"

"Maybe, but the fae don't care about money. They feed off energy. They don't need money or food, or anything, really." She guided the truck down an off ramp and turned into a parking lot. "Here we are."

The hospital was a jumbled complex of concrete

buildings. The tallest stood in the center, a wide five-story tower that looked more like a hotel than a hospital. Other buildings clustered around it like a chaotic pile of giant cinder blocks. Bradley's mom drove through the parking lot to the emergency room entrance, where Kevin waited, talking on his cell phone. He ended his call as soon as he saw them.

"Stay with your sister and Kevin," Bradley's mom said. She hopped out of the truck and ran for the entrance.

"Hey," Kevin said, opening the truck door. "You okay?"

"Yeah," Bradley said. "But Dad's hurt."

His mom emerged from the ER, followed by two hospital workers rolling a stretcher. They moved Bradley's dad onto it and rushed him away. His mom handed the truck keys to Kevin. "Park it and stay with Bradley and Anna in the waiting room. I'll come get them as soon as I can."

"Yes, ma'am."

"Don't leave them. I don't think any more fae are out there," she glanced at the sky, "but I'm not certain."

"Yes, ma'am."

Her expression softened and she touched Kevin on the shoulder. "Thanks."

After she left, Bradley asked Kevin, "You can drive?"

"I'm seventeen, remember? Let's get Anna, and you two can wait here."

Bradley sat on the curb and held Anna while Kevin parked the truck and walked back to join them. Above the parking lot lights, the night sky was clear and dark and dotted with stars. Bradley didn't see any sign of a fae, just the pale half-moon.

"Relax," Kevin said. "There's nothing out there."

"How do you know?"

"If there were two fae, don't you think the other one would have shown up to help in the fight?" He pulled his cell phone from his pocket. "I'm gonna make a quick call before we go in." He pressed a button, held the phone to his ear, then put it back in his pocket. "I can't believe it."

"What?" Bradley asked.

"He's not there. Of all nights, he picks this one to be out. I've been calling ever since I got here, and he hasn't picked up."

"Who?"

"It's not important," Kevin said. He dialed the phone again. "It's Kevin again. Call me as soon as you get this message." He hung up the phone. "Mind if we hang out here for a few minutes? I get terrible reception in there."

Bradley shifted Anna so she was sitting on his other leg. The ER door was just a couple steps away. *If a fae shows up,* he thought, *I should be able to carry her inside quick enough.*

"Any luck with the hatching?" Kevin asked, leaning against the wall.

It took a moment for Bradley to pull his mind away from all that was going on. "No," he said. "You got any more ideas? I've tried all the impossible stuff I can think of."

"Sorry. It just wasn't that tough for me."

Bradley shifted Anna again, glad to have something to think about besides his dad. "How'd you get your body?"

Kevin checked his phone again. "Middle of a fight with my dad."

"You fought with a dragon?"

"My human dad," Kevin said. "The one I'd been left

with as an infant. The guy was a jerk. Always telling me what to do and how to do it. Typical human."

"And?" Bradley prompted.

"The day after I turned twelve, my real dad showed up. He told me that I was a dragon and I didn't have to put up with humans anymore. He said that as soon as I hatched, I could leave with him. Four days later, I was in a fight with my human dad, and boom, suddenly I was a dragon. I went to live with my real dad, but that was a mistake. He just handed me off to Cedrych. I've lived with him ever since."

"What happened to your human parents?"

"Those empty shells got what they deserved." Kevin checked his phone again, then hit the redial button. "Listen," he said into the phone. "This is ridiculous. I've got the package but don't know where to take it. Call me as soon as you get this message."

"Package?" Bradley asked.

"Separate job. I do more than just play bodyguard, you know."

"Oh."

Kevin paced back and forth, alternating between checking his phone and looking at the sky.

"I thought you said you weren't worried about the fae," Bradley said.

"The fae? Why would I–" Kevin stopped pacing. "You're right. I'm nervous, too. Can't be too careful, right?"

Bradley's mom stepped out of the hospital. "Thanks, Kevin," she said. "You can head home now."

"Mom?" Bradley said.

"It's okay," she answered. "The doctors have stabilized him. He should be fine. All he needs is time to sleep."

Kevin checked his phone again. "Unbelievable," he muttered. "Okay," he said, handing her the truck keys. "I hope he gets better soon."

"Later," Bradley said. "Thanks."

"Sure." Kevin walked into the darkness.

"Come on." Bradley's mom lifted Anna into her arms. "Your dad has been moved to the ICU. We can get some sleep in the waiting room."

Bradley followed her deeper into the hospital, up some stairs, and into a small room with chairs and couches. The room had no reception desk or staff, just a no-smoking sign and a coffee machine.

His mom turned off the overhead lights, leaving just a single floor lamp glowing in the corner. She settled herself into a chair, holding Anna close. "Make yourself comfortable," she said, "morning will be here soon enough."

Bradley stretched out on a couch. "Mom, do you think this has anything to do with Chloe's disappearance? I mean, could the fae have been here for her, instead of for me?"

"I don't know." His mom closed her eyes. In the dim light, her skin looked even more pale than usual. "Get some rest, Bradley. I need you to be sharp tomorrow when you're looking after your dad."

Bradley's eyes flew open. "Me?" he asked. "What about you?"

"I need to be with Mrs. Herns."

Bradley sat up. "But–"

His mom opened her eyes and regarded him over the top of Anna's head. "We don't know what's going on, Bradley. Was that fae by itself, or did it have friends? Is it working with Sallson, or is it the one who took Chloe? We just don't know. You said it yourself: what if the fae are just interested in her? You and your dad will be safe enough here."

"You don't know that," Bradley said.

"I know you're scared," she said gently. "So is Mrs. Herns. Her child is missing and she has no idea why. What happens to her if a fae shows up at her trailer? She needs us. She needs me."

"But how can I look after dad? I mean, what if a fae comes here?"

"They won't." She shifted Anna into a more comfortable position. "Remember. During the day, the fae are fragile. They have to use all their power just to protect themselves from the sun."

"Even indoors?"

She smiled at him. "If a fae shows up in his fae form, open the curtain on the window."

"Oh." Bradley felt a little foolish, but still scared. "What about a dragon hunter? They're fine during the day."

"No hunter will come anywhere near you if there's even a chance your dad could wake up."

"Wake up? He's in the ICU!"

"Don't underestimate your father. By tomorrow morning, he'll be able to wake if he needs to. Even from his bed, he's more than a match for any hunter."

"What if you're wrong? What do I do if a hunter or a fae shows up?"

"Call me. I'll be here as fast as I can." She stroked Anna's hair. "Just between you and me, that's pretty fast."

"So, uh," He ran his hand along the edge of the couch, feeling the rough fabric beneath his fingertips. "What does

that make me? Just something to slow the bad guys down? A
. . . a speedbump?"

His mom regarded him for a moment. "Aw, Bradley," she
said at last. "You know I'd never willingly put you in that
position. I love you too much."

"But–"

"Of course," she interrupted with a smile, "I've loved
your father for an awful lot longer."

Bradley's jaw dropped.

"Oh relax," his mom said, blue eyes sparkling in the
dark. "Tomorrow morning, I'll call Kevin to come help.
You're tougher than you think, Bradley. I felt you breaking
through my illusions tonight. That means you're starting to
control your power, starting to hatch. I know you'll keep your
dad safe." She closed her eyes. "Now get some sleep."

Starting to control my power? Bradley stared at the ceiling. *I
don't even know what my power is!*

18

DAD

"**B**radley," his mom said. "The sun's up."

He opened his eyes and yawned, then made a face. His breath tasted like old fish chowder. His mom stood in the doorway of the waiting room, holding Anna in her arms. "Can we see Dad?" he asked.

"He's been moved out of the ICU. The nurse said we should check in downstairs."

"Is he okay?"

"The doctors think so. They've stitched him up, and he's responding well."

Anna woke with a start. "What's going on? Where's Dad?"

"Shh," Bradley's mom put her down. "We spent the night at the hospital. Your father's going to be fine."

"Are you sure?" Anna asked, rubbing her eyes.

"He's getting better now."

Anna pulled her hands away from her face, and looked suspiciously at her mom.

"Trust me!" she said, ruffling Anna's hair. "He'll be fine."

"Can I see him?"

"Tonight, you can. He's sleeping right now. In the meantime, you and I are going to visit with Chloe's mom. No school for you, today."

"Have they found Chloe?" Anna asked.

"Not yet."

Bradley followed them down the stairs. As far as he could tell, his mom hadn't slept at all the previous night. Every time he'd looked over at her, she'd been awake, staring into the darkness as she held Anna. Her eyes had looked unfocused, and didn't blink. He guessed she was somehow watching over his dad.

He'd been up most of the night as well, worrying about his dad and thinking about his parents. They'd been together for hundreds of years. Hundreds. By comparison, they'd only known him for twelve years. He remembered the night of his dream, when his mom had as much as said that if he didn't hatch, they'd abandon him, just like they had their other children.

Just like Abigail.

In the stairwell in front of him, Anna and his mom were talking about the get-well presents they were going to make.

An emptiness crept into Bradley's belly. What about Anna? What if she never hatched? He clenched his jaw. The idea of leaving her behind was even worse than the thought of them leaving him. *They might leave,* he thought, *but I won't.* Human or dragon, it didn't matter to him. Humans weren't just empty shells. Anna wasn't just an empty shell.

They walked out of the stairwell and into a small reception room. "Sign in and go straight to your dad's room," his mom said. "The next visiting hours don't start until later, but the nurse last night said that if you're quiet, you can stay in the room with him the whole day." She gave him a quick hug. "I called Kevin. He'll be here at eleven."

"Another speedbump?" Bradley asked.

She grinned. "Something like that. I'll be back for you around five. Understand?"

"Got it," Bradley said.

A gray-haired lady wearing a straw hat and a name badge that said Midge sat behind the giant desk. Bradley examined her, his heart already pounding at the idea of talking to a stranger. It seemed unlikely that a dragon hunter would work as a hospital receptionist, but that didn't mean she wasn't a fae. *Mom said they make their bodies each morning*, he thought. *They could be anyone.*

"Stop it," he muttered to himself. Talking to strangers was hard enough. He didn't need to imagine they were supernatural killers too.

He took a few deep breaths to steady himself and walked to her desk. "Um, hello."

Midge glanced up from her computer. "Hi, hon. How can I help you?"

"I'm . . ." He clenched his hands to stop them from shaking. "I'm here to see my dad."

"At seven thirty in the morning?" She shrugged. "Okay. Sign in while I get you a bracelet. What's his name?"

"William Nash. He came in last night. A, um, a tree fell on him. I spent the night in the ICU waiting room."

Midge tapped on her keyboard. "You're in the wrong part of the hospital, honey. He's over in room 427. Don't worry. I can sign you in." Behind her, a label slid smoothly out of a printer. Midge stuck it to a plastic bracelet. "Give me your wrist."

Bradley held out his hand and Midge fastened the bracelet around his wrist.

"Go through those big double doors behind me. Turn left, and the main lobby is the third room on the right. That's where the elevators are."

"Thanks," Bradley answered, turning away. He pushed through the doors she'd indicated. The beige carpet stopped at the doorway, replaced by shiny white tile.

Bradley stopped on the tile, a wide smile spreading across his face. *I did it!*

For the first time since leaving Jacksonville, he had talked to a stranger by himself without having a panic attack. He turned left, squeaking his sneakers on the tile, and counted turns until he reached the wooden door to the main lobby. The sound of piano music brought him to a full stop, his hand on the door.

He took his hand away. Someone was playing a piano in the lobby.

"Of course," he muttered angrily to himself. "You didn't think the lobby would be empty, did you?"

He turned back to the door, and put his hand on the knob. *You can do this.*

Pulling the door open a crack, he peeked in.

This lobby also had beige carpet, but with interlocking triangles in burnt orange and blue. A shiny black grand piano sat in the room's center, playing itself.

Bradley's eyes locked on the piano. It was the same size as Mr. Sallson's, but without the huge cabinet extending to the floor. Instead, it looked like a regular piano.

He opened the door wider, but stopped at the sight of a man eating yogurt at the reception desk. Bradley clenched his fists. *He's just like Midge,* he told himself. *Don't get scared. He's a receptionist, just like Midge.*

"Can I help you?" the receptionist asked.

"Um," Bradley said, trying to keep his voice even. His heart was pounding so loud, it sounded to him like a drum accompanied the piano. "I'm looking for the elevators."

The man smiled. "I get that a lot. Let me check your wrist band and I'll buzz you in."

Bradley glanced again at the piano as he walked across the room to the desk.

"Crazy, isn't it?" the man said. "Who listens to player pianos anymore? But someone donated it last month." He examined Bradley's wrist band. "I gotta say, it sounds great."

"Where's the cabinet?" Bradley asked.

"The what?"

"The cabinet where the computer goes."

The man laughed. "The computer's smaller than my hand. We download the music, and it plays."

Bradley remembered all the wires he'd seen under Sallson's piano. Had they been fake? Just camouflage? This piano had plenty of empty space beneath it. *Plenty of room to hold Chloe.*

"You're good to go," the receptionist said. He pressed a button on his desk and the door behind him buzzed and swung open.

Bradley ran to the elevators, hit the number four, and waited impatiently for the doors to open. He couldn't wait to tell his dad about the piano. The elevator opened and he ran to room 427.

"Dad, I–"

He stopped. His dad was fast asleep, with tubes sticking out of his nose and left arm. His breath rattled in his throat each time he exhaled. If anything, he looked even worse than he had in the truck.

There were three chairs in the room, two by the window and one by the bed. Bradley sat next to his dad, and called his mom on his phone.

"Bradley?" she answered. "What's wrong? Are you okay?"

"Yeah, Mom, I'm fine, but–"

"Your dad? Is he okay? Did someone come to the hospital room?"

"No, no. It's nothing like that," Bradley said. "We're all fine. It's just–"

"You're sure?" she interrupted.

"Yeah, Mom."

He heard her exhale.

"Thank goodness," she said. "But I can't talk right now. Mrs. Herns is . . . well, she needs me. I'll call you when I have a moment."

"Mom!"

"Don't worry so much, Bradley. You're perfectly safe, and Kevin will be there in a couple hours. Just call me if there's any trouble. I'm here for you."

Bradley's phone clicked off as his mom hung up.

She's there for me. Yeah, right.

He dialed Kevin next, but his cousin didn't pick up. "Hey Kevin," he said. "Call me as soon as you can."

Wishing Chris had a phone, he started to pace back and forth at the foot of the bed. *I need to hatch.* That was the key to everything. If he could turn into a dragon, everything would be better. His family would be safe, and he'd be able to save Chloe.

But how? He'd tried following Kevin's advice, had attempted every impossible thing he could think of. The only time he'd been even slightly successful was in the swamp, when he'd been swarmed by bugs.

Bugs, he thought. He walked to the window and opened the curtains. *Is that all I have to look forward to? Am I some kind of bug dragon?*

He spotted a fly walking along the windowsill. "Turn," he said softly.

The fly stopped and rubbed its legs together, then continued on its way.

"Turn," Bradley whispered again. Eyes narrowed, he tried to will the fly to turn toward him. *I need to do this,* he thought desperately. *I need to hatch to save my family.* A dull ache started behind his eyes. "Turn, you stupid thing!"

"Hey kiddo," his dad rasped from the hospital bed. Bradley jumped in surprise. "How you holding up?"

"Dad!" Bradley said, spinning. He rushed to him. "How are you? Are you healing?"

"Yeah, but not as quick as I'd like." His dad pressed a button and raised the head of his bed. "You look really bad. Did you get any sleep last night?"

"A little. Listen Dad, I think I discovered something about Chloe. You know that piano that plays itself?"

"Wait." His dad raised a hand. "I can't stay awake much longer."

"What?'

"The healing," his dad said in a voice that slurred and

paused at strange times. "I'm only awake for . . . brief moments. I want to talk about hatching."

Bradley grabbed his dad's hand and held it tightly, scared by the weakness of his dad's voice.

"Between the fae and the hunters . . . We're running out of time. You need to figure out how to hatch. Hearing my story might help."

"Okay, Dad." *Please don't die.* He added silently. *Please.*

"When I was a kid, I wanted to be a knight. Do you know what that means?"

"Sure. Armor, jousting, big swords, tournaments."

"No." Bradley's dad closed his eyes, then winced as he swallowed. "Not those stories. The knights were the ones who . . . who kept you safe when everyone else ran away, the ones who wouldn't let you down no matter what, the ones who'd die to protect you."

Bradley didn't say anything.

"That's what I wanted to be," his dad said. He coughed. "Then I discovered I could be a dragon. That was better than being a knight. For me, turning into a dragon happened as soon as I realized I could be everything that I dreamed of being." He opened his eyes and squeezed Bradley's hand. "What about you? Haven't you ever dreamed of being anything?"

Bradley looked down at his father's hand, but nothing came to mind. "I don't know. Maybe."

"Really? No dreams? No heroes? You read a lot of comic books. Didn't you ever dream of being a superhero?"

"I guess." Bradley paused. "But that's not how things work. There aren't any heroes these days, just people."

"You really believe that?"

Bradley felt his dad's disappointment like a physical blow. The straight set of his mouth, the slight squint to his left eye . . . Bradley had seen it before.

"It's okay, kiddo," his dad rasped. "You'll figure it out." He closed his eyes.

"Wait!" Bradley said. "Are you going to be okay? I mean, I know you said you just need to sleep, but . . ."

"I'll be fine." He squeezed Bradley's hand without opening his eyes, then let it go. "All I need is sleep." He folded his hands over his blankets and fell fast asleep.

Bradley dropped into the chair and stared at the ceiling. *Dad wants me to be a hero. But how?* He still had no clue how to hatch.

According to the dragon book, he had to decide what kind of dragon he wanted to be. His mom had said the key was to find out what he cared most about. His dad had just asked him what he dreamed of being.

He closed his eyes, thinking. Could it be that easy? Did he just have to decide what he wanted? *What do I want?*

The answer came immediately. He wanted to save Chloe.

Standing, he started to pace again. Now that he knew about the piano, he was certain he could save her. He just had to get to Sallson's trailer and break open the fake cabinet. Instead, he was stuck here, watching his dad sleep.

Chloe's more important, he thought. His dad didn't need him.

Even his mom had said it. No fae would come by during the day, and his dad didn't have to worry about dragon hunters. They were just interested in eggs.

He clenched his fists. Every moment he stayed in the hospital was a chance that Sallson would move Chloe out of the piano. He needed to leave, to get out, to save her. The thought built inside his mind until it was all he could think of. He felt trapped, like he was going to explode. His skin tingled, and his face burned.

"Relax, kiddo," his dad said, reaching slowly for the phone.

Bradley jumped. "You're awake?"

"You're too wound up." His dad coughed. "I'll call Mr. Vaega, see if he can stop by with Chris and take you two home for some downtime."

"Okay." Bradley felt light-headed, almost dizzy with relief. "But what about you?"

"I'll be fine. Stay at Chris's place with his dad. Don't . . ."

"I will," Bradley said quickly. "If anything happens, I'll call Mom. She's at Mrs. Herns."

"Good."

Bradley nodded, not trusting himself to speak. Had he somehow wished his dad into sending him home? Or had his dad just seen how tense he was? *It doesn't matter*, he told himself. One way or another, he was going to save Chloe.

19

BEING A HERO

"Okay, guys," Mr. Vaega said, opening the door to his trailer. "It's ten thirty, and class isn't until three. Bradley, I'm starting you in the beginner's group."

Bradley paled, imagining himself in a room full of strangers, all practicing karate.

"You'll be fine," Mr. Vaega said. "The martial arts require discipline. That discipline will help you get past your condition."

"I hope you're right," Bradley said.

"You know I am." Mr. Vaega punched his shoulder lightly. "Now, I've got a ton of paperwork to do. You two behave yourselves."

Chris and Bradley watched Mr. Vaega close the bedroom door.

"Dude," Chris said, once they were alone in the kitchen. "Your dad's the coolest! I can't believe he talked Dad into letting me skip school."

"Yeah," Bradley said, still thinking about how he would deal with a martial arts class filled with strangers.

"What do you want to do now?" Chris asked.

Bradley hesitated. He'd spent the car ride from the hospital trying to figure out how to convince Chris to go with him to Mr. Sallson's. He hadn't come up with anything good. "Did you notice there weren't any cars at Sallson's place?" he asked.

"No." Chris opened the refrigerator. "When I said 'What do you want to do?' I meant 'How about some TV?' or 'What game would you like to play?' I didn't mean 'How can we get arrested?'" He handed Bradley a can of soda, then closed the refrigerator. "How about SiegeStones? We haven't played that in a while."

"Did you see the piano in the hospital lobby when you came to get me?" Bradley asked. "It was a player piano like Sallson's."

"Dude! Give it a rest! We're not going to . . . Wait a minute. I did see that piano."

"Did you see how small it was?" Bradley took a swig of soda. "I asked the receptionist guy. He said the computer was tiny."

Chris looked out the window. "Then what's up with Sallson's piano?"

"Exactly!" Bradley gestured with his soda. "I bet all those wires we saw underneath were fake."

"So, you want to break into the guy's trailer and search his piano."

"Why not? We know he's creepy, and we know he's hiding something."

"How do we know that?" Chris said.

"Remember the file I printed out? It had tons of information about my family: names, birth dates, even places we've lived."

"That is creepy, but still. Remember what happened last time we went there."

"C'mon, Chris! This is our chance. Sallson's car's not in his driveway. Chloe could be in his piano. We've got to check!"

Chris emptied his soda in two long gulps, and set the empty can on the counter. "You know my dad will literally kill us if we get caught, right? I mean, he'll actually end our lives. And if he doesn't, your mom will."

Bradley grinned. "So we don't get caught."

Chris thought for a moment. "Okay. We've got to get there without going by your place or Mrs. Herns'. Let's head out the back, then between the Munoz and Calloway's, and sprint for the fence."

Bradley nodded. Once they reached the fence, they'd follow it around to Sallson's trailer and climb back over. He opened the back door. "I'm first. See you there!"

He walked casually until he reached the green space between the trailers and the fence. After a quick check to make sure no one was watching, he broke into a run. It took him two jumps to reach the top bar of the fence. He was still scrabbling his feet on the metal links, trying to climb over, when Chris arrived.

Chris leaped, grabbed the top bar, and swung his legs over in one smooth motion. Bradley reached the top of the fence, rolled over it, and let himself down. When his feet hit the ground, they slid out from under him and he sprawled in the muddy grass.

"Smooth, shrimp," Chris said. "Real smooth."

"Shut up."

Chris helped him up. "We're kind of in a hurry, here."

"Maybe we'd go quicker if you just gave me a ride," Bradley said. "I mean, you are as big as a horse."

They ran the rest of the way to Sallson's front door. This time, they didn't hear any piano music playing. Bradley, still breathing hard from the run, glanced at Chris, then rang the bell.

"What are you doing?" Chris asked.

"We've got to make sure no one's inside."

There was no answer.

Chris turned to him. "So how were you planning on getting in? Break a window?"

"I was kind of hoping that it would open . . ." Bradley slammed his shoulder against the door and it drifted open. "Ha!"

Chris didn't move. Just like last time, the trailer was dark, its shades and curtains closed. "That doesn't make sense. He should have figured out how to close the door after the last time we broke in."

"He's really old. Maybe he's too weak to pull it all the way closed."

Chris grabbed Bradley's shoulder to stop him from going inside. "Something's not right here. We should get my dad."

"Relax!" Pulling away from Chris, Bradley stepped inside. "See? It's just an empty trailer."

Chris followed, closing the door and setting the deadbolt. "Is it darker than last time? It seems darker."

"Yeah," Bradley said. Chris was right. Last time, they'd been able to see everything in the dim light. This time, the piano was just a large forbidding shadow sitting in darkness. He glanced at the light switches on the wall, but didn't touch them. If anyone was watching the trailer, they'd see the lights turn on.

Together, they ran to the piano and squatted down. Bradley opened the cabinet door.

"I can't see anything," Chris said.

"Me, neither."

Bradley shone his phone light on the opening. In its harsh white glare, he saw the same tangled mess of wires and circuit boards that he'd seen the last time he checked the piano.

Chris grunted. "Nothing."

"It doesn't make sense," Bradley said, sitting back on his heels. "What's all this for?"

"Maybe it's fake." Chris reached in and pushed the wires around. He leaned in closer. "Point the light to the right. There's something back there."

Bradley moved closer and held up his phone. Its light revealed a black metal bar hidden behind the wires. "Is that what I think it is?"

"It's a handle," Chris said, reaching for it.

"Don't pull it yet," Bradley said. "Let's keep looking." He reached in, forcing his hand past the wires, and felt the solid surface behind them. There was a groove in it, a groove that formed the shape of a rectangle. "It's a door," he said, backing away. "We found it!"

"Okay," Chris said. "Here we go." He grabbed the handle, braced his other hand against the piano, and pulled.

Clicks sounded from the trailer doors and windows, and Chris made a strangled gurgling noise, halfway between a scream and a groan. His whole body convulsed, then went limp. The sharp odor of burned flesh filled the room.

Bradley scrambled to his friend. Chris's eyes were closed, but he was breathing. "Chris," he hissed, shaking his shoulders. "Chris!"

It's a trap, Bradley thought looking around the dark room. The whole trailer was a trap. *It's for me*, he realized with a sinking feeling. *If I'd come alone, I'd be the one lying on the floor, helpless.*

He jumped up and ran to the French doors at the back of the trailer. The door handle turned, but the doors wouldn't open.

"Chris," Bradley shouted. If pulling that handle had locked the doors, it had probably also sent a message to Mr. Sallson. "You've got to wake up."

Shining his phone's light on the piano, he spotted a thick black power cord that connected it to the wall. He yanked the plug from its socket.

"Come on, Chris!" He knelt by his friend and shook his shoulder. "Wake up!"

Chris didn't respond.

Frustrated, Bradley shook harder. "Wake up!" *Come on, Chris*, he thought furiously. *Wake up!*

Chris startled awake, then shouted in pain. "My hand!" He rolled awkwardly to his feet, cradling it against his body. "My hand!"

"We've got to get out of here!" Bradley said.

Tears streamed down Chris's cheeks. "Man, this hurts. Oh man-oh-man, this hurts." He ran to the kitchen sink, turned on the cold water and stuck his hand in it. "Ow!" he yelled. "Ow, ow, ow!" The palm and fingers of his hand were burned bright red. Blood seeped from his flesh.

Bradley felt sick. "This whole thing's a trap. The trailer, the piano, the handle . . ." He stopped, looking at the open piano cabinet. The black handle Chris had grabbed was easily visible among the wires. *You don't make a trap without bait,* he thought.

"I can't close my hand." Chris opened the freezer and fumbled for ice.

Staring at the handle, Bradley took a deep breath to steady himself. The piano was unplugged. The handle couldn't still be electrified. He squatted in front of it.

"Dude!" Chris said. "What are you doing?"

"We still haven't found Chloe," Bradley said. "I have to check." He swallowed nervously, then grabbed the metal handle and pulled.

The mass of electronics swung forward, revealing a small dark chamber with Chloe inside, curled into a ball, her eyes closed.

"Chloe!" Bradley shouted in triumph. He snaked his arms under her and pulled her onto the carpet. Her body felt as limp as a rag doll, her skin cold and clammy.

"Is she okay?" Chris asked, cradling his hand.

"I don't know."

Bradley held her gently. *Wake up, Chloe,* he thought. *You have to wake up!*

She didn't.

Car tires crunched on the dirt road in front of the trailer. Bradley and Chris exchanged a glance. "The back doors are locked," Bradley whispered. "They locked when you pulled the handle."

Chris snorted, stepped to the French doors and kicked. Wood splintered and the doors burst open. He turned back to Bradley. "Give her to me. I run faster."

"One-handed?" Bradley tried to lift her, but her body slipped out of his hands.

"Hurry!" Chris said.

"I'm trying!" Chloe slipped out of Bradley's hands again. Unconscious, she seemed twice as heavy as normal.

A car door slammed in front of the trailer. Two more slams followed it.

Bradley grabbed Chloe with both hands and heaved her up over his shoulder, like a sack of potatoes.

The handle of the front door turned and the door rattled in its frame. Bradley froze, watching, but the deadbolt held it closed.

Bending under Chloe's weight, he went out the back door.

Chris followed.

"Go get help," Bradley said as he tried to run. "My mom, your dad . . . anybody!"

Chris strode beside him, still cradling his burned hand against his body. Tear streaks stained his cheeks. "Yeah right, shrimp. Like I'm going to leave you here. Can't you run any faster?"

"She's heavier than she looks!" Bradley tried to speed up.

"Stop!" a voice shouted from the trailer.

Bradley and Chris looked back. Two large men with military haircuts walked toward them. A black-haired woman in a dark purple jacket stood in the broken doorway of the trailer. "Quickly!" she shouted. "Get the egg!"

At the sight of the strangers, an all too familiar fear filled

Bradley. His stomach lurched, and his mouth went dry. *Not now*, he thought. *Please, not now!*

"Aw, crud." Chris turned to face the men. "Run, Bradley."

"D-Don't be an idiot," Bradley stuttered. "There are two of them!"

Chris rolled his shoulders in a move Bradley had seen him do countless times before his matches. "That's why you need to start running."

"But your hand—"

"Listen, shrimp," Chris interrupted, settling into his fighting stance. "You're the one carrying Chloe."

Bradley bit back his answer. Chris was right. *It's not like I could do anything, anyway*, he thought, hating himself. He stumbled into a faster run, Chloe bouncing on his shoulder. Tears gathered in his eyes. Why did he always have to be so afraid? Why couldn't he be like Chris? Just once he wanted to not be afraid, to be the one standing strong.

Behind him, he heard one of the men growl, "Get out of the way, kid."

"Make me," Chris answered.

There was a shout, followed by an "oof" of pain. Without stopping, Bradley glanced over his shoulder. The taller man was on his knees on the grass, holding his stomach with one hand. The beefier man advanced toward Chris, fists raised.

Bradley turned back to his running. He'd never seen Chris lose a fight, but he'd also never seen him fight one-handed. Heart pounding, he stumbled onto the dirt road and headed toward the Herns' trailer.

Shouts sounded behind him again, followed by meaty thunks. Chris cried out in pain. A man cursed.

Panting, Bradley tried to move faster. Running with Chloe was hard. She felt heavier with every step, and her feet banged painfully against his stomach.

He couldn't hear Chris or the men anymore, but didn't dare look back. Every step he took, he expected to feel a hand grab his shoulder.

By the time he reached Mrs. Herns' driveway, he was soaked in sweat, and his muscles were burning. "Help!" he shouted. "Mom! Mrs. Herns! Help!" He stumbled to the trailer's front door and kicked it, still yelling.

Mrs. Herns jerked open the door angrily. "What are you—?"

At the sight of her daughter, she dissolved into tears. "Oh, my God," she cried, taking Chloe. She sank to the floor right there in the doorway, crying and rocking her sleeping daughter.

"Mom," Bradley shouted past them. "Mom, I need help!"

"Wake up, Chloe," Mrs. Herns whispered, kissing her daughter's head. "It's Mommy. I'm here. Wake up, pretty girl. Please wake up."

"Mom!" Bradley shouted again.

"Bradley?" Anna appeared in the den behind Mrs. Herns, her eyes as wide as saucers. "Mom just ran out the back. She said we need to stay with Mrs. Herns and—"

Bradley turned and ran, gulping for air. His legs felt as weak as wet noodles from running with Chloe, but he had to help Chris. He just had to. He leaned forward, willing himself to run faster.

Rounding the corner of the Alder's trailer, he spotted Chris lying in the field, curled into a ball. The two men stood on either side of him. The taller one stood awkwardly on one leg, and blood dripped from his nose. With an angry grin, he gestured to the other man, who grunted and kicked Chris in the ribs.

Bradley screamed as he ran at them, red hot rage surging through him.

The black-haired woman appeared in the shattered doorway on the back of Sallson's trailer. "Get back here," she shouted. "Now!"

"Just a moment," the tall man answered. "We've almost got what we came for."

Beside him, the thicker man crouched like a wrestler, his dark eyes tracking Bradley.

A whisper echoed down from the clear blue sky, like a slight breeze blowing across the grass. "Hush."

The men tumbled to the ground like puppets whose strings had been cut.

Bradley slowed to a stop. *Mom?* He glanced up at the sky, then back to the unconscious men. Beyond them, the black-haired woman disappeared into the trailer.

Bradley dropped to his knees next to Chris. "Are you okay?"

"Did you get Chloe to—?"

The trailer's roof collapsed with a loud whump.

Chris and Bradley both turned their heads to look.

Another whump sounded, compacting the trailer like an empty soda can. Glass, wood, and metal flew in every direction. Bradley threw himself over Chris, shielding him with his body.

A third whump sounded, followed by a bright purple flash. Bradley closed his eyes and covered his head as broken wood, plaster, and glass fell all around him. When he opened them again, Sallson's trailer was completely demolished. Chris was breathing raggedly beneath him. The men on the ground lay motionless, half covered by broken pieces of trailer.

There was no sign of the black-haired woman.

20

PARENTS

"I t hurts," Chris said. "It hurts so bad. It even hurts to breathe."

"I'm calling 911," Bradley said, pulling his phone from his pocket.

As he waited for an answer, a wind ruffled his hair, and he heard his mom's whispered voice. "I'm with you."

A woman answered the phone. "Is this a fire, police, or medical emergency?"

Bradley spoke fast, explaining that Chloe had been found and that they needed ambulances for her and Chris. Once he was sure she believed him, he disconnected and put the phone back in his pocket.

"I think my ribs are cracked," Chris groaned.

"Take him to Chloe's trailer," Bradley's mom whispered in his ear.

Bradley helped Chris stand. "Lean on me. We'll go to Chloe's."

With most of his weight on Bradley's shoulders, Chris took an experimental step. "I think I can do that."

Moving slowly and carefully, they made their way to the dirt road. Together, they staggered down it to Chloe's trailer. Bradley's mom opened the door as they approached. She was barefoot, and wearing her blue sundress. "Oh, you poor boy," she said to Chris. "Take him inside, Bradley."

"Is Chloe okay?" Chris asked.

"She's asleep. Mrs. Herns and Anna are with her in her bedroom." She helped Bradley get Chris to the couch, then brushed Chris's forehead with her hand. "Hush."

Chris's eyes closed and his face went slack.

"Mom!" Bradley said. "You can't do that!"

"We don't have much time," she said. "Tell me what happened."

For the first time in his life, Bradley recognized the power in his mom's voice. She wasn't just asking him to talk. She was compelling him. "It was a trap," he said. "Chloe was in the piano, and when Chris tried to open it, he got electrocuted. If I'd gone there alone . . ."

"Okay." She hugged him tightly. "It's okay. You're safe now, but we have to move quickly. That woman in the trailer was a fae."

"The flash of light!"

"Yes. Her body broke when I smashed the trailer. When the sunlight touched her, it destroyed her." She took a deep breath. "This is proof the fae are working with the dragon hunters, and that means we're in real danger. Not just you, but all of us. We need to stay together. We need to . . . I don't know what. If the fae are coming after us . . ."

Bradley felt her heart pounding through the hug as she stroked his hair. *She's scared*, he realized. *Mom is scared.*

"Chris," she said, pushing away from Bradley, "are you well enough to listen?"

"Huh?" Chris woke up at the sound of her voice. "What? Sure. Sure."

"Good. The ambulance will be here soon."

He licked his lips and nodded.

"Mr. Nash and I don't need the publicity that's coming with this. We don't want it. I don't know what happened in that trailer, but I need it to be clear that you are the hero. You are the one who saved Chloe. You are the one who—"

"But Mrs. Nash, that's not what happened," Chris interrupted. "It was Bradley that dragged me over there."

"Doesn't matter," she said.

Chris opened his mouth to speak, but she overrode him. "Your dad can use this, Chris. With you in the news, his karate lessons will be sold out every day for the next year." She stood up. "You two boys get your story straight, whatever it is. I'll get you some burn cream for that hand."

Bradley smiled weakly at Chris. "How about this: you rescued her, then called me to come help?"

"This is nuts," Chris said. "You should get the credit."

"I can't."

"Okay, okay," Chris said. "What about me being electrocuted?"

"It was a short, some kind of a problem with the wire that zapped you while you were opening the piano. Then the circuit breaker flipped and broke the circuit. You woke up, rescued Chloe, and called me."

"Won't work. They'll see the circuit breaker is fine."

"In that pile of rubble?"

Bradley's mom returned with cubes of ice wrapped in a soft towel. "This might help your hand. Sorry I couldn't find any burn cream."

"Thanks," Chris said.

She patted his head. "I'll call your dad."

After she left, Chris laid his head back on the couch. "Dude," he whispered. "What happened out there? What knocked out those guys and crushed the trailer? Who was that woman in the trailer, and why did she tell those guys to get an egg?"

"I don't . . ."

"And what's the deal with your mom keeping you out of the news?"

"I can't talk about it," Bradley said.

"It's about the stuff you found on Sallson's computer, isn't it?" Chris whispered. "That's who you guys are hiding from."

"Yeah."

"Come on, Bradley. What's going on?"

"I'll tell you later," Bradley said. "I promise."

I swear, he added silently. *I'll tell you everything.*

Mr. Vaega burst through the front door. "Christopher Zhao Vaega," he thundered. "What did you think you were doing?"

Chris flinched. "Sorry, Dad."

Bradley stepped from between them.

Mr. Vaega towered over his son. "Don't you sorry me, boy. I told you to stay in the trailer. Inside!"

Bradley's mom laid a hand on Mr. Vaega's shoulder. "He saved Chloe, Andrew."

Mr. Vaega turned on her. "He—what?"

"Chloe's with Susan now. An ambulance is on its way."

"Ambulance? You said he was hurt, but not—" Mr. Vaega knelt by the couch. He touched his son's shoulder. "What happened?"

"My hand's the worst." Chris tilted it so his dad could see the burn. "But I think I might have a cracked rib. There were two guys, Dad. I dropped one, but the other was too strong, and I couldn't use my right hand. He blew through my block. All I could do was keep them off Bradley."

"He stopped them so I could get Chloe away," Bradley said.

"Oh, Chris," Mr. Vaega squeezed his son's good hand. "I should have been there. Why didn't you tell me? I would have helped."

"I could have taken them, Dad. I could have. But my hand was burned and—"

Mrs. Herns, her eyes brimming with tears, stepped into the room. She held Chloe in her arms, and an overnight bag dangled from her shoulder. Anna stood behind her, shifting her weight from foot to foot. She was wearing a pair of bright yellow plastic sunglasses.

"Can I ride with Chloe to the hospital?" Anna asked.

Bradley's mom shook her head. "The ambulance would be too crowded. We'll go separately in our truck. Why don't you go get some coloring books, so you'll have something to do?"

"I'll get some for Chloe, too," Anna said to Mrs. Herns.

Mrs. Herns tried to smile. "I'm sure she'll appreciate that, just as soon as," her voice caught and she swallowed, "as soon as she wakes up."

"Hurry," Bradley's mom said to Anna. "They'll be here soon."

Bradley sat hunched over at the kitchen table. *I've got to hatch,* he thought desperately. *All this is because I haven't hatched yet. They're after me. The dragon hunters, the fae . . . They're all after me.*

21

LIKE MOTHER, LIKE SON

B radley's dad was fast asleep when they reached his hospital room, but he looked much healthier than before. Tubes no longer stuck out of his nose, and his breathing didn't rattle.

"How long has he been sleeping?" Anna asked. "It's not like Chloe, is it?"

"No," Bradley's mom said. "This is a good sleep."

"He's back to his regular color," Bradley said, relieved. It was one thing to be told that his dad would heal, another to actually see him doing it.

"I told you he'd be okay," his mom said.

"What about Chloe?" Anna asked.

"The doctors are checking her now. As soon as her mom has news, she'll call."

"But—"

"That's all we can do, Anna." She sat on the foot of the bed, and gestured to a chair. "Why don't you watch some television? It won't wake your father if we keep it turned down low." She clicked on the television.

Bradley dragged a chair to the wall, so he could watch too, but not be in the way of his mom.

Aerial footage of Highwater Acres filled the screen, focusing on Mr. Sallson's destroyed trailer. The words "Special Report" glowed red in the bottom corner, partially obscuring the trucks next to the ruined trailer. People in hardhats picked through the rubble, and police were stretching yellow tape around the perimeter. Neighbors stood on the other side of the tape, pointing and talking.

"Wow," Anna said, lifting her sunglasses off her head. "What happened?"

Bradley shook his head. His mom sure had done a number on that place. *Just like in my dream*, he thought. *Just like she did to that village.* He wasn't sure how he felt about that.

The picture changed to a blonde reporter with a very serious expression. She held a microphone in front of old man Alders. Mr. Alders had clearly dressed for the occasion, wearing his blue Sunday suit instead of the sweatpants and t-shirt Bradley was used to seeing him in.

"Yep, I saw it all right," Mr. Alders said. "Woke up when I heard the Nash boy yelling for help. I peeked out my window and saw him carrying little Chloe and shouting. Behind him, the Vaega boy tried to fight some men." He sighed. "Poor kid. He got beat up pretty bad. I grabbed my phone to call the police. Then the Nash boy came running back, and the men just fell over. Darndest thing."

The reporter pulled the microphone back to her own mouth. "That's when the trailer collapsed, when the men fell over?"

"Yes, ma'am." Mr. Alders coughed into his hand. "I've

never seen anything like it. Looked like the hand of God come down from heaven." He shook his head. "The Almighty flattened that place just as sure as I'm standing here."

The reporter smiled at the camera. "I can only imagine. No one has been able to tell me just what happened to the trailer. What exactly did you see?"

Mr. Alders looked at the camera nervously. "Three hard hits. First the roof collapsed, then the walls busted out, then the whole thing just fell apart and there was a flash of purple light."

"Purple light?"

"Yes, ma'am."

"When you say hits, what do you mean?"

"That's what it looked like. It looked like something was hitting that place with a tree, except there weren't any tree— or anything else for that matter. Like I said, it was the hand of God, punishing that man for what he done to that little girl."

Anna whirled around to Bradley. "You were there? You saw it get smashed?"

"Yeah," Bradley said, "It was just like Mr. Alders said."

"Wow," Anna said, turning back to the television.

Bradley bit his lip. Between the mysteriously smashed trailer and the flash of purple light, any fae who saw that broadcast would be heading to Highwater Acres. *They can't all be after me, can they? There must be some good fae out there.*

After the interview, the news cycled through pictures of Highwater Acres, the police cars in front of Mrs. Herns' trailer, and photos of Chloe. Bradley leaned his head back against the wall and let his eyes close. The image of Chris curled into a ball on the grass floated into his mind, followed by Mrs. Herns pleading with Chloe to wake up.

"Look," Anna said. "There's Chris!"

The screen showed Chris on a stretcher being pushed into the back of an ambulance. His dad climbed in next to him, holding his hand. "This was the scene earlier today," the reporter said. "As Christopher Vaega, one of the boys who saved little Chloe, was rushed to the hospital."

"Chris is on T.V.!" Anna said. "He's gonna be famous!"

"I sure hope so," Bradley said. "He earned it."

"We'll be leaving Highwater Acres now, so we can take you to the location of both Chloe and Chris," the reporter said. "Dan is on his way there now, and we'll go to him live right after these messages."

Bradley and his mom exchanged a glance, then he stood and shut the door to their room. His mom closed the window blinds.

"What are you doing?" Anna asked.

"Just making it easier for your dad to sleep," Bradley's mom said, turning off the television.

"What about Chloe?" Anna complained. "Can't we go see her? You said we'd see her when we got here. You promised."

"We will go see her, just as soon as her mom calls. In the meantime, why don't you color something? I'm sure she'll be awake soon."

While Anna dug into her backpack for a coloring book, Bradley dragged his chair over next to her. He tried not to look as worried as he felt. The hospital room was too small for either of his parents to turn into a dragon. *We should still be okay*, he thought. *The fae won't do anything during the day.* He didn't know would happen after dark. With his dad asleep, it would be up to him and his mom to keep them safe.

His phone rang.

"Hey," Kevin said. "What happened? I thought I was supposed to meet you at the hospital at eleven, but you're all over the news."

"Yeah," Bradley said. "We—"

His mom took the phone away from him. "Kevin," she said. "It's worse than we thought. Fae are working with the hunters."

"Hunters?" Anna said, looking up from her coloring book. "Fae?"

Bradley waved her to be quiet and stood close to his mom so he could hear.

"No way," Kevin said. "The fae probably just wanted that girl."

"I don't think so," Bradley's mom said. "I need you to come to the hospital and stay in the lobby. Keep an eye out for anything that looks suspicious. Don't tell anyone what room we're in. If anyone comes our way, call me."

Anna tugged at Bradley's hand. "Who would be coming our way?"

"No one," Bradley said.

"Yes, ma'am," Kevin said. "But have you been online? Kids from the school are posting about Chris and Bradley and how they saved Chloe. A bunch of them are going to the hospital after school. Even some of the teachers. They're making posters."

"Chris *and* Bradley?" she asked. "The television only mentioned Chris. Are you sure they know that both of them are at the hospital?"

"Yes, ma'am."

Bradley's mom closed her eyes for a moment, and then opened them again. "Okay. Get here as quickly as you can." She clicked off the phone.

"What is it, Mom?" Anna asked.

"Hush–" his mom started to say.

"It's nothing," Bradley interrupted, with a glare at his mother. "The fae are like fairies," he said to his sister. "And hunters . . . well, they're the bad guys. It's all a big story."

"Bradley," his mom said warningly.

"She's fine," he shot back at her. *No more hushing*, he thought. *No more turning us off.*

"What was Mom talking about?" Anna asked, suspicious.

"It's just a game Mom's playing with Kevin," he said, trying to stop her questions. "You know, like cops and robbers."

"No really," Anna said to her mom. "What's happening?"

"It's true," Bradley insisted. *Stop now*, he thought desperately. *If you don't stop, Mom will hush you to sleep.*

Anna opened her mouth to say something, then closed it. She shook her head, confused, and went back to coloring.

Bradley looked triumphantly at his mom. *See?* he thought. *All I had to do was talk to her.*

She raised one eyebrow. "You do that almost as well as I do."

All the blood rushed out of Bradley's face. *Oh no!* A sick

panicky feeling filled his stomach. *I didn't mean to . . . I mean, not that way, not by controlling her mind.*

He clenched his fists. *I'm no better than Mom!*

22

TRUST

"You know," Bradley whispered to Anna. "It's okay if you ask questions." They were watching cartoons while their mom talked on the phone. It was Bradley's first chance to talk to Anna privately since he'd willed her to be quiet.

Anna looked at him like he'd lost his mind. "Hush! I'm watching!"

Bradley felt terrible about what he'd done. *Is that what I am? Not a bug dragon after all, but a mind control dragon?* He ran his fingers along the skin of his forearms. They felt as human as always.

Kevin called to say he was in the lobby.

"Cool," Bradley said. "Mom, can I go down and see Kevin?"

Still on her phone, she shook her head.

"Sorry," Bradley told Kevin. "I'm stuck here."

"No problem, cuz. I'll let everyone know you're too

injured to see them. Build up your rep. a little. When you go back to school, you'll be a hero."

Bradley smiled as he hung up the phone. It felt good to be called a hero.

"When can we see Chloe?" Anna asked.

"I don't know," Bradley said. "Mom said they'd call us when she wakes up."

Anna sighed dramatically. "Hospitals are so boring."

Unless I start turning into a dragon, Bradley thought. *Or a hunter shows up, or a fae. Then it'll get pretty exciting.*

None of that happened. Instead, the hours crawled by. Anna watched an endless stream of cartoons. His dad slept. Every hour or so, a nurse stopped by to check on Bradley's dad. Bradley's mom watched each nurse closely, her gaze focused and intense. She wouldn't let Bradley or Anna leave the room, not even to get food. Instead, they ordered a huge lunch for his dad and split it. They did the same for dinner.

That evening, as Bradley played cards with his mom and sister, a nurse knocked on their door and let himself in. "Sorry to interrupt," he said, "but Mr. Vaega asked me to stop by."

"Chris's dad?" Bradley put his cards down. He had seen so many nurses today that they no longer triggered his fear of strangers. He still felt a moment of panic when each one arrived, but that was it. "How's Chris do . . .?"

The question died in his throat. The nurse's eyes didn't look right. They were too shiny, and the pupils seemed slightly out of place. *Like two glass eyes*, he thought, *just like Mr. Sallson's.*

He stood up quickly, his mouth dry, his heart pounding.

"Chris is fine," the nurse said. "In fact, he asked if you could come visit." He leaned forward and smiled sympathetically. "He's going a little stir crazy, if you know what I mean."

Bradley didn't answer, couldn't answer. He was frozen with fear. The nurse's eyes were like Mr. Sallson's eyes.

"Can I come, too?" Anna asked, putting her cards down. She turned pleading eyes on her mother. "I want to see Chris!"

"I don't see why not," the nurse said.

"Mom—" Bradley's voice came out barely louder than a whisper. His hands shook, and he was having trouble breathing.

"Not tonight," his mom interrupted. "We're all too shaken up over what happened today. Please tell Mr. Vaega that Bradley'll be down first thing in the morning."

"Y . . . Yeah," Bradley said. *Didn't his mom see the nurse's eyes? Why was she being so calm?*

"Are you sure?" the nurse asked. "A little company could be just what Chris needs."

"Maybe tomorrow," Bradley's mom answered firmly. "Tonight, I want Bradley close by."

The nurse pursed his lips, considering. He stared at Bradley's unconscious dad, then his eyes drifted back to Bradley's mom.

She stood, arms folded. The polite smile she'd been wearing faded away, and her eyes glittered with an angry blue light.

The nurse nodded. "If you change your mind, just send him down. Chris is in room 311." He left, closing the door behind him.

Bradley's heart still pounded in his chest. He turned to his mom. "Didn't you see his–"

"Shh. Anna, dear, I think it's your turn."

Anna looked at her cards. "Bradley, do you have any fives?"

Bradley tried again. "Mom, his eyes–"

"*Whisper.*" The word sounded soft and clear to Bradley, as though his mom were standing behind him and whispering directly into his ear. The sound wasn't real, he knew, just an illusion that only he could hear. "*Be as quiet as you can, so you don't frighten Anna. I will hear you.*"

"Didn't you see his eyes?" Bradley breathed, barely moving his lips.

"*They looked fine to me.*"

"Do you have any fives?" Anna repeated.

Bradley ignored her. He looked away from his sister, and whispered to his mother, "but they were . . . wrong, just like Mr. Sallson's."

"*Mr. Sallson's eyes looked strange? You should have told me.*"

"I thought they looked strange to everyone. What does it mean?" His mouth was still dry, but the panic he'd felt earlier had faded. Had it just been another anxiety attack? Maybe the nurse was the same as everyone else. Maybe he had imagined the eyes being wrong.

"*Maybe,*" his mother said, "*your human eyes are interpreting what your dragon self is sensing.*"

"I don't know what that means."

"*If you're right about Mr. Sallson and the nurse being fae, then you can do something neither your father nor I can. You can spot a fae.*"

"No way!"

"*What other explanation is there?*"

"Bradley!" Anna said. "I asked for fives. Do you have any fives?"

"Um," he scanned his cards. His sister hadn't heard anything he or his mom had said. "No. Go fish."

"Aw!" Anna pulled a card off the top of the deck. "I like playing with Chris better."

"*If the fae have found us, we have to leave.*" His mom stood up. "*Catch your sister.*"

Bradley lunged forward to catch Anna as she slumped in her chair. "You can't do that!" he yelled at his mom. "It's not right!"

"It is what it is," his mom said, speaking normally again. She moved to the window, drew the curtains back, and picked up a chair. "Now be quiet."

"You can't be serious." Bradley backed away, shielding Anna with his body.

His mom smashed the chair through the window. The glass broke, but it made no sound, and the pieces vanished as they fell to the parking lot outside. Using the chair, she knocked out the glass shards that still clung to the window pane.

Bradley's mouth dropped open.

"I wish Antleen was here, or your granduncle Li," she said. "We should have called him right away. He's a healer." She pulled the tubes out of her husband's arms.

"Stop!" Bradley said. "Are you crazy? He needs those!"

"No choice." She lifted Bradley's dad, slung his body over her shoulder, then held out her hand. "Come on."

Bradley shook his head.

"Listen," his mom said "If that man was a fae, the only

reason he left was because he didn't think he could defeat me. He's coming back, and he'll bring friends."

"Friends?"

His mom stepped up onto the window ledge. "If we stay here, we die."

"But—" Bradley stammered.

Still holding his father, she jumped. Both of them vanished into thin air.

"Bring your sister. I'll catch you."

Bradley picked up Anna and stepped to the window. As far as he could see, the night air was empty. There was no way of telling that his mom was there.

"Trust me."

Carrying Anna, he climbed onto the ledge, then stopped. He was four stories up, looking down at a half-empty parking lot. "I can't."

"I can force you, if that would be easier."

"I . . ." Bradley held his sister as tightly as he could. He shook his head. "I can't."

"Jump!"

Bradley took a deep breath. His mom wasn't forcing him, she was asking him. He jumped.

Invisible dragon talons caught him, cold and hard as metal, and he and Anna vanished. He still felt his sister in his arms, but he couldn't see her. He couldn't see himself, either.

Beneath him, the hospital fell rapidly away as they accelerated upward through the night sky.

"You're safe," his mom said. "I have you."

Eyes glued to the countryside below, Bradley didn't answer. He was so high up that the cars looked like toys. Trees and houses sped by in a blur, and soon they were approaching Highwater Acres. "We're going home?" he asked.

"It's not safe to be outside." She lowered Bradley to the ground. He and his sister tumbled gently to the grass, turning visible as they fell.

He sat up. "This is the first place they'll look for us!"

"Probably, but this is more than just our trailer. We have to keep it safe."

Brushing off Anna, he stood. "More than just our trailer? What do you mean?"

"Hurry. Get inside before they show up."

Bradley fumbled his key out of his pocket and opened the front door, then carried Anna inside and put her in the green recliner. As he turned, he saw his dad lying on the couch.

Mom must have turned human and brought him in behind me. He looked around, but didn't see her. She was still invisible.

"Lock the front door," she said. "And close all the curtains and blinds. I'll make sure that anyone who looks at this trailer will think it's empty."

Bradley saw the sliding glass door to the back porch open and close. Moments later, the trailer creaked and rocked. *Mom*, he thought. She was sitting on the trailer, watching for enemies and maintaining the illusion that the trailer was empty.

Bradley walked through the trailer, closing curtains and locking doors and windows.

Mr. Sallson was only the beginning, he realized. *The fae are after us.* He adjusted Anna in the green chair so she could sleep more comfortably. *But why? Why are they working with the hunters? What did we ever do to them?*

His phone rang, but before he could answer, his mom whispered, "Turn it off. Stay silent and stay awake. Trust nothing. They are looking for you."

Hands shaking, Bradley sat down at the kitchen table. *They're looking for me*, he thought. *This is all because of me.*

23

A DARK NIGHT

By midnight, Bradley had moved to the kitchen counter, where a small gap in the curtains let him see outside. Highwater Acres looked the same as it did every night: dark and quiet. Clouds hid the moon and covered much of the sky, but a few stars still shone through.

In the den, his dad and sister were still asleep.

Outside, a cloud moved beneath the other clouds, drifting steadily closer toward him. Something about it didn't look right. He concentrated on it, squinting and clenching his jaw. *See it*, he thought. *See what's really there.*

The cloud faded into Kevin's blue-skinned dragon body, which would have been impossible to see in the night sky, if not for his giant golden eagle wings. He landed in the front yard. "Bradley?" he called, lowering his dragon head to peer in the windows. "Aunt Gayle? Are you guys in there? Everyone's worried about you. They're going crazy at the hospital."

Bradley moved to the door to let him in, but stopped before opening it.

"Sh." His mom's voice sounded in his ears. "Stay hidden," she said. "Stay silent."

Kevin knocked on the door, hard enough to rattle it in its frame. "Are you hiding?"

Bradley stepped back. Maybe it wasn't really Kevin. That would explain why his mom wanted him to stay quiet. He returned to the looking out the kitchen window and concentrated on seeing through any illusions. All he saw was Kevin.

"Come on, Bradley," Kevin said. "Are you in there? How am I supposed to be a bodyguard if you don't let me know where you are?" Bradley heard him walk around the trailer, then watched his oversized dark shadow slide across the vertical blinds that covered the sliding glass door.

Once he was back out front, Kevin spread his wings and flew away.

As Bradley watched his cousin disappear into the night sky, a movement across the street caught his eye. Mr. Sallson stepped out from behind the wreckage of the tree struck down by the fae's attack the previous evening.

That's why Mom didn't answer Kevin. She knew Sallson was watching!

The old man watched Kevin fly away, then moved closer to examine the trailer.

Heart pounding, Bradley backed away from the kitchen window.

A beam of brilliant white starlight shone through the front door.

Bradley ran to the den, grabbed his baseball bat, and stood in front of Anna, shielding her.

The light vanished, leaving a round smoking hole in the door. A small but intense white glow floated through it: the fae in its natural form.

Bradley watched, frozen in place by fear. *How can I fight that?*

"He can't see you," his mom whispered.

The light floated through the den, then down the hallway. When it reached Bradley's bedroom door, it flashed and turned into Mr. Sallson. The old man looked around one more time, then opened Bradley's bedroom door.

Sweat dripped down Bradley's forehead. If the fae saw through his mom's illusion, it would be up to him, him and his baseball bat. He squeezed its handle tighter.

Mr. Sallson emerged from his bedroom, then went into Anna's.

We're not here, Bradley thought, trying to add as much power as he could to his mom's illusion. *We're not here!*

Mr. Sallson walked past him again, through the kitchen and into his parent's room. Then he came back to the kitchen and dialed the phone. "They're not here."

There was a pause.

"I'm standing in their kitchen. This is not an illusion. We'll just have to . . . wait a minute." He moved his hand as if he was picking a piece of paper off the counter.

He thinks he's reading something, Bradley thought. *Mom's making him think he found a clue.*

"They left a note for Kevin," Mr. Sallson said. "It says he should meet them in Miami, at the Fontainebleau hotel." He listened, then spoke again. "I'll meet you there. With the father injured, now still is our best chance to get the egg."

He hung up, took another look around, then changed back into a floating ball of light and flew out through the hole in the front door.

Bradley lowered the baseball bat and sank to the floor, holding his head in his shaking hands.

24

SWAMP VERSUS SKY

B y the time morning arrived, Bradley was exhausted. He sat on the floor, leaning against the couch where his dad slept, and watched the sun glow around the edges of the curtains.

"We made it," his mom said.

Bradley turned his head tiredly toward the hole in the front door. He didn't really expect to see her there. During the night, he'd grown accustomed to hearing his mom's voice, even though he couldn't see her. "Are you staying outside?"

"No. Go get some sleep. I'll be in shortly."

"Sleep," he repeated. The thought sounded better than he'd ever thought possible. He walked into his bedroom, kicked off his shoes, and stretched out on his bed. "What about Anna and Dad?"

"I'll be right here."

Bradley closed his eyes and fell fast asleep.

Several hours later, he woke to the sound of his sister laughing. "No, Daddy! That's not how it works!"

He pushed himself up on his elbows and checked the time. The clock read ten minutes past three, and the sun was shining through a gap in his curtains. The not-so-distant roar of diesel engines and heavy construction equipment filtered through the trailer walls, as a crew worked to clean up Sallson's trailer.

"Not like that, either!" his sister said.

He walked into the den. His mom was asleep on the green recliner. His dad sat on the floor, wearing pink beads in his hair and pointing Anna's toy hair dryer at her. A wave of relief washed over Bradley. His dad was back to his old self, laughing and healthy.

"He's awake!" his dad said, pointing the hair dryer at him. "Welcome back, sleeping beauty."

"Me?" Bradley said. "You've been out for two days!"

"Yeah. It was a good sleep, too."

"Does this mean it's time for the picnic?" Anna asked, grabbing the toy hair dryer. She wore a pair of sunglasses shaped to look as if a bright blue butterfly had landed on her face and she was looking out through its wings.

"Yes." Bradley's dad stood. "Why don't you carry the blanket? I'll get the basket." He touched his wife gently on the shoulder. "Hon. It's time to go."

She yawned and stretched.

"Picnic?" Bradley asked. *When the fae are after us?*

"In the swamp." His dad winced as he pulled the beads out of his hair. "I promised Anna we'd have a picnic in the swamp."

"But what about—"

"Just grab the thermos, and let's go to the raft."

"My raft?" He looked at his parents. His mom was wearing her blue sun dress, and his dad had on a pair of navy-blue shorts and a gray t-shirt. Both wore beach sandals on their feet. *They're dressed so they can change into dragons.*

"Come on!" his dad said.

Still yawning, his mom handed him the thermos. "Listen to your father."

The construction sounds faded as they walked into the lush green wilderness of the state park. Mosquitoes buzzed in the air, and lizards rustled through palmettos. Frogs splashed in the distance.

Bradley led the way beneath the moss-draped branches, glancing back occasionally. His dad had Anna on his shoulders, followed by his mom, who had slung an empty backpack over her shoulder. When they reached the raft, Bradley looped the guy line around his wrist, bent over, and pushed the raft into the river.

He and Chris had spent months building their raft. It was made of logs roped together, with boards nailed to the top to make a flat surface. Beneath the logs, they'd built a small wooden framework around a dozen or so empty plastic milk jugs, sealed closed with superglue. Chris had said the air in the milk jugs would help the raft float. Bradley hadn't been so sure, but he couldn't argue with the results.

Once it was in the water, Bradley straightened. "Um," he said. "I'm not sure it will hold all of us."

"Sure it will." His dad put Anna down, then jumped onto the raft.

"My turn!" Anna shouted, leaping after him.

The raft tilted dangerously before leveling out, several

inches lower than before.

"Really dear," Bradley's mom said with a wink. "You worry too much." She put a hand on his shoulder for balance and stepped onto the wooden planks.

The raft sank deeper into the brown water. "If you say so."

Bradley retrieved the paddles from where he kept them tied to a tree and stepped carefully onto the raft. It sank lower, so low that their feet were almost level with the water around them. Bradley handed one paddle to his dad and pushed off the bank with the other one. "I hope we don't meet any alligators."

Afternoon in the swamp was a time of green shadows and brilliant colors. Where the sunlight broke through the canopy, it dazzled the water and painted the leaves yellow and bright green. Flowers turned their heads toward it and dragonflies flitted through its light, snatching mosquitoes out of the air. Where the sun didn't reach, deep shadows transformed logs and cypress knees into strange, otherworldly things.

"Where are we going?" Anna asked.

"It's a surprise," her mom answered. "Now why don't you close your eyes and relax. We'll be there soon enough."

"A nap?" Anna asked. "On the raft? No way!"

Bradley leaned into his paddle, quietly keeping them in the middle of the river. As he guided the raft, his mom started to sing her favorite lullaby.

"Dreams to sell, fine dreams to sell. Angus is here with dreams to sell." Her voice was soft and low, but Bradley felt the subtle power within it, the gentle irresistible urge to sleep.

Anna yawned and sat down.

"Hush now wee bairnie and sleep without fear, for Angus will bring you a dream, my dear."

Bradley glared at the water.

"What's the matter?" Bradley's mom asked once Anna was fast asleep. "You don't like Scottish lullabies?"

"I don't like what comes with them," he snapped. "It's not right. You shouldn't put her to sleep like that. It's no different than hitting her on the head with a hammer."

"Maybe we should just stop them from asking questions, instead." She put her hands on her hips. "Would that be better?"

"I didn't do that on purpose!"

"Enough," his dad said from the front of the raft. "I don't like it either, but we can't leave her home, and we sure can't have her awake for the Gathering."

"The Gathering?" Bradley echoed.

"That's right," his mom said. "Now could you please turn around?"

"Why?" Bradley said.

"Because your mother asked you to," his dad said.

"Fine," Bradley said, turning, but I don't see why—" The raft tilted suddenly and Bradley lost his balance. His dad caught his shoulder and steadied him before he fell overboard.

"What's going on?" Bradley pushed away from his dad and looked around. "Oh."

His mom was gone. In her place were her sandals, sun dress, and the empty backpack.

His dad picked up the clothes, put them in the backpack, and slung it over his shoulder. "Don't bother," he said as Bradley stared at the sky. "She's in full stealth mode. I don't think there's a creature alive that can see her right now. At least," he added thoughtfully, "I hope there isn't." He reached for the paddle. "I'll take a turn, now. I know where we're going."

Bradley handed over the paddle and sat cross-legged on the wet boards. He picked up Anna. "Are you okay with how Mom puts Anna to sleep?"

"To be honest, no." His dad paddled the raft forward. "It's a sky dragon thing, playing with people's minds."

"Well, I'm glad I'm a swamp dragon," Bradley said.

"I wish," his dad said. "That thing you did with Anna? Getting her to not ask questions? And with me? Making me send you home with Chris? Total sky dragon. Swamps are way more straightforward."

"Oh."

"I've been telling your mom for years that you were going to be a swamp dragon," his dad said as he steered them down a branch in the river. "Your green eyes and small size both come from me. It only made sense to think that you'd also be a swamp dragon, like me." He shook his head. "She's never going to let me hear the end of this one."

Bradley sighed. He wanted to be like his dad, too. He brushed a wayward hair out of Anna's face.

"Not that it matters," his dad continued. "A dragon's a dragon. That's what's important. Sky dragons aren't that bad. After all," he said, "I married one, didn't I?"

Bradley didn't answer.

His dad looked over his shoulder at him. "Swamp or sky, you're turning into one heck of a dragon, kiddo. That move to go rescue Chloe with only a human as backup? Pure swamp dragon."

Bradley blushed. "Thanks."

His dad continued paddling, guiding the raft along the branches of the river. Bradley watched the swamp glide past. When they reached a sunlit hummock, his dad laid his paddle on the raft and bent down to pick up Anna. "This is the place."

Bradley lifted the picnic basket and stepped carefully off the raft. His dad grabbed the guy line and jumped ashore, then dragged the raft up out of the water, pulling it with one hand as if it were weightless.

"Wow," Bradley said. Even knowing his dad was a dragon, it seemed impossible for him to be that strong. None of the other dragons he'd seen had been that strong in their human forms.

"Come on." Still carrying Anna, his dad took strode up the hill. "I want to get to the Gathering before Helene."

Bradley hesitated. The ground felt firm enough beneath his feet, but the hill was covered with long grasses, and Bradley knew what lived in long grasses: snakes. Carrying the picnic basket in one hand, he lifted a paddle with the other and poked the grass ahead of him as he walked. "What is a Gathering, anyway? I mean, I know what the word means, but you say it like it's something special."

"It's an old tradition, a way for dragons to come together to talk. In a Gathering, old transgressions are ignored and violence is prohibited. Think of it like meeting under a flag of truce. Your mother called this one the night I went to the hospital."

Bradley heard something slither away from his paddle. He waited until it was quiet before taking another step. "Wouldn't it be easier at the trailer?"

His dad laughed. "All those dragons in our trailer? No way. Outside is best. Even if it weren't, we can't be sure the trailer isn't being watched."

"I thought Mom tricked the fae into going to Miami."

"She did, and she kept us hidden as we left our trailer. We can't be too careful, though. Your mom's checking out the swamp now, making sure we haven't been followed."

The hill they climbed stood slightly taller than the trees around it, but was broad and gently sloped, with no discernible peak. When they reached its rounded top, Bradley dropped his paddle and put down the picnic basket. The sun felt warm and relaxing, and the cloudless blue sky overhead called to him in a way he never remembered experiencing. "Who's coming?"

"Do you remember your uncle Cedrych and aunt Luanna? They have a big family. If anyone can help us, it's them. Antleen'll be here, too, and Kevin. I'm hoping my uncle Li can make it also . . . Ah," his dad said, pointing. "There's our first arrival."

Bradley followed his dad's finger and spotted a dragon flying toward them above the treetops. *No*, Bradley thought, *that's not a dragon*. It was a huge flat stone disk with a person standing on top of it. He shaded his eyes and squinted, watching the figure get closer.

The rock rider wore jeans and a brown leather bomber jacket. A pair of old-fashioned flying goggles covered her eyes, and a white scarf rippled in the air behind her. She balanced easily on the giant rock, holding a walking stick in her right hand.

Bradley laughed out loud. Even from this distance, he recognized Antleen.

25

THE GATHERING

The wide rock floated to a stop directly above Bradley and his dad. As they backed away, it settled onto the grass. Antleen pulled off her flight goggles and unwound the scarf from her neck. "Hey, Bradley. Hey, bro. We the first ones here? Where's Gayle?"

"She's around," Bradley's dad said, gesturing to the clear blue sky. Holding Anna with one arm, he stepped onto the rock to give her a hug. "It's good to see you again. It's been too long."

The top of Antleen's stone platform was covered with several inches of rocks, each about the size of a golf ball. "Did you fly that all the way from Ocala?" Bradley asked, stepping carefully onto the rocks.

"Could have," she said, giving him a quick hug. "Do you like it?"

"It's huge!"

Antleen laughed. "Your mom told me how you saved

Chloe. Good job." She glanced mischievously at her brother. "I particularly love how you made your own dad send you."

"Yeah," his dad said sourly. "That won't be happening again."

Bradley grinned. "Why aren't you in dragon form?" he asked.

"This is more fun. It's a little harder to stop people from seeing me, but I can do it."

"Time for the rules," Bradley's dad said to him. "First: stay off Antleen's rock, and be ready to hit the ground if you see her get angry."

"Angry?" Bradley asked, suddenly uncertain.

"Most dragon families aren't quite as friendly as what you're used to," his dad said. "Second rule: don't talk unless you're asked to. You and Kevin are too young to be here, so stay quiet."

Antleen held Anna while Bradley's dad removed his sandals and shirt and put them in the backpack. He added Antleen's flight goggles and scarf, then took Anna back into his arms and stepped off the rock to face Bradley. "You're in charge of your sister."

After a quick check for snakes, Bradley sat cross-legged in the grass. His dad rested Anna on his lap.

"She's getting bigger," Antleen said. "Won't be long until she's hatching, William."

"I hope so," Bradley's dad said, setting the backpack next to him.

Antleen gestured with her chin to the north. "Here comes Cedrych, and it looks like Li's with him."

"There's Kevin," his dad added, pointing in a different direction.

Bradley concentrated on the empty blue sky. *Focus*, he thought. *See them!*

Kevin came into view first, flying with slow eagle-like strokes of his wings. A black duffel bag dangled from his talons. Next, Bradley spotted a huge flying snake undulating through the air. Its sinuous body glistened blue and green, as though dripping with water. As it came closer, Bradley saw six legs tucked up against its body, with clawed feet curled into fists and an over-sized head that looked vaguely horse-shaped.

Finally, he spotted the third dragon, a black-scaled creature straight out of a fantasy painting. About his dad's size and shape, it soared on giant wings that flapped slow and strong. Silver highlights around its scales flashed in the sun.

"Can you see them?" Bradley's dad asked.

"Yeah."

"Good. Now pretend that you can't. Never give up an advantage, especially with dragons. Let them think you still don't have the focus to see them."

Bradley shielded the sun from his eyes as he pretended to search the skies. The trio landed in the trees, but he kept up his performance, looking from cloud to cloud.

"Down here," Kevin called, walking up the hill.

Bradley did his best to look startled. Kevin wore his loose blue and red swimsuit and a surf shop t-shirt, but was not wearing his normal illusion of youth. If anything, he looked even older than his seventeen years, with dark tired circles under his eyes. Behind him walked a short gray-haired man with a big belly. He wore black sweatpants, an over-sized Chicago Bears jersey, and a pair of blue flip-flops. Bradley hadn't seen his uncle Cedrych in years, but he was easy to recognize.

The third person was new to Bradley: an elderly Chinese man in a sea-green kimono and matching slippers. *That must be Dad's uncle Li*, Bradley thought. He braced himself against the usual wave of fear at meeting a stranger, but for once it didn't come. Instead, all he felt was a slight thrill of nervous energy.

"Hey Cedrych," Antleen said, one hand on her hip. "Where's Luanna? Is she okay?"

Cedrych reached the top of the hill and stopped a pace from the rock. "She was too busy to come. She told me to pass along her kindest regards." He coughed. "Or something like that."

"She can't still be angry," Bradley's dad said. "That was eight years ago."

"Yeah, well," said Cedrych. "She is."

"I'm sorry. Once this is over, I'll come to Chicago and try to make it right." He shook hands with Cedrych and Li. "It's good to see you both."

"Gayle told us you needed help protecting your son," Cedrych said. "She's around here somewhere, I assume?"

"Yes," Bradley's mom said without appearing. "I'm keeping us all unseen. This Gathering will be as private as I can make it."

"Why all the secrecy?" Cedrych said. "It's not like we haven't dealt with hunters before."

"Indeed." Li raised a wrinkled hand toward Bradley. "You are the egg that's in danger?"

"Uh, yeah," Bradley said. "I'm Bradley." He carefully

moved Anna into the grass beside him, then stood up. "Nice to meet you."

"Nice to meet you, as well. I am Li, the husband of your grandfather's sister." His eyes moved up and down Bradley, then he gave a small nod and turned to Bradley's dad. "You were right to call us. He will be a powerful dragon."

I will? Bradley's heart sped up. Li was the guy who wrote the dragon book. If anyone would know, he should.

Kevin, standing several paces back with his hands jammed into his pockets, rolled his eyes.

"Is this all of us?" Li asked.

"Yes," Bradley's dad said.

"What about your father? If your egg is in danger, he should be here."

"He and I aren't on the best of terms."

"Enough with the chit chat," Cedrych interrupted. "Why are we here? And don't say it's just because of an egg." He glanced at Bradley. "No matter how powerful it may be."

Bradley's dad pulled folded pieces of paper out of his back pocket and handed one each to Cedrych, Li, and Antleen. "An organization of hunters has targeted our family. Bradley stole a file from them. It included this list."

Cedrych examined the page in his hand. "This goes back over two hundred years."

"The rest of the file includes more details," Bradley's dad said, "including places and birth dates. Look closely."

"My name's here." Cedrych squinted as he read the list. "And Luanna's."

"As is mine," Li added.

"They missed some of us," Bradley's dad said. "Helene's name isn't there, and neither is Kevin's. But it does include several children Gayle and I had, unhatched eggs we thought safe to abandon."

Abandoned eggs. The idea still made Bradley feel sick. He looked down at his sister lying in the grass. *I won't leave you, Anna.*

"Your turn, kid," Cedrych said to Bradley. "Let's hear it. Who'd you steal this list from?"

"It started when Chloe was kidnapped," Bradley started. He told them everything that had happened, focusing on his two trips to Sallson's home and including the purple light that had flashed when the trailer was destroyed.

Cedrych whistled. "The fae?" He looked at his brother. "How'd you get *them* mad at you?"

"I didn't."

"It's clear they're working with the hunters," Li said. "That black-haired woman in the trailer proves it. The question is why."

"Okay, everyone," Antleen said. "My turn."

She paused, waiting until all eyes were on her, then spoke. "Some fae have learned how to use the *gallu draig.*"

A moment of shocked silence followed her pronouncement.

"That's impossible!" Kevin blurted out.

"You ever heard of Max?" Antleen said.

"The hunter that kidnapped you?" Cedrych said.

She nodded. "He was a fae. He couldn't use the *gallu draig* the way we do, but he could draw—"

"Max was a fae?" Bradley's dad interrupted. "How could . . . but he never . . . What?"

"He fooled us all," Helene said, "but he was a fae, and he figured out how to pull the *gallu draig* out of eggs."

"Why would he?" Li asked.

"Because it's energy," Helene answered. "Thousands of times more powerful than light, but still consumable. A fae that can pull it into himself becomes much more powerful than other fae."

Bradley's dad rubbed his forehead. "Fae that are dragon hunters. You should have told us."

"Until today, I thought Max was the only one. I never heard about any others, and believe me, I've searched. If there'd been any indication that another fae could do this, I would have told everyone I knew."

"This means the fae are against us," Cedrych said.

"No," Helene said. "Not all of them."

"How do you know?" Li asked.

"I just . . . I just do."

"Helene," Bradley's dad said, his voice gentler than the others. "You should have told me."

"For as long as I've been alive, dragons have been ignoring fae," Li said. "Have the fae been preparing to move against us? To enslave us?"

"They've probably just been quietly stealing our kids," Cedrych said, glaring at Helene. "I can't believe you didn't say anything!"

"Max was just one fae," Helene said. "He's the only—"

"Clearly not," Cedrych interrupted. He shook his head. "So typical."

Several stones raised off Helene's platform and started spinning slowly around her. "What would you have done? Start a war with the fae?"

"Stop it," Bradley's dad barked. "This is a Gathering."

The rocks paused, and then dropped. "I did what was

right," Helene said. "You know what our father would have done if he thought a fae had taken me."

"He would have gone to war," Bradley's dad said, nodding. "Nothing would have stopped him."

"Better to go to war than have our kids be stolen," Cedrych said.

"Stop bickering," Li said. "The most dangerous foe we've ever faced is before us. We cannot afford to fight with each other." He looked at the list in his hand. "This explains how far back the file goes. The fae are ageless. They could have been tracking us for centuries."

"I didn't sense any *gallu draig* in Mr. Sallson," Bradley's mom interrupted, her voice floating bodiless around them.

"You wouldn't have," Antleen said. "The fae convert it to light energy, making it a part of them."

"Great," Cedrych said sarcastically. "So we can't even spot them. How are we supposed to defend against creatures that are indistinguishable from humans?"

"Worse," Bradley's mom said. "They can create whatever body they like. They could be birds or cats, or anything. We wouldn't know."

None of them can spot a fae, Bradley thought. *All these powerful dragons, and I'm the only one that can see the fae.*

"We fight," Bradley's dad said, starting to pace. "I need to research how to change my scales so they'll stop those light beams. Maybe they can be reflected or absorbed. Cedrych, I'll need you to—"

"William," Cedrych interrupted, holding up a hand. "I'm not staying."

Bradley's dad stopped. His face stilled.

"This paper has my family's names, too," Cedrych said.

"None of us are safe. We need to go back home and warn everyone."

"Bring them here. We'll stand together."

"No."

"Gayle and I are your best shot, Cedrych. You know that. If any of us can beat the fae, it's us."

"This is too big a fight," Cedrych said. "Even for you. Going up against just one fae almost killed you, and you're the toughest of all of us. No. I have to get back to Chicago and prepare my family. You're on your own."

Bradley's dad turned to Li, his voice intense. "Stay with us, Uncle. With your healing and Gayle's illusions, we can win this fight."

Li didn't answer for several breaths, but then he lowered his eyes and bowed his head. "I'm sorry, William," Li said. "But Cedrych is correct. The five of us would not be enough. I have other family to warn and gather. We must all look to our own, to prepare—"

"Look to our own?" Bradley's dad roared. "Why do you think I called this Gathering? Individually, none of us are safe! We need to come together. We need to stand, together."

"The fae have tracked us," Li said. "But we do not know who they are, or how many there are. The prudent course is investigation. We cannot strike at an enemy until we know its face."

They're scared, Bradley thought. *They're so scared they're running away.* "But we do know one of them," he said quickly. "We also know they want me. Use that. I can be the bait. We can catch them."

His uncle Cedrych shook his head. "Won't work. Your

trap might get a few, but we don't know how many are out there. Our families would be at risk for reprisals."

"What about my family?" Bradley's dad said. "How do I fight them and protect my family at the same time?"

"Stop being so dramatic," Cedrych said. "Just go hide somewhere. It's what you've been doing for the past twelve years, anyway. You should be good at it by now."

Bradley's dad flinched as if he'd been struck, and all the color drained from his face.

"Be careful, Cedrych." The voice of Bradley's mom slithered around them, low and rough.

Cedrych jumped in surprise, then frowned. "Lay off it, Gayle. You won't break the rules of—"

"Try me." Her voice was flat and hard. Cedrych looked around, his expression uncertain.

A cloud of rocks floated up from Helene's platform, hovering around her.

Cedrych backed up a step.

"Here's an idea," Kevin said. "Why not hide Bradley until he hatches? Uncle William, you and Aunt Gayle stay and fight the fae while he tries to hatch. If you both stay here, the fae'll think Bradley's with you and won't search anywhere else. All you gotta do is stall for time while Bradley hatches."

Granduncle Li looked thoughtful. "Interesting! William has never been happy with hiding. It's likely your enemy knows that. Use their expectation against them."

"No," Bradley said quickly. He couldn't handle another scene like he'd had in the trailer, watching helplessly while his dad fought. "I can help. I want to help."

"Don't be stupid," Kevin said. "You're just a battery for

the fae." His voice had a condescending edge that ignited an angry fire deep within Bradley. "You're a danger to whoever you're with."

"I am not," Bradley grated. "I'm hatching. I am. It won't be long."

"It's not a bad idea, Bradley," his dad said. "With you safe, your mom and I can fight."

"I don't want to hide!" Bradley said.

"Why don't we take him back to Chicago with us?" Kevin asked Cedrych.

"No," said Cedrych. "My name's on the list, which means they're watching our family, too. Sending him with us won't do any good. What about you, Helene? You're not on the list."

"Not a good idea," Antleen said.

"Why not?" Bradley's dad asked. "We just need to move him away from us."

"It's not that I don't want to," she answered, her stones dropping to the platform, "but I'm nowhere near the fighter you are. If the fae show up, what am I supposed to do?"

"Hide," Bradley's mom answered. "If they find you, run back to us. It won't be long. Please, Helene. I would take him if I could, but he could take weeks to hatch, and I can't keep him invisible that long. You and Kevin are the only ones not on the list, and Kevin's been here these past days. It's likely he's been spotted."

"How can I get him away from here? I don't do invisible, Gayle."

"I can keep you unseen long enough for you to get away."

"I can't," Antleen said. "You don't understand . . ." She

stared at Bradley and Anna, her expression bleak, then took a deep breath and blew it out.

She's tired, Bradley thought. *Tired and sad.*

"Okay." Antleen reached into the backpack and withdrew her flight goggles and scarf. "But if I'm going to do this, I better get going. Bradley, I'll be back in a little while. Pack whatever you need."

The rock platform beneath her feet trembled, then raised off the ground and carried her swiftly away.

"That's that," Cedrych said. "No hard feelings?"

"That depends on how this turns out," Bradley's dad said.

The two men stared at each other for several heartbeats before Cedrych turned away. "Come on, Kevin," he said. "It's a long way back to Chicago."

"Shouldn't I stay with Helene to help guard Bradley?"

"No," Cedrych said. "They're hiding, not fighting."

"I can hide with them," Kevin said. "Come on. They hired me to be a bodyguard, and I haven't done anything yet."

"If a fae finds them," Cedrych said, "you won't be any help at all. I know your power, Kevin. You don't stand a chance against a fae."

"But—"

"He's right," Bradley's dad interrupted. "We're betting on secrecy, and fewer people are easier to hide. Thanks, Kevin, but you're not the dragon for this job."

Kevin's jaw clenched, then he turned to follow Cedrych down the hill.

Li inclined his head to Bradley's dad. "I understand how you must feel, but this plan is a good one. Bradley will be safe in his aunt's care, and I will return as soon as I can."

"You honestly think we'll last that long?"

Li flinched, and his head bowed more deeply.

"Pass that list to my father," Bradley's dad said. "He should know what's going on."

Li nodded and walked down the hill.

Bradley turned to his dad. "What was all that about Kevin's power?"

"Each dragon has a specialty, a power that comes naturally. Kevin's is . . . Well, he deals in physical sensations. That won't help against the fae. Not much, at any rate. They don't feel things the way we do."

"Oh." Bradley knelt down next to his sister. "What are we going to do about Anna?"

"You noticed, huh?" his dad gave a disgusted grunt. "To them, she wasn't even worth mentioning." He paused, thinking. "She'll have to go with you."

"What about you and mom?" Bradley asked.

"We'll have to stay together, rest during the day so we can fight at night. Your mom'll quit her job and I'll close the shop. It's probably for the best. No way to tell how long this thing will last."

"I can't just run away, Dad. You know I can't."

"The whole point of this plan is to buy you time to hatch. Now that we know what's coming, your mother and I will put up a good fight."

"You don't sound very confident," Bradley said.

"Without the others . . ." his dad trailed off, then gave a forced shrug. "If the fae attack in numbers, we'll have to run. Don't worry. You should still be safe."

"Dad!"

"Just focus on hatching. Once they don't have an egg to steal, they won't have any reason to keep bothering us."

Great, Bradley thought. *No pressure. Just hurry up and hatch before the fae wipe out your whole family.*

26

GOODBYES

B radley's mom woke Anna once they were back on the raft.

"You said we were going to have a picnic," Anna said.

"I'm sorry," Bradley's mom said. "We wanted to, but we have to get back. We'll have a picnic on the raft."

"On the raft?"

"Sure!" Bradley's mom opened the picnic basket and pulled out their red and white checkered picnic blanket. "Help me spread it."

"We've never had a picnic on the raft before," Anna said as she grabbed one end of the blanket.

Bradley and his dad stood on either side of the raft, using their paddles to push off against the muddy river bottom. They had a clear blue sky overhead, a cool breeze, and the gentle sound of water lapping all around them.

"Let's eat," his mom said, upending the picnic basket onto the blanket. PBJ sandwiches wrapped in wax paper tumbled out, along with Girl Scout cookies, plastic cups, and a pile of carrots.

"Youngest gets first pick!" Anna shouted, lunging for the food.

Bradley watched. *This could be our last picnic. If I don't hatch quickly enough, or if the fae find us . . .* He stopped the thought. They were moving as fast as the raft would go.

"Go on, kiddo," Bradley's dad said. "I can keep us moving on my own."

Bradley forced himself to smile as he stowed his paddle, then moved forward to pour himself a cup of lemonade. It tasted ice-cold and delicious, sweet and tart all at once. Out of the corner of his eye, he spotted Anna sneaking a cookie into her sandwich. Behind her, his mom smiled and pretended not to notice. She gathered together some food for his dad, then took a turn at the paddle.

Anna flopped on her back. "That was awesome."

"I'm glad," Bradley's mom said, but her voice didn't match the words.

Anna raised her head. "What's wrong, Mom? You sound sad."

Bradley and his dad exchanged a glance.

"Well," Bradley's mom answered, giving her paddle to Bradley, "I'm just sorry that we didn't find what we were looking for."

"What was that?" Anna asked.

Bradley's dad quietly took up the other paddle, and the raft increased its speed.

Bradley's mom looked as sad as he had ever seen. "Courage," she said at last. "I thought we'd find it growing on a hill, but I was wrong."

Anna looked at Bradley, confused. "Courage?"

He shrugged and pretended to look confused. He hated lying to his little sister.

She stood, her eyes on her mom. "Are you okay?"

"I'm fine, dear. Why don't you help your dad paddle?"

Anna went hesitantly to her father, and soon she and her dad were having a splash fight.

Bradley's mom watched the sky, her eyes distant and unfocused. *She's keeping us hidden and safe*, Bradley realized. *Always. That's what she's always doing. It's what she's been doing ever since I was born.*

They arrived at the trailer just as the sun was starting to set. "Get packed, kiddo," Bradley's dad said to him. "Make it quick."

"But—" Bradley started.

"There's no time to argue. The sun's almost gone."

The sun's almost gone. Bradley ran to his room and grabbed his duffel bag. Would the fae attack tonight? How much time did they have?

"Pack?" Anna said. "What for?"

"He's going on a trip with Antleen," Bradley's mom said. "Doesn't that sound like fun? You should go, too."

"Well . . ." Anna said. "I would, but I want to see Chloe. Can I see Chloe first?"

"No dear, but she'll be out of the hospital when you get back. Why don't you go with Antleen? Come on. I'll help you pack."

"I really want to see Chloe." Anna trailed after her mom.

Bradley tossed the dragon book into his duffel, then grabbed handfuls of clothes and shoved them on top. He couldn't stop thinking that the fae were closing in. *They're probably hiding in the bushes across the street, just waiting to attack.*

"Not the best packing job," his mom said from his doorway.

Bradley jumped. "Mom! Don't you need to get outside to hide us? You know, like last night?"

"We still have time." She leaned on the door frame. "Besides, this is different than last night. Your dad's both awake and angry." She chuckled. "Honestly, I feel a little sorry for the first fae that shows up."

Bradley zipped his duffel closed. "Do I really have to go?"

"Yes. Everyone's counting on you. If you can't figure out how to hatch . . ."

Bradley groaned.

"Don't worry. I know you can do it." She took a deep breath. "Also, while there's still time, I wanted to say I'm sorry."

"Sorry? What for?"

"I was the one who told you that Sallson wasn't dangerous."

He swallowed, fighting back a rush of tears. *She's apologizing because she doesn't think she'll see me again.* "It's okay."

"Go see your father," she said. "He's got something to show you."

Bradley found his dad in his parents' room, sitting on the bed, which had been pushed to the far side of the room. He stopped in astonishment. There was an open trapdoor in the floor, directly underneath where the bed usually sat. Through the hole, Bradley saw gold bars gleaming dully. He moved closer, his mouth suddenly dry. The bars were stacked side-by-side with no space between them, a dusty yellow brick foundation beneath the floor. "Is that gold?"

"Yep."

"But we're not rich," Bradley whispered, his eyes glued to the gold. More than anything, he wanted to reach down and touch it, to pick up a piece and hold it close. "We live in Highwater Acres. You're a car mechanic. Mom waitresses at a diner."

"Whine, whine, whine. Our life isn't bad. I like working on cars, your mom loves the gossip at the diner, and you and Anna are happy, well-adjusted kids."

"But we could be *rich* kids!" Bradley knelt by the hole in the floor. This close, the gold seemed to have a smell. He inhaled deeply. The odor was warm and intoxicating, even a little dizzying.

"It's not your gold," Bradley's dad said. "It's mine."

Bradley couldn't take his eyes off the precious metal. His heart thumped. "How much is there?" he asked.

"Three layers of bricks under the whole room, everything your mom and I have accumulated over the centuries."

Bradley reached down to touch the gold bars. They were cold and slightly damp, but tingled under his fingertips. "This is why Mom brought us back to the trailer last night," he said. "It's . . . it's your dragon hoard."

"Gold is important to a dragon. It stores *gallu draig*. What you're looking at is a giant battery, one that your mom and I have spent centuries charging. It helped your mom last night, and it will help us fight the fae tonight."

"Wow."

"If something happens to us, you need to know it's here."

Bradley jerked his gaze from the gold to his dad. "What?"

"If something happens to your mom and me, Cedrych's family will be here as quick as they can. You'll have to beat them here to get it. There are no rules when a dragon dies. Whoever gets the gold, gets it." He closed the trapdoor. Its top was carpeted to match the rest of the room, and it had no visible handle. "Now give me a hand with this bed."

After they dragged the bed back into position, his dad put an arm around his shoulders and guided him out of the room. "I'm not going to have to keep my door locked when you come back, am I?"

"What?" Bradley's voice cracked. "No. Of course not."

"How's our little egg?" his mom asked from the kitchen. "Still an egg?"

"Yeah," His dad answered. "I don't know if I should be happy or not."

"Be happy." Bradley's mom pulled him into a hug. "We don't want him to be *that* kind of dragon."

Bradley glanced back toward his parents' room. *They thought the gold might make me hatch*, he thought. He shivered, remembering how it had tingled under his fingers. *I wonder if it almost did.*

His mom let go of him. "We should get going. Antleen'll be here in a few minutes." She turned her head. "Anna, time to go!"

"What about the fae?" Bradley asked. The sun had set, which meant the fae would be at their full strength.

"Let us worry about that." His dad held out a hand. "Phone."

"Why?"

"I can't track it, but I know people who can, and I'm sure the fae do, too."

Bradley handed over his phone.

Anna backed out of her room, dragging her backpack. "I just added a few things." She had dark green camouflage sunglasses pushed up over her hair. "Could you carry it?"

"Sure." Bradley heaved it up over his shoulder and picked up his duffel.

"You two have fun with Antleen," his mom said. She kissed each of them goodbye. "Silly me. I just remembered that I forgot my purse in the truck." She winked at Bradley and left through the front door.

Bradley's dad knelt and pulled them into a group hug. "Take care of your sister, Bradley, and mind your aunt. But more importantly, focus." His eyes locked on Bradley's. "Do you understand? You have a job to do."

"I know," Bradley said. "I'll do it."

"And you," his dad said to Anna, bumping noses with her. "You cause as much trouble as you can, okay?"

"Hooray!" Anna shouted.

"Now get out of here." Bradley's dad opened the front door. A dented old blue Ford Sedan was parked out front.

The night air was cool and fresh and filled with the rustlings and splashings of the swamp. The moon was larger than it had been the night Bradley's dad was attacked, not quite full, but almost.

Anna shivered. "Who's that?"

Bradley glanced over his shoulder. He wasn't certain, but he thought he saw a dragon-shaped shimmer in the night sky. *Mom's keeping us hidden.* Anyone watching probably couldn't even see that the door to the trailer had opened, let alone see the car. "Come on," he said to Anna. "Antleen's waiting."

The car's passenger windows had smoked glass, impossible to see into. As Bradley and Anna approached, the passenger door swung open and Antleen leaned toward them. She wore a fedora, overcoat, and black sunglasses, and had a black bristly mustache on her upper lip.

"This mission," she said to Anna, "is top secret. Where's your disguise?"

Anna pulled her camouflage sunglasses down over her eyes. "Got it." She climbed into the booster that was in the back seat.

"And yours?" Antleen said to Bradley.

"I'm working on it," he said, sliding onto the front seat. "Believe me, I'm working on it."

27

ON THE RUN

As they drove away from Highwater Acres, Antleen took off her sunglasses and mustache. She handed them to Bradley. "Too itchy."

Bradley put them in the glove compartment.

Antleen nodded toward the windshield and murmured. "Can you see her?"

Bradley concentrated on the sky. The almost-full moon had a haze around it, a ring of wispy light that made it look like a giant round eye peering out of the sky. The stars seemed cold and distant, like frozen rain drops.

See her, Bradley thought.

A pain pulsed behind his eyes, spreading through his head as he strained to see.

Gradually, a vaguely dragon-shaped outline of faint light appeared, soaring above them. It was visible, he had no doubt, only to him. He smiled.

"She's hiding us," Antleen said.

Bradley nodded. As fun as Antleen was making their

flight, he knew exactly how dangerous it was. The fae were after them, the same fae that had put Chris in the hospital and almost killed his dad.

As they swung onto the highway, Antleen lifted a half-full coffee cup from a plastic holder clipped to the dash. She took a long sip and put the cup back, then glanced at him. "Try to relax, Bradley. Worrying won't help."

"Stay safe," the voice of Bradley's mom whispered through the car, loud enough for them all to hear. "Come back to me when you can."

Tears sprang to Bradley's eyes. He wiped them away quickly before Anna or his aunt could see.

"Mommy?" Anna asked, her voice quiet.

No one answered.

"Hey," Anna said more loudly. "Did you just hear Mom?"

"I sure did," Antleen answered. "You never told me she was magic."

"I . . ." Anna said. "Na-ah! You didn't hear her. You're tricking me."

Antleen laughed. "That's just what Bradley used to say."

Bradley leaned his head against the seat. Despite everything that had happened, he still didn't have any idea how to hatch. Seeing the dragons at the Gathering had been downright easy, though, so he hoped he was getting closer. *And I made Anna stop asking questions at the hospital,* he remembered, *and I made Dad let me leave the hospital.*

Those thoughts made his stomach roil. If that's what sky dragons were all about, he wasn't sure he wanted to be one. *What if I don't like the dragon I'm turning into?* The idea made him nervous. *Maybe that's the real reason that some dragons don't hatch.*

The miles rolled past his window as he thought about the dragon he wanted to become. Antleen and Anna played game after game, calling out letters on signs, making rhymes, even telling each other a story, one line at a time. Eventually, Anna drifted off to sleep. Bradley looked sharply at his aunt.

"Relax," she said. "I'm swamp, not sky. I don't do the sleep thing. She's just a little girl riding in a car."

"Where are we going?" Bradley asked.

"I have a cabin in Georgia, surrounded by wilderness, on the edge of the Okefenokee. Virtually no one knows about it, not even your parents."

"Sounds like a good hiding place," he said, trying to keep the bitterness from his voice.

"We've got water and electricity, but that's it. We left our phones with your dad, and there are no roads, computers, or TVs. It'll be just us and the trees. Nothing to distract you from hatching."

Bradley sighed. "I just wish I knew how."

"It wasn't easy for me, either," Antleen said.

"Mom says I have to figure out who I want to be," Bradley said. "Kevin says I should try impossible stuff. The dragon book says I need to discover what I need, whatever *that* means, and Dad says I need to follow my dreams." He took a breath. "But I don't have any dreams!"

Antleen pressed her lips together for a moment. "For me, it was all about finding the one thing."

"The one thing?"

"Yeah. The thing that was most important to me. Once I had that, everything else just kind of happened."

"Is that why the dragons I've seen are all so different? I mean, Mom, Dad, Kevin and Granduncle Li don't look anything like each other."

Antleen nodded. "What we want shapes us. Your mom wanted to stay safe and be left alone. She ended up invisible and able to control people's perceptions, to keep them from seeing her. Your dad wanted to be a defender of the weak, so he's huge and strong."

"And you?" Bradley asked. "What's your one thing?"

"None of your business. I will tell you my primary power, though." Her coffee cup floated up to her lips and she took a drink. "I'm telekinetic."

Bradley watched the cup as it flew back to the cup holder, remembering the rocks that had spun around his aunt at the Gathering.

"So?" she asked. "Any idea what your one thing might be?"

"I don't know." Bradley's mouth tasted sour. His stomach felt like it did when he didn't know the answers on a test. He had no idea what his one thing was. All he knew was that he had to hatch, that every minute he stayed an egg was another minute his family was in danger.

"How did you get back from The Gathering so fast?" Bradley asked.

Antleen grinned. "I dumped the giant rock on the far side of the swamp, then rented this thing." She tapped the steering wheel. "After that, all I had to do was pick up some supplies."

"You said you had a lot to do."

"I wanted to leave before any of the others." She looked at him, all humor gone from her face. "There's more going on than we know, Bradley. Too many of these pieces don't fit together. We need to take every advantage we can get."

Bradley opened his mouth, then closed it again.

His aunt was talking about not even trusting her own family.

He looked out the window. *It's all on me*, he thought. *I have to hatch.*

28

THE CABIN

They drove all night, then parked the car behind an abandoned shopping center. Anna woke, and Antleen pulled a frame pack and her walking stick out of the trunk.

"What's with the walking stick?" Bradley asked. Between trying to hatch and worrying about the fae, he was exhausted. "You had it at the Gathering, too."

"It helps me focus," Antleen answered. "It grounds me when I need to . . ." Her eyes slid to Anna then back to Bradley. "Move things."

"Move things?" Anna echoed.

"Yes." Antleen waggled her eyebrows dramatically.

Anna laughed. She had switched to her rainbow sunglasses, the ones with the bright blue lenses that reflected the sky when she tilted her head.

"Now," Antleen said, shouldering her pack, "we hike."

She led them into the weeds, following no trail that Bradley could see. They hiked through the Georgia back country, crossing streams and hummocks. Mostly, they stayed under the cover of large hardwood trees. When Anna got tired, Antleen carried her on her shoulders, pointing out landmarks as they walked.

After a couple hours, Bradley gave up on trying to figure out his one thing, and switched to attempting one impossible task after another. Flying didn't work. Neither did levitating. He couldn't read his sister's mind, or send her any thoughts. He willed some birds to come down to him from the trees. They ignored him.

Shortly before the sun set, Antleen stopped and shrugged off her pack. Anna's backpack rolled onto the grass beside it. "We're here."

"Here?" Bradley asked. They were standing in a swampy clearing beside a dark brown river. "I thought you said there was a cabin."

Antleen pointed. About fifty yards away, tucked beneath a stand of giant sprawling live oaks, stood a worn log cabin with a wooden porch. Spanish moss hung all around the little building, draping over its metal roof and clinging to its walls.

"Cool," Anna breathed, taking off her sunglasses to get a better look.

Antleen opened her pack and pulled out a carabiner of keys. "I think so."

The wilderness had almost completely reclaimed the cabin's wooden porch. Vines covered its railings, bushes grew through its wooden slats, and tall grasses screened the latticework beneath it. Of the whole cabin, only the brick chimney seemed to have resisted nature's advances. The rest of it looked more like a plant than a building.

Antleen unlocked the front door. "Why don't you two relax while I cook dinner?"

"Sounds good," Bradley said. He dropped his duffel and stretched out on the hammock.

Anna pulled a lollipop from her pack and climbed up next to him. "My legs hurt."

"Mine, too." He listened to the crickets calling in the early evening air. A wind rustled the green canopy of leaves and moss around the porch. The place was so peaceful that he could almost forget he was hiding from hunters who wanted to kidnap him and steal his power.

No, I can't, he corrected himself. *It's all on me. I've got to stay focused.*

Anna snuggled against him and sucked on her lollipop.

Bradley stared at the moldy ceiling. He still had no idea what his "one thing" might be. All he'd come up with was not being scared of strangers, and that wasn't much of a power.

Knock, knock, knock. Pause. Knock, knock, knock.

Anna sat up. "Did you hear that?"

Heart pounding, Bradley sat up also. Who could be knocking? He swung his feet to the porch floor.

Knock, knock, knock. Pause. Knock, knock, knock.

"Antleen," he whispered to the open door of the cabin.

She poked her head out. "Yeah?"

"Someone's here. Listen!"

Knock, knock, knock. Pause. Knock, knock, knock.

Antleen smiled. "I think you can handle this one yourself." She nodded at the tree growing against the porch. "Why don't you climb up and check?"

"Can we?" Anna took off her sunglasses and leaned over the railing to look up.

"Just don't fall," Antleen said, going back inside. "That would be bad."

Knock, knock, knock. Pause. Knock, knock, knock.

"It's a woodpecker," Bradley said, feeling embarrassed.

"What did you think it was?" Anna asked, climbing off the porch and into the branches of the tree.

Bradley followed.

They worked their way carefully up, trying to climb as quietly as they could, until they were even with the rusted edge of the metal roof.

Knock, knock, knock. Pause. Knock, knock, knock.

Anna craned her neck around, then pointed through the Spanish moss. Bradley peered between the gray branches of the tree and spotted it: a flash of red feathered head, a glimmer of a black back.

The woodpecker hopped sideways around the tree and out of view.

Knock, knock, knock. Pause. Knock, knock, knock.

"That is so cool," Anna said.

"Yeah," Bradley said.

They stayed in the tree for a while, hoping to get another look, then climbed back down. On the way, Bradley's nose caught a familiar smell wafting up from the cabin. Spicy-hot, but at the same time pungent and heavy, it set his mouth to watering.

Chili. His aunt had made chili. He raced into the cabin.

Antleen sat on the floor by the fireplace, reading a book. A cast iron pot hung over the fire, with his aunt's brick-red chili bubbling and spitting within. Thick chunks of meat floated among the beans. Bradley leaned over the pot, breathing in the sweet onions, spicy chili peppers, and rich beef. He licked his lips. "That smells delicious."

Antleen handed him a metal bowl and a large spoon. "Have at it."

"Ewww," Anna said. "It's disgusting!"

His aunt laughed and opened the refrigerator. "I've got some cold macaroni and cheese, waiting just for you."

Wrapping his hand in his sleeve, Bradley used the ladle hanging from the side of the cauldron to scoop up the thick hot goo and plop it into his bowl. "Got any cheese?"

"Of course." Antleen tossed him a wedge of cheddar. "Here at casa Antleen, no request is too extreme."

Anna laughed.

After shredding a couple inches of cheese onto his dinner, Bradley looked around for a seat. The cabin's main room doubled as both the living room and kitchen, but the only furniture was the couch his sister occupied. He dropped cross-legged to the floor.

"Not bad, huh?" Antleen said. "I'm glad the chimney still works. I much prefer cooking on a fire to using the stove." She stretched. "You guys'll sleep out here. I get the bedroom."

"I call the couch," Anna said.

Bradley sighed.

Two open windows, one behind the couch and one beside the front door, provided a slight breeze, but not nearly enough to clear out the smell of musty wood, smoke, and chili. Bradley took a steaming bite and dug in his pack for the dragon book.

"What's that?" Anna said.

"New book I got." He flipped it open and found a painting of a blue butterfly hovering over a field of dead grass. Below the painting were the words *It's not what you can do that's important. It's why you do it.*

Anna put her sunglasses back on. "Weird book. It looks like it's made out of wood."

Bradley turned his back to her. "Go bug Antleen, Anna. I'm busy."

He flipped to the last page of the book. The whole page was painted black, except for three words, their letters visible as bare unpainted paper: *Who are you?*

I'm the guy that has to hatch, Bradley thought with a sudden burst of fear. *Cause if I don't, my parents are going to die.*

29

A MIDNIGHT VISITOR

K nock, knock, knock. Pause. Knock, knock, knock.
Bradley woke with a start and scrabbled to his feet. Antleen's rhythmic snoring drifted in from her bedroom. Anna slept on the couch. Moonlight shone through the windows of the cabin.

Stupid woodpecker. Bradley yawned and stretched.

Knock, knock, knock. Pause. Knock, knock, knock.

He froze, mid-stretch. The knocking sounded like it was on the front door. He moved closer. Maybe the wood was old, and had bugs in it?

He grasped the doorknob, then hesitated. What if it wasn't a woodpecker? *It's not like anyone else would be out here.*

Knock, knock, knock. Pause. Knock, knock, knock.

On the other hand, what if it was somebody? *Stop being so scared!*

Before he could talk himself out of it, he yanked open the door.

A tall red-haired man in a leather jacket stood on the

porch, the same man Bradley had seen talking to Mr. Sallson in Highwater Acres. His skin was unnaturally pale, and his eyes seemed strange, as though he was looking through Bradley instead of at him.

Fae.

Bradley froze, terrified. He clutched at the door with shaking hands. "I . . . I . . ."

"Bradley," the man said.

Bradley's mouth moved, but no sound came out. He swallowed and tried to force himself to breathe.

Behind him, Antleen's bedroom door creaked open. "What's going on?"

He turned toward her. "F . . . F . . . Fae!"

Antleen was barefoot, wearing sweatpants and a rumpled t-shirt, but she held her walking stick in her right hand. She crossed the room in four quick strides, and put herself between Bradley and the man. "Max," The name came out in one long sad syllable.

Bradley's eyes shot to her face. Max was supposed to be dead.

"What are you doing here?" Antleen demanded, her knuckles white where she gripped her walking stick.

"Warning you."

"I told you what I'd do if you ever came back," Antleen said.

"Not at night, you won't." Max tilted his head toward Bradley. "Even if the moon wasn't shining, I have all his power to draw on."

Bradley felt like he'd been punched. *Kevin was right. All I am is a battery.*

Antleen glared at Max. "You said you'd leave us alone,"

she said. "Three years ago, that was the deal. I let you live. You promised to leave."

"I did leave," Max said. "But I've been called back by someone I can't ignore."

"Why—?" Bradley's voice came out as a terrified squeak. He squeezed his eyes shut. His heart was pounding so loud he could barely hear his own words. *Antleen is here*, he thought. *You can do this*. He opened his eyes. "Why can't you ignore him?" he asked.

"Power," Max said, his voice flat and emotionless. "He's been collecting dragon eggs and trading their power to build an army. He has countless followers—fae, humans, even some dragons. When he calls, I have no choice but to listen."

"You promised," Antleen repeated.

"You shouldn't have taken Bradley after the Gathering. Once they knew you had him, they came straight to me."

"How did they know?" Bradley asked.

Max and Antleen didn't respond. Their eyes were locked on each other.

"Join us," Antleen whispered to Max.

"What?" Bradley's voice cracked in astonishment.

"Helene," Max said, his voice surprisingly gentle.

"You know how strong William and Gayle are," Antleen said. "You know what I can do. Imagine the four of us together. We could stand against anyone."

"It's too late." Max stepped back. "Sallson's on his way here. He expects my help."

Sallson. Bradley's fists clenched as raw rage burned away his fear. "You're lying! He didn't call you after the Gathering. I saw you with him last week. You've been working with him the whole time."

"You are mistaken."

"No, I'm not!" Bradley said. "Antleen, you have to listen. He's lying! He's not—"

An invisible force hit Bradley in the chest and shoved him back into the couch. He landed next to Anna, who had her blanket pulled up so it covered everything but her wide frightened eyes.

"Stay quiet," he whispered to her. "It'll be okay."

"Why?" Helene asked Max. Her eyes scanned the broken pieces of sky visible through the leaves. "If Sallson's on his way, why warn us?"

"Because we had a good couple of centuries," Max answered softly. His voice caught, ever so slightly. "And I wanted to say goodbye."

Before Antleen could respond, Max returned to his fae form, a golf ball-sized reddish-golden light. The light darted off the porch and zipped away into the night sky.

Bradley watched his aunt's eyes track it until it disappeared.

30

ONE LAST CHANCE

Antleen closed the door. "I'm sorry I shoved you, Bradley" she said, "but I needed to ask him more questions."

"Three years ago?" Bradley hissed, scrambling to his feet. "He was the dragon hunter who tried to grab me, wasn't he?"

His aunt nodded.

"You said you'd taken care of him," Bradley said. "You told Mom you took care of him!"

"I thought I had. I was wrong."

"You don't get to be wrong," Bradley shouted. "You can't be! This is too important."

"What's going on?" Anna asked. "Who was he? Where'd he go?"

Antleen put down her walking stick and gathered Anna into a hug.

"No," Bradley shouted again, waving his arms. "Answer

me! Why didn't you say something? Why didn't you tell us Max knew we were here? Why did you agree to hide us?"

His aunt looked at him, her eyes wet. "Don't you understand? Max just saved our lives."

"He . . ." Bradley stopped. It didn't make sense. Max was the enemy, the bad guy. He was both a dragon hunter and a fae—and now his aunt was crying?

"He said he was leaving," Antleen said softly. "Three years ago, he swore." She kissed the top of Anna's head. "I'm sorry. I'm so, so sorry."

"Don't cry, Antleen," Anna said, hugging her. "It's okay."

"But," Bradley shook his head. "Max has been alive all this time, and you knew?"

"Yes," Antleen said, putting Anna down. "He was . . . a friend." She wiped her eyes with the back of her hand. "Then he tried to take you, three years ago." She shook her head. "I should have . . . but he swore he was leaving. I let him go."

"We're dead." Bradley dropped onto the couch. "We're all dead."

"What?" Anna said, clutching her blanket.

"No," his aunt said. "Just the opposite."

"But he kidnapped you," Bradley said.

"Kidnapped?" Anna said, "like Chloe was?"

"I was never kidnapped," Antleen said. "He and I ran away together. I invented the kidnapping story to keep your grandfather from getting angry with me. After my 'rescue,' Max and I went in different directions, but we still saw each other whenever we could." She shook her head. "That all ended three years ago."

Centuries, Bradley thought. *He was her boyfriend for centuries.*

"Antleen," Anna said, tugging at her sleeve. "I don't understand."

"There's no time, little Annabear." Antleen headed for her bedroom. "Close the curtains, Bradley. Block out the light however you can."

Bradley and Anna chased after her. "Why?" Bradley asked. "What's your plan?"

"Sallson will be here any moment. We don't want him to see inside." She slid an ax out from beneath her bed. "Now get out there and seal the curtains."

"Can you beat a fae?" he asked. "I mean, with your telekinesis? Can you just grab him?"

"No. When they don't have a body, they're just energy. There's nothing for me to grab on to. Close the curtains. I want Sallson to think we're hiding in here. Hurry. We don't have much time. He may already be outside."

Anna's eyes were wide and scared. "Antleen?"

Bradley ran to the den and pulled the curtains closed. "If you can't beat him, what are we going to do?" A crash sounded from his aunt's bedroom, followed by the sound of splintering wood. He grabbed a towel and stuffed it around the edges of the window, where the curtain didn't cover, and moonlight was streaming in. He remembered his mom saying that the fae could use any amount of light, that they were strongest at night, under a moon.

"What's going on, Antleen?" Anna asked. "What are you doing?"

Bradley dropped the towel he was working with, then fumbled to get it back in position. He imagined Sallson right outside the cabin, watching him. His hands shook and he dropped the towel again.

"Our adventure is getting a little scary now," Antleen said to Anna as she continued to chop the wooden floor with the ax. "But it'll be all right. Bradley, are you done yet?"

"No," he yelled. "I can't get the towel to stay. It won't stay!"

Antleen stuck her head around the door. "It'll have to do. Get in here."

"Down you go, both of you." She gestured to the hole she'd made in the floor. It was dark and smelled wet. "I'll pull the carpet over after you're in."

Anna grabbed Antleen's hand. "No," she cried. "I can't. It's too dark."

The hole was only about three feet deep, not even tall enough for Bradley to sit up in. He'd have to be on all fours in the muck. "I can't, Antleen. I can't hide again. Let me help. Please. I know I can help!"

"My sunglasses!" Anna dashed into the den.

"Listen," Antleen said, grabbing a blue and green silk kimono from under her bed. "I might be able to handle this Sallson guy, but not if he's using your power against me."

"But I can help!" Bradley said.

"Then help from under the porch. The crawlspace goes all the way to the front. If you think you can do something, do it from there, but stay hidden."

Anna returned with her pink plastic sunglasses. They weren't covering her eyes, but were up over her hair. "Can't we stay with you, Antleen?"

"I'm sorry, Anna." Antleen hugged her.

Bradley stepped down into the hole and reached for Anna, but she clung to her aunt with both hands. "No, no, no!"

"It's okay," Bradley said. "I'll be with you. It's just like hide-and-seek at home."

Come with me, Anna, he thought. *I'll keep you safe.*

Anna let go of her aunt and grabbed him in a fierce hug. Holding her with one arm, he dropped to all fours in the mud. Above him, Antleen pulled the rug over the hole, then dragged something heavy on top of the rug.

The air beneath the cabin pressed in around them, smelling of dirt and decay. Bradley held Anna to his chest with one hand and crawled awkwardly through the blackness. She clung to him like a monkey, her arms and legs wrapped around his torso, her face pressed tight to his chest. Wet mud soaked through the knees of his pajamas.

Something slithered across Bradley's hand. He squeezed his eyes closed and froze.

Please don't let it be a snake. Please don't let it be a snake.

Overhead, he heard the cabin door open and bang shut. Footsteps creaked on the front porch, then all was quiet. Bradley forced himself to stay calm. *Antleen wouldn't run out on us,* he told himself. She wouldn't leave them under the cabin all by themselves.

He listened, but all he could hear was his and his sister's breathing.

"What's wrong?" Anna asked.

"Nothing," he said, shaking his head. His aunt had told him to watch from the latticework. She wouldn't have done that if she was just going to run away.

He started crawling again, then banged his head into a wooden post.

Beneath him, Anna gave a little whimper.

"Shh," Bradley breathed into her ear. "We're almost to

where we can see, but we have to be super quiet." He crawled slowly to the front of the porch, where weeds and grass grew through the wooden latticework. The ground was firmer there, almost dry.

"I'm going to let you down," he whispered to Anna. "We can watch through the holes. Just be careful to stay back. Don't let your fingers or nose poke through the wood, and watch out for snakes."

She nodded and went to her hands and knees beside him.

Bradley inched forward and looked into the night. The field in front of the cabin stood empty: no Max, no Sallson, no Antleen. The woods were quiet. He let out a breath. *Maybe Sallson isn't coming.* Maybe Max had given them enough time to find a new hiding place.

Then, between one breath and another, Mr. Sallson appeared in a patch of moonlight next to an oak tree. He still wore his same tattered old clothes, still looked the part of the harmless old man.

Fear and anger raged through Bradley. His blood pounded in his ears and his hands trembled. Sallson was responsible for everything: Chloe being kidnapped, Chris getting electrocuted, Bradley's dad almost dying. It was all because of Sallson.

31

ANTLEEN

A nna clutched his arm. "It's—"

Bradley clamped his hand over her mouth. He shook his head and waited until he saw that she understood before releasing her.

Mr. Sallson's gaze swept over the cabin, then the trees above it.

Every fiber of Bradley's being wanted to charge out of his hiding place, to burst through the latticework and beat the old man with his bare fists.

Control, Bradley thought fiercely. *Focus.*

He kept his breathing quiet, and stayed absolutely still. *There's nothing here*, he thought, trying to project to the fae. *The cabin is empty. The dragons have fled.*

Moonlight streamed down on Mr. Sallson, but no breeze disturbed the trees around him. No insects chirped in the trees. No frogs called out from the river. The night seemed to be holding its breath.

A rock floated silently up from the riverbank, silhouetted

in the silver moonlight. It hovered for a moment, then flew at Mr. Sallson.

Before the rock could hit him, Sallson transformed into a golf ball-sized white light that hovered in the darkness. Bright as a spotlight, it illuminated the whole forest around it. The rock flew past it to hit the side of the cabin.

Fae, Bradley thought, looking at Sallson's true form.

"He turned into light!" Anna whispered.

Bradley reached out to hold her hand, but didn't take his eyes from the scene before him.

Antleen, in human form, appeared above the river, riding a giant rock just like the one she'd ridden to the Gathering. She'd changed from her sweats and t-shirt into the blue and green kimono, and her hair was pulled into a tight ponytail. She stood straight-backed, holding her walking stick in front of her.

Bradley felt tears forming in the corners of his eyes. His dad was a giant combat dragon, and he'd almost died facing a fae. What chance did Antleen have?

The stone platform floated into the field toward Sallson, and Antleen raised her left hand. A small cloud of rocks rose from the platform to swirl in front of her.

A beam of white light shot from Sallson toward her. It burned into the cloud of stones, but didn't reach Antleen. She smiled and put both hands back on her stick. Thousands of rocks rose around her, forming a larger and much more formidable dome of swirling stone.

Antleen lowered herself to all fours, and her body changed, flowing into the shape of a four-foot-long turquoise dragon. Dragonfly wings sprouted from her back, sending the kimono fluttering to the rock beside her. A ridge of upright scales, sky-blue and edged in black, sprang down the center of her neck and ran to the base of a long tail that grew to more than double her length and had a nasty looking black stinger on its tip. Her wings moved in an iridescent blur of motion, raising her several inches from the rock platform, but keeping her within the dome of wildly spinning rocks.

Bradley's mouth dropped open. Antleen looked nothing like any dragon he'd seen before. She was delicate and beautiful, not at all suited for fighting.

Anna clutched at his arm. "Where'd she go? What happened to Antleen?"

"Shh!" Bradley hissed, angry with himself for losing focus. *I need to help Antleen.* He looked around the forest, but couldn't think of any ideas. *I can't just watch. I have to help. But how?*

Sallson flew a lightning fast circle around the floating maelstrom of rock, firing white beams of light from every angle. They struck Antleen's whirling stones over and over, sometimes sizzling through as many as five or six of them, but never reaching the dragon at their center.

Rocks from Antleen's platform flew at Sallson, turning and spinning after him as he darted between trees.

Bugs, Bradley thought. It was the only trick he knew. It wasn't much, but maybe it would help. *Attack the fae!* he thought, projecting all his hate and need and anger, trying to muster the same focus he had used to see through his mom's illusions. *Attack!*

Stones and light flew back and forth between the fae and the dragon. Sallson's beams couldn't pierce Antleen's shield, and her rocks were too slow to catch Sallson.

Attack! Bradley's head ached from the strain of trying to command the bugs. He knew they were out there, could sense them somehow, but they weren't responding.

The battle among trees was a chaotic swirl. The glowing fae darted around Antleen's spinning dome of rocks, casting erratic shadows in every direction.

Bradley squeezed his eyes closed to concentrate harder. *Why aren't they attacking?* He clenched his teeth. *I made Anna stop asking questions. I made my dad send me to Chris's. Why can't I command these bugs?*

"Oh, no," he whispered. *I'm turning into Mom.*

"What?" Anna whispered back.

"Nothing, nothing. Shh." Bradley swallowed, suddenly cold. *It's not right. I shouldn't be forcing them to do what I want.*

"Bradley?" Anna asked.

Is this what I've always done? I made Dad send me to Chris's. I made Chris go with me to Sallson's. I made Anna stop talking.

He opened his eyes and looked at his sister. *I can't do it,* he thought. *I don't want to do it.* He felt like he was going to throw-up. His aunt was going to die, and there was nothing he could do to stop it. *I'm not like Mom. I'm not.*

Anna tugged at his hand. "Let's go find Antleen."

Blinking back tears, he shook his head. Even though his concentration had slipped, he still felt the bugs around him. He felt other life forms, as well, birds and rats and squirrels and more others than he could count. All of them were scared, hiding from the battle that was lighting up the night.

I'm sorry, he thought. *I'm sorry. I never should have tried . . . I just . . . I just wanted to save my aunt. She's a good person. Really good. She's . . . I just wanted to save her.*

Something slithered past him. He jerked in surprise, but stopped himself.

Silent motion fluttered in the trees.

"Owls," Anna breathed.

They lined the branches of the trees, turning their heads to track the fae.

A squirrel ran up a tree trunk and flung itself into the air, front legs spread wide. Sallson zipped out of the way and the squirrel tumbled to the ground. It scrambled up the nearest tree and chased after the fae, jumping from branch to branch.

They're answering, Bradley thought with a rush of excitement. *They're here to help!* He renewed his focus, concentrating on his connection to the animals. Each was independent, with its own fears and hungers. Together, they felt like a galaxy of dim stars around him, a community of strangers. *Strangers I'm not afraid of.* Bradley wanted to shout with triumph. *This is me! This is who I want to be!*

On the forest floor, a raccoon reared up, grabbing at the fae. The light darted up, then looped around a tree and fired another beam of light at Antleen.

Her platform dipped suddenly, then started lowering to the ground. The rocks stopped flying at the fae, and tightened into a smaller dome around her.

Was she hit? Bradley wondered. *Is that why her platform is dropping?* He focused every ounce of his willpower on his new friends. *Now!* he thought. *We need you!*

The owls spread their wings and dove out of the trees, claws extended. Sallson dodged them, darting at impossible angles. The birds pursued, flapping and banking, cutting off the fae's flight and anticipating its moves.

"Come on," Bradley muttered. The owls had distracted Sallson from Antleen. He wasn't firing at her anymore. That was a start, but it wasn't enough. Bradley needed one of the owls to make contact. His dad had said that disrupting the light would kill the fae. He was pretty sure an owl claw would do the trick.

Antleen's platform sank lower and lower, then settled on the ground.

Run, Bradley thought desperately. Sweat dripped from his forehead. The owls hadn't come anywhere near the fae. *Please Antleen, just run. He won't find me here. You don't have to fight him.*

But as Bradley's focus wavered, he lost his connection to the animals. The owls abandoned the chase. He struggled to call them back, but their own fears were too great. One by one, they veered off and vanished silently into the darkness.

Sallson spun around trees and through branches. He renewed his attack, firing beam after beam at Antleen.

None of the beams penetrated the rocks, but it would only take one lucky shot to end the fight. *No,* Bradley thought. *Please, no.*

Inside the whirling rocks of Antleen's platform, the blue dragon picked up the walking stick with its two front claws and lowered its tip.

As the point of the stick touched the rock, the forest floor exploded. Dirt, rocks, and twigs shot skyward, a raging torrent of muck that ripped the leaves from the trees. Mud streamed up out of the river, raining down water as it flowed upward into the sky.

Sallson darted over Antleen's platform, into the only piece of sky not filled with dirt. From there, he blazed down white beams of light toward Antleen. Her dome of stones shrank to a dense disk of swirling rocks that floated always between her and Sallson.

And all around the two of them, mud and rocks and branches whooshed upward from the forest.

Sallson pressed his attack, firing again and again. Several beams pierced Antleen's defenses, but each time her dragonfly wings moved her sideways and out of their path.

Bradley and Anna pressed their faces to the latticework. It was like trying to see through an upside-down waterfall of mud, one that grew darker and more clouded with each passing second.

Bradley looked up and gasped. The sky overhead was filled with a huge cloud of mud. The stars could barely be seen, and the moon that had been so bright was a dim brown color.

Above the platform, Sallson continued to fire beam after beam of bright white light.

Antleen's whirling shield of stones slowed and grew more sluggish. A beam burned its way through and branded her left shoulder. She tightened her shield, putting more stones between her core and the fae.

The dirt continued to darken the sky, until the moon and the stars disappeared completely, leaving the fae as the only source of light, a hard white glow that grew dimmer with each beam it fired.

The rush of dirt from earth to sky stopped.

She's done it, Bradley thought. *Sallson has no more light to use.*

The dragon and the fae faced each other in almost complete darkness. Sallson, little brighter than a spent flashlight bulb, flew slowly around Antleen. Her shield, reduced to a few dozen stones still rotating between them, moved with him, protecting her.

Cut off from the moonlight, Sallson appeared out of energy. Likewise, Antleen was spending all her effort maintaining the ceiling of dirt. Neither could attack.

Bradley placed his hands on the latticework, staring at the dim light that was Sallson. *Now's the time she needs my help the most.*

He reached out with his thoughts again, trying to reach the owls. There was no response. He concentrated harder, focusing his energy until the back of his eyes pulsed with pain. *Attack the fae!*

Behind her shield of stones, Antleen scraped her teeth together and belched. Fire roared out in a bright hot wave. Bradley shielded his eyes. When he looked again, all was darkness. He couldn't see his aunt, couldn't see the forest, couldn't even see Anna lying next to him.

"Is it–?" Anna started.

"Shh," Bradley hissed. Sallson had either run away or been killed. There was no way to tell, but if Antleen thought she was safe, she wouldn't be keeping the mud cloud overhead. He moved his mouth next to his sister's ear and spoke as quietly as he could. "We have to wait until daylight."

"I'm scared."

"I'm here, Annabear," Bradley said, trying to sound as much like his dad as he could. "It's okay. We just have to stay quiet. That's all."

Time crawled by. Mosquitoes buzzed around them. The musky smell of old mud and cabin mold grew stronger.

Bradley's arms cramped. Anna stretched out in the dirt beside him, pillowing her head on her arms.

At last, the sun peeked over the horizon, turning the dirt-filled sky a weird shade of orange-tinted mud.

Antleen stood on her stone platform, human once more and wearing her kimono. She leaned heavily on her walking stick.

Bradley banged his hands against the wooden latticework. Once, twice, and then on the third try it broke free. He scrambled out of the muck, Anna close on his heels.

"We did it!" he shouted.

Antleen picked her way through the pile of stones and walked toward them. The forest around her looked like some sort of unearthly battlefield, with its leafless trees and torn up earth.

Bradley gazed at his aunt. "You are amazing," he said. "I can't believe it!"

She leaned on her stick. Sweat plastered her hair to her head and streaked the sides of her face. Her eyes had deep shadows beneath them. "Looks like we won."

Anna ran to her and took her hand. "Antleen," she said, "why's the sky muddy?"

"Because," Antleen patted her hand, "I don't want to get it all over me. I'll let it down once we're inside."

"Or not," Max said from the front porch of the cabin.

Bradley spun. The fae looked exactly the same as he had on the porch: tall and pale, with short red hair and a brown leather jacket.

Antleen pulled Anna behind her. "Get out of here, Max. It's over. Sallson's gone, and I won't let you take Bradley."

"I think you will," Max answered, stepping back under the roof of the porch.

A beam of reddish-gold fae light, so bright it seared the eyes, fired from Max's left hand and through Helene's midsection. She gasped, clutching at her stomach, and collapsed to the ground.

Anna screamed.

The fae smiled at Bradley, mocking and confident. "Hello, again."

Bradley's mouth went dry and his hands started to shake. *No*, he thought, *this can't be happening.* His breath came in short little gasps.

Dirt fell from the sky and slammed into him, driving him to the ground. Sticks and rocks bounced off his back, and foul-smelling muck poured over him. He struggled to all fours, keeping his head down.

All the mud and debris that Antleen had raised into the sky was falling.

"Bradley!" Anna yelled. "Bradley!"

"I'm. . . I'm okay," he stammered, covering his mouth to keep the mud out. "Stay with Antleen!"

Mud continued to fall, breaking branches and splattering off the cabin roof. Through the torrent of brown fluid, Bradley could just barely see his aunt and sister. Anna was stretched out on top of Antleen, who lay motionless.

Tears mixed with the dirt coursing down Bradley's face.

Antleen!

The weight of the mud drove him the rest of the way to the ground. Shaking with fear, he put his hands over his head. There was nothing else he could do.

32

NO MORE

W hen the mud finally stopped falling, Bradley straightened, bruised and shaky from the pounding. Max stood on the porch, arms folded across his chest. Antleen lay on the ground a few feet away, Anna on top of her. Both were half-buried in muck.

"Anna?" he called.

"Antleen's hurt," Anna answered. "She's not moving!"

"It'll be ok—" Bradley gasped as a wave of fatigue hit him. He stumbled, dizzy with the sudden loss of energy.

"Good thing you're here," Max said. He raised his right hand toward Bradley and made a twirling gesture.

The rest of Bradley's strength left him. He swayed on his feet, struggling just to breathe. *No,* he thought. *No, no, no! This can't be happening.*

"Without you here to recharge me," Max continued, "without your *gallu draig,* I never could have risked using so much power during the day." Max flicked a piece of dirt from his sleeve, then repeated the twirling gesture with his hand. "Without you here, there's no way I could have killed your aunt."

Bradley dropped to one knee, then to all fours. Max was taking his *gallu draig*, and there was nothing he could do about it. *Antleen*, he thought. *Antleen, I'm sorry I didn't hatch in time. I'm so, so sorry.*

"Thanks to you and Helene," Max continued. "Sallson is gone, and I have all the power I could want. You're strong, Bradley. You could last for twenty or thirty years. Maybe more."

Bradley felt more of his *gallu draig* being drained away. His sight dimmed and his whole body trembled.

"Poor scared little Bradley," Max taunted. "At least now you won't have to worry about strangers." He laughed.

Bradley's limbs gave out. He sprawled in the wet mud, too weak to even turn his face away from the dirt. *Max is what I've always been scared of*, he thought. It wasn't strangers, after all. He just hadn't known because his memories had been erased.

"No!" Anna screamed. "Get up, Bradley! Get up!"

Bradley tried to answer, but he couldn't make his mouth work.

"He's too weak, little Annabear," Max said. "One day, you'll understand. You're only a few years from hatching yourself."

Fresh tears seeped out of the corners of Bradley's eyes. *He's going to take her, too, keep her until she starts to hatch. I can't . . . I can't let him do that.* His skin prickled with heat. He closed his eyes, searching for the strength he needed, the strength he knew that his dad would have had.

Mom wouldn't give up, he thought. He remembered his

mom's expression when she had faced the fae in the hospital, remembered her words when she had left the trailer to help his dad. *Playtime's over.*

Clenching his teeth, he struggled to get his arms and legs beneath him. *I can't be afraid anymore. Anna needs me. Antleen needs me.*

"That's a good boy," Max said. "Keep making that *gallu draig* for me."

Eyes still closed, Bradley remembered Chris staying behind to fight the men at Sallson's trailer. *Just like Dad*, Bradley thought, *just like Antleen.* They had all sacrificed themselves to protect him. All his life, he'd been protected by his family and friends.

"No." Bradley clenched his fists. The mud squished warm and wet between his fingers as he pushed himself up to all fours.

He heard his father's voice, spoken from a hospital bed and echoing in his head ever since, *haven't you ever dreamed of being anything?*

"No," Bradley repeated. He hadn't dreamed of being anything. He'd never thought beyond his own panic attacks. But now he dreamed. Now, he dreamed of being as brave as his parents, as brave as Chris. He dreamed of being brave enough to save his sister.

He opened his eyes.

Anna lay half-buried in dirt and debris, sobbing on Antleen's still body.

It's my turn to protect someone, Bradley thought fiercely. *Anna needs me.*

Max stood on the porch, a mocking smile on his face.

"No more," Bradley gritted through his teeth.

"Excuse me?" Max said.

"No more fear," Bradley said. "No more hiding." Rage flared to life deep within his belly. He inhaled a ragged breath and felt it burn through his lungs. The prickling in his skin intensified to a painful heat. *I will not let Max take Anna.* The determination to save his sister shone clear and bright in his mind, driving away his fatigue. He clung to it with all his willpower. *I will not.*

"You think I'm beaten," he said, raising his head to glare at Max, "a pathetic little nothing who's run out of guardians." The anger in his belly boiled hotter and spread. It met the cold, desperate determination of his mind, and he felt an electrifying jolt of energy surge through him. He stood, filled with a single purpose that left no room for weakness. "No more."

Max raised a hand toward Anna. "Don't make me kill her, too. You've already given me more than enough energy to do it."

"No!" Bradley shouted. The last remnants of fatigue left his body, replaced with an overwhelming sense of power. It rippled through his muscles and skin, reshaping them. His clothes tore away as his body grew and changed shape. Wings erupted from his back, and he felt his face elongate. His heart pounded in his chest, deep and resonant. "I will not let you!"

Max stepped back, no longer smiling. His head tilted up to meet Bradley's gaze for half a heartbeat, then he jumped off the porch and ran into the destroyed forest.

Bradley's roar echoed through the trees. He pawed the ground with deep red claws, then flexed his burgundy wings and leaped into the sky. As he flapped higher, his awareness expanded, encompassing the life all around him.

Down in the river, alligators crawled up the banks, their slow dangerous minds filled with curiosity. In the trees and sky, hawks turned their sharp eyes toward him, then spread their wings to fly at his side.

The emotions and thoughts of thousands of creatures, from the smallest gnat to the largest bear, spread out through his mind like a giant star map. He felt connected to each and every one, like he'd known them all his life, and they him.

Protect my family, Bradley thought fiercely. *Attack the fae!*

Beneath him, down among the leafless trees, a cloud of mosquitoes enveloped Max. A rattlesnake darted through the mud to strike the fae's ankle. Rats and squirrels clambered up his legs. A hawk raked his scalp. Alligators lumbered up from the river, grunting. To the north, a pair of coyotes turned and loped silently in his direction.

All we have to do is break the body, Bradley thought. *The sunlight will do the rest.*

He watched Max struggle clear of his attackers, then sprint through the trees. The fae was light on his feet and fast, but no match for even the slowest of his pursuers. He staggered under their teeth and claws, then spun, putting his back to a tree. His eyes raised to meet Bradley's, and he raised both hands.

A beam of intense red-gold light burst forth.

Bradley flinched, but the light splashed off the red-gold scales of his chest. His mother's words danced in his ears, every bit as clear as the night she'd spoken them, *your body will be whatever you need it to be.*

He tilted his head back, opened his massive dragon jaws, and gave another roar.

Answering his call, the beasts of the forest swarmed over Max, biting and slashing. The fae shoved away to run, but an alligator's jaws clamped down on his leg.

There was a flash of reddish gold light, and the fae was gone.

33

NEW FRIENDS

B radley swooped down to pick up his torn clothes, then landed with them behind the cabin and changed back into his human body. He was surprised at how natural and easy it felt to change shape. Mostly, though, he was worried about Antleen. He picked through the clothes that had ripped off when he changed into a dragon. The shirt was the most intact. He tied its pieces around his waist and used his shredded jeans as a makeshift belt.

As he hurried to the front of the cabin, his sister scurried away. "You're a dragon!" she squeaked.

Bradley knelt by his aunt. He sensed her energy, a determined pulse in the web of life to which he was now intimately connected. "Antleen," he whispered, touching her shoulder. "What should I do?"

She opened her eyes. "I have to concentrate," she said. "I'm not your dad. I have to do this the hard way."

Antleen moved her hands away from the hole in her gut to show him. Bradley caught his breath at the sight of the wound. His aunt was using her telekinesis to control her own flesh. She was keeping the stomach acids from leaving her stomach and forcing the blood to flow and the organs to function. The sheer complexity of what she was doing boggled his mind.

Overwhelmed, he sat back on his heels. "Anna," he said. "We can't move her, not even to the cabin."

"You're a dragon," his sister repeated.

"Yeah, but not a very good one. I wasn't supposed to let you see me. I forgot to think about not being seen."

Anna stared at him.

"It's a secret." He stood and took her hand. "Can you keep it a secret?"

"Umm . . ." She pulled her hand away with a grin. "Nope. Just wait 'til I tell Chloe!"

Bradley sighed. "Go get some blankets for Antleen. Maybe we can build a tent or something. And water, she needs a water."

Anna didn't move. "You should put some pants on."

"What?"

"You're naked."

He blushed. "No, I'm not."

"You're wearing your shirt like a dress."

"Okay, okay." Bradley ran into the cabin for a pair of shorts and a t-shirt. When he came back out, Anna was wiping mud off her aunt's face.

He took a moment to consider his options. Flying for help was out of the question. He couldn't leave Anna out here all by herself. He also couldn't move Helene. He glanced at the river. *Maybe I could build a raft.*

Pulses of life dotted his consciousness: snakes, insects,

rodents, lizards, bears, even some of the larger trees. He felt like he stood in the center of a bustling city of friends.

Protect, he urged silently. *Protect her.*

A snake, tan with vivid black stripes and a large rattle on the end of its tail, slithered through the grass and leaves to drape itself across Antleen's legs. It raised its head at Anna and shook its tail.

Anna shrieked and ran to the porch.

Us, Bradley amended quickly, trying to focus on the three pulses of life that he knew were Anna, Antleen, and himself. *Protect us, please.*

The snake quieted. Birds landed in the tree branches overhead, cocking their heads at each other and chirping suspiciously. A muddy raccoon ambled out of the bushes and squatted on its haunches by Antleen's shoulder.

This is what I've always wanted, Bradley thought. Now that he was connected to all the life around him, there would be no more strangers. *No more being afraid*, he thought. The idea made him almost giddy.

Antleen opened her eyes. "Bradley?" she asked. "Are you doing this?"

"Just some help," he answered, "to keep you safe while you heal. Is there anything else we can do? A pillow, maybe?"

She smiled and closed her eyes. "I knew you could do it. I knew you'd find your body."

A squirrel walked along the porch fence to Anna, then hopped onto her shoulder. Anna stood very still, eyes wide.

"But now you have to leave," Antleen said. "Sallson and Max might be gone, but you heard what Max said. Sallson has an army. You can bet more fae'll be here tonight. Fly back to your parents. Take Anna. Focus on not being seen."

"No," Bradley said. "We won't leave you like this."

"There's nothing you can do," Antleen said.

"Then you better heal faster," Bradley said.

"Yeah," Anna nodded. "You need to get better."

"But—"

"If you keep talking," Bradley interrupted. "I'm going to tell the raccoon to sit on your face."

"Don't make me laugh." Antleen smiled and closed her eyes. "I can't laugh."

When she didn't say anything else, Bradley sat on the top step of the porch. Anna settled next to him.

"What now?" she asked.

"I don't know. We can't move her."

"What she said about tonight, about an army . . . Can you fight them all?"

Bradley took a deep breath. He couldn't make a mud cloud like his aunt, or illusions like his mom, and he was nowhere near as tough as his dad. At night, he doubted he could beat even one fae, let alone an army. If they were still there when night fell, they were as good as dead.

None of that was what his little sister needed to hear. With his new senses, he felt the panic behind her words, understood exactly how hard it was for her to keep from collapsing into helpless tears.

He put his arm around her. "Not a problem," he lied. "I got this."

She eyed him suspiciously. "You're not scared?"

"Me?" he grinned. "Nah. You know me. I'm not scared of anything."

She snorted. "I wish Mom and Dad were here."

Bradley patted her arm awkwardly. "Me, too."

"Can you call them?"

"No," Bradley said. "Dad made me leave my phone at home." *Wait a minute,* he thought. *Maybe I can call them.*

"Anna," he said. "I'm going to turn into a dragon again, okay?"

"Right here?"

"Um, no." He looked around. "I'll go behind the cabin. I'm gonna fly a little, but I'll stay overhead, so I'll be able to see you. Can you stay with Antleen?"

She bit her lip, but nodded.

Now that he knew how, changing into a dragon was as easy as standing up. He walked behind the cabin and took off his clothes. Wings stretched out from his shoulders and he fell forward on to all fours. His arms and legs bulged into powerful dragon legs, with curved red claws on each foot. He felt his head stretch into a shape very much like his dad's.

Anna peeked around the cabin. "You've got a lizard face," she said, laughing.

"Aren't you supposed to be watching Antleen?" he asked.

"Yeah, but . . . you're a dragon. I had to see."

"I have to call Mom. Go back to Antleen."

"You look kinda like a lion, but with snake skin instead of fur and your tail's an alligator tail, but not green. Show me your wings."

Sighing, Bradley straightened his wings out for her to see. He wasn't as big as his dad, closer to the size of an ice cream truck than an 18-wheeler, but his wings felt like they were much bigger, tremendous sails of translucent red flesh that tucked against his body when he wasn't using them. "I look like a sunset, don't I?"

"No," she said. "More like orange and raspberry sherbet swirled together."

"Great," he said sarcastically. "I always wanted to be a sherbet dragon. Now, go back to Antleen."

He spread his wings and jumped into the air. He felt comfortable in the sky, more graceful than he'd ever been on land. He flew higher and higher, until Anna and Antleen looked like tiny dolls next to a toy cabin, and the broad river beyond them was just a thin brown line. Spreading his wings wide, he began a slow circular gliding descent.

His mom had been right. In his dragon body, he had more power than he'd ever imagined. He could sense every living creature for miles around. *Now, I just have to reach Mom.* He concentrated on picturing his mom, trying to remember what it felt like to be close to her: the scratchy polyester of her mustard-colored uniform, the warm feel of her hugs, the flash of her blue eyes when she was angry. Something flickered on the very edge of his perception. It felt like a dragon, but it was too faint for him to be sure.

Help, he thought. *We need help.*

Nothing responded.

He closed his eyes and emptied himself into the need for help, projecting as far as he could, hoping against hope that his connection to his parents might somehow let them hear. *Help us.*

When he opened his eyes again, the ground was much closer than he'd expected. He flapped his wings hard and landed behind the cabin with an impact that shook the ground. He changed back into his human body and pulled on his clothes.

"Are you okay?" Anna asked, poking her head around the cabin.

"Yeah," he answered, embarrassed. "I'm still new at this."

"Did you find help?"

"Not sure. I shouted as loud as I could."

"Wasn't very loud," Anna said. "I didn't hear anything."

"Get some water," Bradley said, checking on Antleen. She was still fast asleep. "For when she wakes up."

"Okay . . ." Anna trailed off, one hand on her head. A horrified expression came over her face. "My sunglasses! I lost my princess sunglasses!" She spun around, looking for them, but mud and rocks and broken branches covered everything.

"You're never gonna find them," Bradley said. "They're gone."

"Aw, man!" Anna stomped into the cabin. "Chloe gave me those."

Bradley sat down next to his aunt and pulled the edge of her kimono over the wound, making sure that the fabric didn't touch the damaged flesh. *At least I can keep the bugs out of it.* He could feel their interest, but they were staying away.

"That's how I'm different than Mom," he murmured. He wasn't controlling the bugs. Instead, they were responding to him as if he were a friend, choosing to protect Antleen instead of being forced to.

Mom, he thought. Had she heard him? If not, what should he do? *I have to find some way of getting Anna to safety.*

An alligator, at least twelve feet long from nose to tail,

crawled up out of the river and walked into the clearing. Bradley watched it stretch out in the sun on the other side of his aunt. The raccoon glanced at it, then trotted to the steps of the cabin and sat down.

Maybe Anna can hide under the cabin with a couple alligators, Bradley thought. *I'm not an egg, anymore. Maybe the fae won't care about me.*

Anna backed through the door, balancing a box of crackers, two bags of potato chips, and a glass of water. She wore a pair of blue and white striped sunglasses, with pink-tinted lenses. She stopped abruptly at the sight of the alligator. "Bradley?"

"It's all right," he said. "He's here to help."

A black bear poked its nose around a tree and made a noise halfway between a groan and a whine. Anna tossed it a bag of chips, then ran past the raccoon to Bradley, sloshing water with every step. Two other bears appeared out of the trees, and the three of them tore into the bag.

A spark of life blazed into Bradley's awareness, high above. He looked up and saw Kevin's golden-feathered body diving out of the sky toward the area behind the cabin.

Relief washed through Bradley.

We're saved.

34

KEVIN

K evin walked around the cabin in his human shape, wearing his blue swimsuit and white surf shirt, and carrying a backpack on his shoulder. He still wore the illusion of his younger self, though Bradley could easily see through it now. The real Kevin was older, with blonde stubble covering his jaw line, and a thin scar down the side of his neck.

Anna peered over the tops of her sunglasses. "Kevin?" she asked.

"I can't believe how fast you flew," Bradley said. It hadn't even been ten minutes since his call for help.

Kevin shrugged. "I wasn't that far away." He looked around the clearing, his eyes pausing on the alligator, then stopping on Antleen. "What happened?"

At the edge of the trees, the bears stopped pawing the chip bag and pointed their noses at Kevin.

"It's kind of a long story," Bradley said. "We took care of Sallson and Max, but–"

"What do you mean you took care of them?" Kevin interrupted, walking forward.

A black bear lumbered into his path. It whuffed through its nose and shook its head from side to side.

Kevin backed away, almost stepping on a rattler that had slid noiselessly out from under the cabin. He hopped sideways.

The snake coiled, and its rattle began to shake.

Fear and mistrust emanated from the creatures around Bradley. "After Antleen got Sallson," he said slowly, "Max attacked her. I hatched and . . ."

"You hatched?" Kevin asked.

Bradley didn't answer. He felt four more alligators climbing up the banks of the river. Two hawks landed on the roof of the cabin, their eyes bright and focused.

"You beat Max?" Kevin said. "Yeah, right."

Bradley didn't say anything. Kevin sounded like he knew Max. If that were true, something was very wrong.

"He did, too!" Anna said. "I saw him. He's a dragon!"

"It's okay." Bradley laid his hand on her shoulder, his mind racing. What had Kevin meant when he said he was close by? Why would he have been close by? "You're right," he said. "I didn't do it all by myself."

"Who helped?"

"It doesn't matter," Bradley said. "What's important is that you're here, and we need help. Antleen's hurt. Mom said Granduncle Li is a healer. Maybe you could go get him."

Kevin looked back at Antleen lying motionless on the ground. "I'll split it with you."

"Split what?"

"Her hoard. You show me where it is and I'll split it with you. Then I'll go get Li."

Anger burned through Bradley. "No!"

"Not even to save her? Don't be greedy, cuz. You don't even know how to use it, and Li could heal her. It wouldn't be a problem for him."

Bradley clenched his fists as the pieces of the puzzle clicked together in his mind. Only the dragons at the Gathering had known that he'd gone with Antleen. Of those, only Kevin was here. "You're the one who betrayed us," he said. "You told Max I was hiding with Antleen. You sold us out!"

"He's working for Max?" Anna said, moving behind Bradley.

"This is just business." Kevin shrugged. "They get eggs, I get gold. It all works out. Now how about it? I'm offering you half her hoard, and the chance to save your aunt."

"I don't know where it is."

"I bet your aunt does," Kevin said. "We could ask her."

"No," Antleen said, her voice still weak. "Don't trust him!"

"That's what you say *now*," Kevin interrupted. "But for how much longer?"

Antleen's body went rigid. Her eyes flew open and she gasped.

"Pain." Kevin laughed. "It can do amazing things." He grinned at Anna. "It's my specialty. Want to try?"

Her mouth dropped open and she shook her head.

"No!" Bradley shouted. "Stop it!"

"Or what?" Kevin asked. "What are you going to do, *cuz*?"

White-hot agony exploded in Bradley's head, a pressure inside his skull so intense it blurred his vision. When it faded, Kevin stood in front of him in dragon form, with flashing blue eyes and feathers that glowed golden brown in the morning light.

Anna screamed and ran into the trees.

"Smart girl," Kevin growled.

Bradley's muscles spasmed, dropping him to the ground and curling him into a stiff painful ball. The pain was so intense he couldn't think clearly, couldn't change into his dragon body. *Help*, he thought desperately.

A surge of aggression answered him. The bears reared up on their back legs. The alligators charged across the clearing, their jaws wide.

Kevin leaped into the air and pumped his eagle wings to gain altitude. "That the best you got?" he shouted. "Animals?"

The pain in Bradley's head doubled. His stomach heaved and he threw up.

"What is it, Bradley?" Anna shouted from under the trees. "What's wrong?"

Bradley reached out blindly with his mind, diving deeper into the life around him, losing himself in the creatures of the forest. The pain receded as his consciousness spread out among his new friends.

We're one, he thought. *We'll face this together.* He exhaled and a cloud of insects converged on Kevin's eyes: mosquitoes, black flies, even gnats.

Kevin exhaled through his nose, blowing them away. "Bugs?" he said. "Really?"

Dimly, Bradley felt the pain increase in his body. It didn't bother him. He wasn't in his body.

He was in the hearts of the eagles that soared down to rake Kevin's back, in the beaks of the mockingbirds that ripped at his wings, and in the stingers of the wasps that drove themselves over and over again into the dragon's belly.

Kevin roared and twisted in midair, snapping at the birds. He lashed his tail back and forth and swept his great talons through the creatures attacking him.

Through a hawk's eyes, Bradley saw his own body on the ground, convulsing helplessly under the waves of pain Kevin sent toward it.

Anna huddled beneath the trees, tears streaming down her face.

We are together, Bradley thought. His vision became a swirl of color and motion, as he saw through the eyes of owls and falcons that joined the assault on the golden-winged dragon. Sparrows and crows winged up from the trees, as well. Some targeted the creature's smooth skin, others its wings or eyes. Kevin flapped higher, circling to an altitude beyond the reach of even the eagles.

He'll come back, Bradley thought, *be ready*.

The birds and insects regrouped. They formed circles in the sky below the dragon, waiting for it to return. On the ground, alligators and black bears moved to the bodies of Antleen and Bradley.

Kevin dove, claws extended. The birds met him in midair, ripping at his blue skin as he plummeted past. Insects filled his nose and eyes.

Now, Bradley thought. *He's distracted.*

An alligator fastened its jaws onto Bradley's leg and

scrabbled backward, dragging him into the trees. Another did the same with Antleen.

Bradley reached out to the sparkling, terrified mind of his sister. *Run, Anna.*

Anna sprinted to the cabin porch and dove beneath it, pushing through the hole in the latticework that Bradley had made earlier.

Kevin landed hard in the mud in front of the cabin. "Give up," he panted.

The bears charged, grunting and chuffing. Kevin roared and they dropped heavily to the ground, their bodies writhing in pain.

Their pain coursed through Bradley's awareness even more keenly than his own. He took it from them and fed it into his own body's twitching agony.

Kevin moved toward the trees, his bright blue eyes gleaming as they searched the shadows. "Where are you?" he hissed.

Behind him, the bears rolled to their feet. Their lips peeled back in snarls.

"How are you doing this?" Kevin said. An alligator lunged for his foot, but he caught it in his mouth and flung it away.

The bears slammed into Kevin, clawing and biting. Rats and squirrels leaped out of the trees onto his back. A rattlesnake struck his leg.

Kevin roared in frustration.

Bradley continued to intercept the waves of pain that Kevin sent, redirecting them into his own body. A loud crack filled his ears. He ignored it. *Together*, he projected toward his friends. *We are together. I will keep the pain away.*

Insects swarmed Kevin's eyes, and hawks dove down to rake his back. Coyotes loped out of the trees, snapping and snarling.

Spreading his wings, Kevin shook off his attackers and launched into the sky. Dark red blood dripped from his blue skin, and his left eye was swollen shut. His wings were ragged with broken feathers. Birds continued to swoop and dive around him, gashing his back and belly with their talons.

Kevin sent more pain at his assailants, but Bradley drained it away, taking it all into his own body. Kevin flapped higher, his left wing badly torn by the bears, until he was higher than any of his assailants could fly.

He circled, searching the forest with keen dragon eyes.

Bradley was looking through the eyes of the eagles, and they saw what Kevin saw: a clearing filled with bears, alligators and snakes. He, Anna, and Antleen were nowhere to be seen.

Kevin roared in frustration, folded his wings and dove, only to be met once again by birds and bugs. Spreading his injured wings, Kevin banked and flew away north.

Bradley's awareness stayed inside his defenders until Kevin passed out of sight.

One by one, the alligators stretched out in the mud around him. The bears walked to the food Anna had dropped. The birds and bugs drifted back down to the ruined tree branches.

Relief flooded through Bradley. His cousin was gone, at least for the moment.

Thank you, he projected. The words felt inadequate, but they were all he had. *Thank you.*

He pulled his awareness back into his own body.

Pain hit him like a wall of fire. His chest and back burned, and his head ached so intensely that he couldn't keep his eyes open. He cried out, or would have, but his throat was ragged and dry, and all that emerged was a gasping little croak.

Tears coursed down his cheeks.

All the pain he'd shielded the animals from was in his own body, and it had twisted and tortured his flesh. His legs were the only part of him that didn't hurt. He couldn't feel them at all.

Antleen lay on her back next to him. Her face had an unhealthy gray tint to it, and blood stained the front of her kimono. They lay by the river bank, under a copse of leafless mud-covered trees. Alligators lounged nearby, watching in every direction. Bradley heard the bears in the clearing, pawing their way through the bags of chips and the box of crackers that Anna had dropped.

"Are you okay?" Antleen asked. "I heard something crack."

He remembered the cracking noise when he'd taken the pain from the animals. *That was me*, he thought. *I broke my body*. "How . . ." he swallowed hard, trying to stop his tears. "How are you?"

"Not good. When the alligator dragged me, I couldn't keep my focus. I lost a lot of blood. I don't know how much longer I'll be able to keep this up."

"Bradley!" Anna shouted from the cabin. "Where are you?"

"What do we do?" Bradley whispered. He couldn't get a deep enough breath to shout to his sister. *Even if I could*, he thought, *there's nothing she can do*.

"I've got nothing left," Antleen said. "I'm sorry, Bradley."

Mom, Bradley thought, closing his eyes. *I did it, Mom. I hatched.* His brain felt tired and fuzzy.

"Come on, Bradley! Where are you?" Anna said. "I have Kevin's phone. It was in his backpack when he turned into a dragon."

Bradley's eyes flew open. "Here," he rasped. "I'm here!"

He heard her running footsteps, then a little "oh" sound as she saw him lying among the alligators. He lifted his head. "I'm hurt," he said. "I can't move. Call Mom and Dad."

She started dialing.

Bradley laid his head on the ground and closed his eyes.

35

CHILI

B radley woke in the hammock on the cabin's front porch, surrounded by the familiar hot smell of bubbling chili. The porch light glowed overhead, and the singing of crickets and frogs filled the night air.

He sat up abruptly, rocking the hammock. "The fae! We have to get out of here! Anna!"

"Relax," his mother said. She sat on the porch steps, wearing her blue sundress and holding a newspaper.

"But—"

"Your dad and I are here" she interrupted, standing, "and you have hatched. The fae won't be coming anywhere near us." She smoothed his hair away from his forehead. "I'm so proud of you. My own little sky dragon."

Bradley rubbed the small of his back. The last thing he remembered was lying paralyzed in the mud. Now, he could feel his legs again, and they ached. Deep purple bruises marked where the alligator had grabbed him. He flexed his hands in the moonlight, remembering. "Where's Antleen? Is she okay?"

"She's inside, making chili," his mom said. "Uncle Li healed both of you while you slept."

"So, it's all over?"

"At least until Anna starts to hatch. We'll deal with that when it comes, if it comes."

"What about Anna?" Bradley challenged. "What if she doesn't hatch?"

"You're so much like your father," she said, eyes shining. "We won't leave her. We'll stay with her as long as she stays with us."

"Why?" Bradley asked. "What changed?"

"I did. After we left the Gathering, I realized that Cedrych and the others weren't the only ones who lacked courage. All those dirty looks you gave me, all that resentment . . . you were right. If your sister doesn't hatch, she'll have to deal with having dragon parents, and we'll have to be brave enough to stay with her as she grows old."

"That's . . . You're . . ." Bradley gave up on trying to talk and just hugged her.

"Besides," she added. "Your dad's convinced she's going to hatch into a swamp dragon. He really wants a swamp dragon."

"Great," he said, drily, pulling back. "That's just great."

Bradley's dad banged through the front door and lifted him into a hug. "Helene tells me that you took down both Max and Kevin."

"Oof," Bradley said. His dad's hug was really tight. "Sort of. Kevin got away. I'm not sure about Max. I think he's dead. There was a flash of light."

"Don't worry about Kevin," his mom said. "I talked to Cedrych and Luanna. They'll take care of him. Believe me."

"As for Max," his dad released him, smiling. "If he's alive, you'll get him next time."

"William!" his mom barked. She pointed her finger at Bradley. "You stay away from Max. Do you understand me? I don't know what'll happen with the fae next, but I don't want you involved."

"Typical sky dragon," Antleen said, balancing two bowls of chili as she stepped onto the porch. "Always avoiding trouble."

Bradley's mom turned a level gaze on her. "You mean, instead of dating it?"

Antleen blushed.

"Kevin was a traitor all along," Bradley said. "He was the one who told Sallson I was hiding with Antleen. He told Max, and Max told Sallson right where we were."

"And then Max tried to double-cross everyone and take you for himself." Antleen handed him a bowl of chili and kept the other for herself. She sat down on the porch with it, her back against the wall. Bradley sat on the hammock, holding his bowl on his knees.

"Why didn't Kevin just grab me at school or something?"

"Her," Antleen said, nodding at Bradley's mom. "He never knew where she was, never knew if she was watching."

"But," Bradley said to his mom, "you weren't around when I was at school. You were at work."

"Silly egg." She ruffled his hair. "The only time I've been at the diner this past week was when I knew you were with your father. I spent most days overhead, keeping watch."

"So why hire Kevin at all? Why get me a bodyguard if you were there the whole time?"

"I wanted someone else for the hunters to focus on, someone to slow them down for me."

"A speedbump?"

She smiled. "Something like that."

"Except when Dad went into the hospital," Bradley said, remembering. "That's the only time Kevin knew for sure where you were. That's why he was on the phone! He said he had a package but he didn't know where to deliver it." He shook his head. "It was me. I was the package."

"But Sallson wasn't answering his phone," Bradley's dad said. "He probably wasn't even wearing a human shape. After seeing what your mom and I did to the fae that attacked me, he was probably hiding."

"Excuse me, children." Li's quiet voice carried from inside the cabin. "You have awakened a little one who is quite interested in seeing her brother."

"Sorry, Uncle Li," Bradley's dad said. "Send her out."

Anna ran onto the porch, unicorn sunglasses perched on the top of her head. "Guess what, Bradley? We're all dragons! It's not just you."

Bradley laughed. "I bet I'm the only sherbet dragon."

Anna put her hands on her hips. "That's what you look like! It's not *my* fault."

"That's enough," Bradley's dad interrupted. "You've seen that your brother's okay. Now back to bed with you."

"Wait! Not yet!" She dodged her dad's arms. "Did you tell him yet? Can I tell him?"

"Tell me what?" Bradley asked.

"Chloe's mom called. She's awake!"

Relief washed over Bradley.

"The docs are keeping her in the hospital for observation," his dad added, catching Anna. "Come on, you. It's time for bed." He carried her into the cabin.

Bradley scooped a big spoonful of chili out of his bowl and stuffed it in his mouth. It tasted rich and thick and spicy, just the way he liked it.

"Well." His mom stood and brushed off her knees. "I imagine you two have some things to talk about." She glanced up at the night sky. "I'll be right inside if you need me."

Bradley and his aunt ate without speaking for several heartbeats after the door closed. He gazed out at the forest. The bare tree branches, stripped of their leaves when Antleen had sent the earth into the sky, were coated with a thick layer of mud. They looked eerie and otherworldly in the moonlight.

Antleen spoke first. "He wasn't always like that, you know."

"Max?"

She nodded, still looking at the trees. "When we ran away together, he was dashing and heroic, and, well . . . different. I didn't even know he was a fae. Nobody did." She put her bowl on the floor beside her and leaned her head back against the wall. "We saw each other every thirty or forty years after that. Nothing serious, but special all the same. Then, about a hundred years ago, he told me that he had discovered how to use the *gallu draig*, how to make it a part of himself. I should have told someone, but he didn't want me to start a war. He was right, too. It would have been bad."

"Like it's going to be now?" Bradley asked.

She sighed. "Yes."

"How did he go from telling you about his power to trying to kidnap me?"

She shook her head. "I don't know. When we saw him on our camping trip, when he showed up to take you, I was so shocked . . ." She trailed off.

"I don't remember," Bradley said, trying to keep the bitterness out of his voice.

"No." She looked at him. "I wish you did."

"What happened after I hit him with the rock?"

"Your mom and dad took you away. I went back and found him. The sun was still out, and he had very little power left. I should have killed him then, but he swore that he was leaving, that he'd stay far away from you, and that he'd never try to steal another dragon egg."

Bradley ate another spoonful of chili. "He lied."

"If I'd known, I never would have brought you here. Max was one of a very few who knew about this cabin."

They ate quietly together, listening to the unnaturally quiet night. Bradley felt the life of the forest pulsing at the corners of his mind, thousands of consciousnesses of varying levels of complexity. In their center, his family sparkled like bright stars.

"Well," he said as he put his empty bowl down on the floor. "I'm glad Max was as big a slimeball as he was."

She snorted. "Why's that?"

"If he hadn't betrayed Sallson, if he'd worked with him to attack you, we'd have been in trouble."

"Yeah," Antleen said. "Looking back, his plan was pretty clear. He wanted me to fight Sallson, so that whoever won would be weak enough for him to kill. Then he could take you and Anna."

"I can't believe you ever fell for him."

Antleen slapped him gently on the back of his head. "Your mom gets to say that. You don't."

She stood and brushed her hands off on her jeans. "Enough about Max. It's time to move on. It's time for the big question."

"The big question?"

"You know: the big question. What's your one thing? Your focus? What let you find your body?"

"Oh, you mean *that* big question." Bradley grinned.

"Out with it, you little runt. What is it?"

"It's . . . It's tough to explain."

"Come on."

Bradley looked out at the trees, suddenly embarrassed. "It's just . . . For the past three years, I've been afraid: afraid of strangers, afraid of panic attacks, afraid of snakes, afraid of what kids at school think when they see me have a panic attack . . ." He looked down at his chili. "All that time, you guys protected me. Last night, it was my turn to protect someone, my turn to not be afraid." He shrugged self-consciously. "I think my one thing is you guys."

"Wow," Antleen said. "You really are like your dad."

36

SECRETS REVEALED

"You're not going to believe this." Bradley stood on the raft, paddling it through the swamp. In the back of his mind, he felt life all around him: snakes, fish, frogs, alligators, birds, turtles, and more bugs than he could count. Farther away, he sensed Anna and Chloe playing in the yard, while his parents drank iced tea with Mrs. Herns.

"Yeah, yeah. You've said that already." Chris sat on the wooden boards, his hurt hand wrapped in white bandages. Bradley knew that his ribs were wrapped as well. It would be some time before Chris returned to doing anything even remotely athletic.

"I'm just warning you so you don't fall off the raft, that's all."

"I get it," Chris said. "You brought us all the way out here where nobody can possibly hear, so let's hear it. What's the big secret? And why are you wearing a bathing suit? You planning on swimming in the swamp?"

Bradley smiled and put down his paddle. "You sure you're ready?"

"Yes, already! Get on with it, shrimp."

Bradley leaped into the air and spread his arms. Wings sprang out of his shoulders and spread wide to catch the swamp air. His body swelled and changed. Red-gold scales covered his skin, and he felt an alligator tail extend from the base of his spine. "That's dragon shrimp, to you."

Chris's eyes went wide, and his jaw dropped.

"What do you think?" Bradley flapped higher. "I don't look like sherbet, do I? Anna says I look like sherbet."

"Ya . . . you . . ."

"Cause I don't think I look like sherbet." Bradley, roughly the size of an ice cream truck, landed on the branch of a live oak. It bent under his weight.

"You're a dragon," Chris said.

"Yeah, but not a very good one. I'm not supposed to let anyone see me."

"You're a dragon!" Chris repeated, standing.

"Yep," Bradley said. "Don't tell anyone."

Chris stared at him for several heartbeats, then a slow smile spread across his face. "Can I have a ride?"

ACKNOWLEDGMENTS

Writing a book may seem like a solitary task, but it is not. I'd like to gratefully thank Rebecca Stanborough, Linda Dunlap, Terri Chastain, Geri Throne, Mary K Swanson, Dawn Rosner, and Gayle Guernsey for all their help and encouragement.

Thanks also to Leanna Crossan for her amazing cover illustration, and to Ghislain Viau for designing the cover.

Thank you all!

ABOUT THE AUTHOR

Patrick Matthews is a writer and game designer who lives in Central Florida. When he's not writing or playing, he can usually be found exploring the roads, searching for new adventures with his wife and two boys. You can learn more at www.pat-matthews.com.

facebook.com/PatrickMatthewsAuthor

twitter.com/OrlandoPat

instagram.com/patmatthews42